WHISPER HOUSE

An Emmie Rose Haunted Mystery Book 4

DEAN RASMUSSEN

DARK VENTURE
PRESS

Whisper House: An Emmie Rose Haunted Mystery Book 4

Dean Rasmussen

For more information about this book, visit:

www.deanrasmussen.com
dean@deanrasmussen.com

Whisper House: An Emmie Rose Haunted Mystery Book 4

Published by: Dark Venture Press

Cover Art: Mibl Art

Developmental & Line Editor: C.B. Moore

❀ Created with Vellum

Diego clutched the flashlight and paused in the doorway. Michelle was standing perfectly still in the middle of the room, facing away from him toward the closet and leaning sideways. Her nurse's costume looked almost real from behind—the scrubs probably *were* real—but the sexy white lace arm sleeves gave it away.

"Getting spooked?" he asked.

She shuddered at the sound of his voice and glanced back, her eyes full of confusion. "What?"

"See something in there?" Diego grinned and took a few steps forward.

She shook her head. "Not really."

"Is the house already getting to you?"

She smiled nervously and turned around, switching off the phone in her hand. "Not me. I'm looking forward to it."

Diego gestured with his head. "You're missing out on all the fun in the next room. Sterling mixed a drink for you."

She nodded with a blank expression. "He's the best, isn't he?"

"You're a lucky girl."

"I..." She glanced around the room.

"Saw something in the closet?"

She paused, then shook her head. "No."

Diego gestured to the phone in her hand. "Are the others on their way?"

She glanced down at it, then tossed it onto the bed. "I'm sure they'll be here soon."

Sterling and Jennifer appeared in the doorway. Their costumes couldn't have contrasted more. He was a zombie with professional makeup applied by an artist earlier that morning in Minneapolis, and she was the Disney Princess Jasmine, complete with real gold bracelets and a diamond necklace.

Sterling was holding two drinks in his hand with a wide grin. "What's going on in here? You messing around with my girl?"

Diego stepped away from Michelle suddenly and played up the guilt for his friend. "I... We..."

Jennifer hurried over and grabbed Diego's arm, painfully yanking him away by his elbow. "He's mine."

"So possessive." Diego rubbed his injured muscles, then slipped his arm around Jennifer's bare waist.

Sterling extended one of the drinks to Michelle. "I got your favorite, babe."

She accepted it and stepped beside him. "We know each other so well."

"Oh, there it is." Sterling plucked the phone off the bed and slipped it into his pocket without checking it.

Diego raised the flashlight. "Are we ready to get started?"

"Where are we going, Captain?" Jennifer adjusted his pirate's hat and clutched his arm.

"It's Halloween in a haunted house, so we're hunting for ghosts, Jen. You're not scared?"

"Not really."

"You're shaking."

She chuckled. "I'm trying to shake some sense into you."

"Won't work." Diego eyed Sterling's torn clothes and gruesome makeup, featuring a long gash running from his left eye down to his neck. "A face only a mother could love."

Michelle frowned. "I think he looks quite... handsome." She cuddled up to him.

"And her opinion is all that matters," Sterling said.

She patted his chest. "My sweet man."

"Okay," Diego said in a low, ominous voice, "let's begin."

"Where?" Jennifer asked.

Diego glanced at Michelle before facing the closet and pointing at it. "There."

"Why there?"

Diego gestured to Michelle. "Because *she* saw something."

"I didn't say that."

"You said it with your eyes." He stepped over to the closet door and opened it slowly. The wood creaked as it opened. Perfect. The house was living up to the hype, so far. "If you see or hear anything strange, point it out. There *are* ghosts in this house."

"... according to the house's owner," Sterling added between sips of his drink. "The same lady who gladly took your money to rent this *haunted* place."

"It's not just her word." Diego aimed the flashlight at Sterling's face. "Did you read the stories? Lots of people have heard things here. Whispers."

"I'm not getting my hopes up," Jennifer said.

"Don't spoil it, Jen," Diego said. "Just keep your eyes open."

"Seriously," Michelle said, "you promised us we'd see some ghosts tonight."

"I *implied* that you might. No guarantees."

Diego led them into a closet and closed the door behind them. In the darkness, they stood shoulder to shoulder, and he took the opportunity to wrap his arm around Jennifer's waist, pulling her closer. She didn't resist.

"I don't think your plan is to scare me," Jennifer whispered.

Diego shushed her, then raised his voice. "Do you hear that?"

"That's my stomach, D," Sterling said. "It wants more alcohol."

"No," Diego whispered, "it's a spirit."

Jennifer let out a long, annoyed sigh.

"You're all going to die," Diego whispered.

Sterling spoke up, "I suppose we all *are* going to die someday."

"Tonight…"

"Is that supposed to scare us?" Michelle laughed. "Jennifer, rein him in."

Jennifer pulled on Diego's arm. "You'll need to do better than that."

"Listen, it's called Whisper House for a reason, seriously. The owner said a woman died in the house."

"How did she die?" Sterling asked skeptically.

"I forgot to ask. But I read that her ghost follows guests around and whispers in their ears, luring them into closets just like this one." Diego moved up against Jennifer's ear and whispered, "Hold still now. This won't hurt at all. Your delicious little neck is…"

His flashlight caught sight of a face in the darkness. He gasped.

Jennifer laughed and followed his gaze. "A little jumpy?"

The face was his own, staring back at him from a full-length mirror set inside an ornate porcelain frame. "Another mirror. What the hell's up with all of those?"

Jennifer moved toward it and looked at herself. "I'm guessing the previous owners were a bit vain."

Michelle fumbled with the door. "I'd like to get out now. I'm claustrophobic."

"Sure, babe." Sterling helped her to open the door. The darkness of the closet gave way to broad ambient light coming in through the unshaded window across the room. The sun had gone down, but a shade of dark blue stretched across the evening sky and the moon was full.

Diego led them toward the hallway. "Nothing in there except four drunk fools."

"When are we going to see some real ghosts?" Jennifer asked. "Can we use the Ouija board now?"

Diego checked the time on his phone. "It's not even eight o'clock yet."

Jennifer groaned and gestured to the window. "It's dark out."

"Shouldn't we wait until midnight to use it?" Sterling asked.

"No." Diego grinned. "You're thinking of Cinderella. We can use that thing anytime, day or night. The spirits are always ready to speak with us."

"Then let's do it now, before the others get here."

They gathered again downstairs in the area that the owner had described as the séance room. There wasn't anything particularly special about it, except for the circular shape and odd designs covering the walls.

Jennifer had placed all the snacks and drinks along one wall in the room. A large sheet of cake sat at the end of one table, decorated in a Halloween theme with 'Happy Halloween!' written in orange frosting over the top.

Diego took a seat along the far wall, placing the Ouija board between himself and Jennifer. Sterling and Michelle sat together on the opposite side with their hands stretched out toward the board, ready to go.

"Something better happen with this, or I suggest you get your money back," Sterling said.

"I've seen these things work before," Jennifer said. "It's a lot of fun, but there's no way to predict what it will say, if anything."

Diego rolled his eyes. "So it's kind of like a trip to the zoo where sometimes you see the animals stepping out of their cage and that's a big thrill, but then the rest of the visit you see nothing and realize it's kind of a scam."

"Well, dammit," Sterling said, "it's Halloween, and this is the night when all the ghosts supposedly come out to celebrate, so let's see some celebrating."

Michelle and Sterling almost simultaneously held up their drinks and then clinked them together. "Hell, yeah."

Something banged up stairs. Not a whisper or a voice or any ghostly apparitions. Just a loud thump and then nothing.

Sterling and Diego looked at each other at the same time.

Jennifer gasped. "What was that?"

Diego held his breath. The room went silent as all of them turned their gaze toward the stairs. Nobody moved for several seconds.

Sterling broke the silence. "Probably just something fell off a shelf."

Michelle got up suddenly, her chair scraping over the wood floor, and Sterling followed her a moment later. Both of them stopped in the doorway of the seance room and gazed toward the top of the stairway.

"Is someone up there?" Michelle asked.

"Nobody's up there." Diego scoffed.

"The spirits?" Jennifer looked at him with wide eyes.

He shook his head. "We haven't even started yet."

Michelle glanced back with narrowed eyes and glared at Diego. "Did you set this all up? Is this a practical joke?"

Diego rolled his eyes. "I want to see ghosts just as much as you do. I wouldn't waste our time on a practical joke. I paid good money to rent this place with the intention of seeing some spirits. Some *real* ones. So..." He beckoned Sterling and Michelle to come back to the table. "... let's say we start this thing."

Diego picked up the board's planchette and put his fingers along its edges. Jennifer joined him.

"C'mon guys," Jennifer said, "I want to make something happen. Don't you?"

Michelle turned back, nodded, then returned to the table with a solemn face. Each of them put a few fingers along the edge of the planchette, and it began moving in a counter-clockwise motion.

Sterling stayed near the doorway with his gaze locked on something out of sight. In his hyper-realistic zombie outfit, he truly looked dead.

"So, how does this thing work?" Michelle asked.

"No idea," Diego said. "We just ask it some questions and it moves around." He looked up at Sterling. "You going to join us?"

Sterling turned his head a little, although he didn't look away from whatever had caught his attention at the top of the stairs. "Don't you guys want to know what that noise was? That's why we're here, right?"

"It's like what you said, Sterling," Jennifer said without conviction. "Something probably just fell off a shelf."

Sterling shook his head slowly and furrowed his brow. "It's weird."

"What's weird?" Diego asked.

Sterling didn't answer. His mouth hung open, still staring at the same spot.

Michelle turned her head toward the wall suddenly, and her smile vanished. She removed her fingers from the Ouija board.

Jennifer leaned toward her friend. "You okay?"

Michelle met Jennifer's gaze. "Sure," she said softly.

"Let me... go have a look." Sterling walked off. A moment later, his footsteps thumped up the stairs.

"If you see any ghosts," Diego shouted, "have them come down for a drink."

Jennifer groaned. "That's disrespectful."

"They're *ghosts*, my princess! Since when do they need respect? They can't hear us anyway, right?"

"He'll come back and scare us." Michelle looked toward the doorway as if expecting Sterling to return at any moment. "I know it. He's just as bad as you, Diego."

"I'm the worst." Diego nodded and smirked before closing his eyes halfway with his chin up as if going into a trance. He focused again on the Ouija board. "Let's begin again, my children."

Jennifer and Michelle joined him in moving the planchette.

"I'd like to ask the spirits a question. Is a princess allowed to marry the undead?" Diego asked mockingly.

Jennifer jabbed her elbow into his side. "Don't ruin it."

Michelle pulled her hands away and stood up suddenly. "I should check on Sterling."

"What for?" Diego broke from his disingenuous trance. "He'll come back down in a minute."

Michelle rubbed her fingers and gazed fixedly at the floor. "I need to go to him."

Jennifer gestured to the Ouija board. "No, please don't go. Mustn't keep the spirits waiting. Put your fingers on this with us. It's working."

Michelle shook her head. "Later." She stepped over and grabbed the silver cake cutter from beside the Halloween cake, staring at it with a confused expression.

"You hungry?" Jennifer asked.

Michelle didn't answer.

"A woman with a knife is always a scary sight," Diego said.

Michelle stepped toward the door and nodded. "He's up there alone."

"If you see any ghosts, maybe you can wave it through their bodies to scare them down here."

Michelle didn't laugh. She left the room.

Diego shook his head and continued playing with the Ouija board. "She won't be back."

Jennifer laughed.

"She's been shaking in her shoes since she walked in the door," Diego said. "But I guess that's the whole point. What fun is a haunted house if you aren't scared, right?"

"She's really worked up," Jennifer said with a concerned expression.

"Just a ghost newbie. Hasn't done anything like this before."

"And you're an expert?" Jennifer grinned.

"At least I know how to work this." The planchette moved beneath their fingertips, forming incomprehensible words at first, then making out a few obscene ones next, stopping after each one to laugh hysterically and take another drink. They continued for several minutes, with each new word more absurd than the one before, until the final letter of one word appeared within the planchette's hole. *Truth.*

Diego stopped and considered the word they had formed. "What the hell? Where did *that* come from?"

"Nobody wrote it, Diego. It just happens naturally."

"Bullshit. None of this happens naturally. It's just an enter-taining toy. I made all the words appear just now, except... that last one. You do that?"

Jennifer shook her head with a straight face. "Not me."

"You're pranking me now." Diego glared at her suspiciously.

"No." She looked toward the door. "They're awfully quiet up there."

Diego shrugged. "It doesn't matter."

"Sure it does." She leaned toward the door and shouted, "Michelle?" Her voice echoed up the stairs. Nobody answered her.

But something else hung in the air within the moment's silence, a soft whisper in the distance as if someone were gossiping about them from behind the wall.

A chill shot up Diego's neck and bristled the back of his hair. The whispering continued, even as he met Jennifer's gaze. He could tell by the look in her eyes that she'd heard the same thing. He lurched to stand, knocking the Ouija board and planchette across the table, then circled around and hurried out toward the stairway.

"What's going on?" Jennifer asked, her voice tight and weak. "I... think we should go."

Diego knew what she meant. Not to go upstairs, but instead to leave the house, and not in an hour, after exploring the source of the sounds, but *right then*, that minute.

"We will." Diego charged up the stairs with Jennifer following him, calling out Sterling and Michelle's name. The hell with it. They would tease him for being scared, so caught up in the moment that he'd forgotten it might be just a practical joke and his friends would be waiting up there somewhere ready to jump out and humiliate him with a good laugh.

"That's fine," he mumbled along the way. "We'll all have a good long laugh and a few more drinks. That sounds like a nice, fun evening."

But that voice he'd heard... so *real*, as real as his heart pounding now in his chest. This wasn't just being scared anymore, this was terror. He'd never felt such panic in his life. He had to get Sterling and Michelle out of there. Get them all out of there.

"Sterling... Michelle..." he called out.

Still no answer as he searched through each room for them, finally approaching the doorway to the room at the end of the hall. There was no answer as he stepped past another damn mirror hanging in the hallway, as if anyone needed to see themselves every five minutes. And still no answer as he got to the bedroom and saw them.

Michelle stood over Sterling as he lay sprawled out on the floor, covered in blood with his eyes wide open. It didn't look real at first, with Sterling's shredded clothes and makeup obscuring the reality of what had happened. But fresh blood oozed from Sterling's wound where the cake knife had struck him near his heart. His mouth gaped as if she'd thrust it into him a moment before a scream had escaped his throat.

She didn't seem to notice them when they first arrived in the room. Her stare was fixed on Sterling's lifeless body while her hands extended toward him, facing up, as if waiting to embrace him. Blood had spattered over her arms and chest.

Jennifer screamed.

Michelle turned slowly to face them, staring at her hands in confusion and shock. "I... I don't know why I did that."

I t was hard to believe.

Finn hadn't just taken them on a simple beach vacation. That would have been more than enough. Instead, he had flown them all the way to Mexico, then rented a sleek car and booked them into a one-bedroom villa that Emmie and Sarah would share during their stay. The sprawling slice of paradise was larger than the bottom floor of her house, it seemed. And she couldn't help wondering how much all of that had cost him.

After they'd arrived, thankfully, he'd gone to his room, a white Spanish-colonial villa across the patio from theirs, and let them settle in. Sarah had gasped at all the amenities—a robe and slippers, complimentary shampoos, oils and creams in glass jars, an exotic fruit basket, an enormous walk-in closet and even more enormous marble bathroom. Emmie had curiously turned on the crystal lamp next to her side of a bed and read about all the activities available in the hotel and in Cabo San Lucas.

"Did you know that Jennifer Aniston stays here?" she had asked Sarah. "How much do you think Finn makes as a contributing editor, anyway?"

Sarah looked up from her open suitcase with a big grin. "I know, right?" She walked over and sat on the edge of the bed.

"It's weird, isn't it, when we still discover things about each other that we didn't know? Feels like I've always known the two of you."

Emmie opened her mouth to agree with her friend, although the words slipped away when Finn's whistle told them he was waiting for them outside. He had promised to have them on the beach before sunset. The three of them trooped down a series of sunbaked steps to a private inlet featuring the dark blue waters of the Pacific, sunbeds on the sand and dramatic, desertic rock formations to the side—shielding them from the "lower class," probably.

And they had pretty much lived like royalty the past few days. It was amazing to be away from the grim December weather of Minnesota and in the clear, golden air of Baja California instead. But she remembered with a shudder that their flight to the frozen tundra of the north and reality would leave tomorrow morning.

It all would have been heavenly, if only Emmie had managed to stop looking at her phone in disbelief, wondering why she wasn't getting any calls or emails requesting her freelance design services. Her freelance income had never reached that of a regular full-time job, but lately it had dropped off to where she wondered if her phone was broken.

She was checking her messages again when Sarah's squeal filled the air and Emmie looked up to find her friends in the water together.

Sarah must have just fallen from Finn's shoulders backwards into the sea. She emerged laughing and pushing back her hair, and he didn't lose the opportunity to keep her afloat with one arm around her. Oh, the old excuse of the water, "I need to help you here," so that a naked arm could go around a naked waist. And Sarah looked comfortable in his embrace.

Good for you, girl. Have some fun.

But it was more than fun, wasn't it? They were falling in love.

The thought gave Emmie a pang high in her stomach.

The attraction between them had grown slowly but surely, and in the week they had been there, it had taken a leap and a bound.

In that week, both had changed.

For one, after two days when Sarah had worn a modest one-piece swimsuit worthy of the Olympic team, she had finally appeared at dinner wearing a white halter dress that performed a miracle: It made Finn stop talking in the middle of a sentence.

Emmie looked in the same direction of his mesmerized gaze and saw Sarah approach, and the thought occurred to her: *Sarah's beautiful.*

She had always thought her friend pretty, with her small features and big eyes, but now she was something else. Tanned, wearing gold hoops she had bought in town, the purple ends of her hair tucked in a bun, the dress showing off her figure—Sarah was breathtaking.

And she had taken Finn's breath away. He stood and waited for her to sit, and Sarah didn't call him silly or make any jokes. She only blushed. Another miracle: Finn obviously didn't remember (or care) what he and Emmie had been talking about. He kept throwing looks at Sarah all night; looks that lingered, too.

Also, for a guy who was careful never to go beyond a couple of glasses of anything, he drank a bit too much. Trying to build up courage?

He walked them up the steps quietly and waited until they got into their room as if some predator—or ghoul—could come and eat them. Finn had grown quiet and even solemn, and that must mean something big.

Sarah hadn't said anything either. She had just wished Emmie good night when they were in bed, and then she had fallen asleep smiling.

Who falls asleep smiling? Only children—and Sarah.

Now barefoot servers clad in white shirts and Bermuda shorts were preparing the beach, as they did every afternoon, which meant that soon it would be time for sunset drinks on the shore, a ritual they had observed every day so far. The staff smoothed the sand with brooms and straightened the sun beds, all set at a fair distance from each other so different groups or couples in this exclusive environment didn't bother each other. They brought floating candles for her side table and a vase of the same hot-pink flower that surrounded their villa.

Emmie lay in the sunbed and looked at the two empty places next to her.

She had thought it would be different. That was the truth. She had thought that Sarah and Finn would spend a lot of time by her side. Her sunbed would be in the middle, between them, and they would talk, laugh, tease each other. They would explore those rocks and caves nearby, go to town for food adventures and shopping, sleep in hammocks.

They had done all that. But often in the last four days, the beds to her right had sat empty.

She looked at her phone again, this time at the image gallery. She had taken photos of her friends, and now she scrolled through them for proof she didn't need. There was Finn, looking handsome in a white linen shirt and jeans and smiling at Sarah; she glowed as she smiled back at him, a flower he had just given her stuck behind her ear. There they were, visiting churches, riding horses, even dancing.

To be fair, it *was* Emmie's phone, and she had taken the photos, so it made sense that she wasn't in them, but Sarah had also stopped doing the natural thing: grabbing Emmie's phone to take pictures of her, too. And Finn had stopped bothering to take pictures of the two women. Or a selfie with the three of them huddled together.

She had to go back several days to find pictures of her with them.

The night before they had walked on the beach, and the air had been fragrant and deliciously cool, but also heavy with things that were not happening between her friends because Emmie was there.

They must have been longing for her to scram... and she didn't.

She looked at them again, with their joyous, wet faces glimmering in the sun, their cheeks almost touching as they floated. When they looked at each other, Emmie laughed out loud.

They aren't falling in love, fool. They're in love already.

You are the third wheel.

You are stopping their happiness. Keeping them from each other.

They want each other, not you.

Tears sprang to Emmie's eyes as she chided herself for being a self-pitying and melodramatic idiot. *What if they like each other? Isn't that great? Two people you love, finding happiness?*

No, no, no. We were supposed to all be together. The three of us. A team.

Her mind went into overdrive.

Sarah will go live with Finn in Caine House, and I will be alone. Not even Alice is there anymore. I will see them less and less, just like here.

They will be too busy loving each other to care about ghosts or about anything.

And as if on cue, almost in front of her, someone in the water began to splash incessantly, bobbing up and down. The sea was flat here, but there was still a lifeguard staring out from his wooden tower. But he wasn't charging into the water to save the drowning person.

What the hell?

There were no other guests on sunbeds or on shore, and none of the staff seemed to notice.

Emmie's heart sank. It was another lost spirit, caught in the eternal loop of drowning, with no way to move on unless someone like her rescued their soul, or until the spirit accepted death and moved on without help.

An agony spread through her, seeing that desperate

drowning spirit. She glanced at her friends, but they hadn't looked her way in ages. And she had had a couple of mai tais before, so perhaps it wasn't the best idea to swim out to the spirit.

Sarah should be here to do this with me.

More splashing and pleading; it would drive her crazy. It was a man, and wearing a bathing cap. The event must have happened decades ago.

The man cried in a hoarse voice, but Sarah's laugh drowned his pleas.

It was too much. Emmie rose from the sunbed and walked with purpose to the water. *I'll do it alone. I can do it.*

Emmie moved out into the water and swam toward the struggling spirit. She could hear him calling out a name in Spanish, which faded and rose with the waves that crashed against her face.

She called to him and their eyes met briefly. So much pain in that desperate stare.

After reaching him, she touched his hand, feeling the icy fingers grip her wrist.

But he sank suddenly, pulling her down with him. She hadn't had time to catch a full breath and his grasp dug into her flesh. Within the murky silence, she struggled to free herself, pushing and kicking him away. Nothing else she could do. No way to help him beneath the waves.

She broke free after twisting sideways, then dashed toward the surface again, just as she reached the last of her shallow breath.

Gasping for air after breaking through above the waves, she waited for him to resurface. Maybe she could still lead him over toward Sarah, and her friend could help to release him from his agony.

But after a few minutes, it was clear that he wasn't going to come up again. She headed back to shore.

Out of breath and with her wrist aching where the man had

gripped her, she climbed out of the water and returned to her spot on the beach.

"Would you like some drinks now, or will you wait for your friends?" the very polite server asked her in good English.

She composed her face and took a couple of breaths before turning with a smile to say, "I'll wait for them."

"Sure," the man said, and moved away silently.

Emmie fell on the bed, exhausted and frustrated. Where had the ghost gone? Would it return? And why wasn't Sarah with her, so they could help the poor spirit?

Why wasn't Sarah ever with her now?

Bitterness swelled in her chest. *Enjoy Finn, girl, before he starts staring at someone else.*

Her phone rang just then, startling her. She grabbed it with cold, wet fingers and glanced at the notification that popped up on her screen. A Minnesota number, although she didn't recognize it. She let the call ring until her voicemail kicked in. Almost certainly a telemarketer or someone trying to sell her a car warranty or urging her to get her computer cleaned of viruses for the ultra-low price of only ninety-nine dollars. She would lose it if a telemarketer dared to bother her at that moment. And if it was anything to do with her freelance business, she would call them back after listening to the message.

Finn and Sarah were returning now—the golden couple, their arms almost touching as they walked together in her direction, too engrossed in their talk to look at Emmie. They were like an ad for the destination: *Come to Cabo San Lucas and be this beautiful and in love!*

Still, why had she thought that Finn would play with Sarah's feelings? Why was she being so cynical and bitter about her friends? She was happy for them—really. Really, she was.

But the situation now reminded her of her days in Green Hills as a teenager, spending an afternoon at the lake with her friends but feeling so far out of place. The odd woman out.

Odd. Maybe she could put that one word on her gravestone

to sum up her life. She pondered that thought for a moment—but all three of them were odd, weren't they? A triangle of oddness.

Her phone rang again, making her start once more. It was the same number; maybe an urgent call for freelance work? She couldn't take the chance to ignore it, so she answered.

"Hello?" Her body tensed, waiting for the unmistakable slick pitch of a salesperson to begin.

"Emmie? Emmie Rose Fisher?"

"Yes?" Hearing her full name jarred her a little, but she kept quiet.

"This is Jason Reeves. I don't know if you remember me?"

Jason Reeves? Didn't ring a bell. "Not really," she said warily.

"Well, we knew each other, ages ago."

"How did you get my number?" she said, not really believing him.

"Thing is, I read the story online, about how you helped track down and stop the serial killers Grace Hyde and Zelda Hyde."

Oh, one of those people. Another ghost enthusiast. She prepared herself to cut the conversation short, but he barreled on.

"I'm really interested in talking with you about a job."

Job. She moved her ear closer to the phone. "Okay…"

"An opportunity, I mean. And it would be dealing with something you can do. Something of a psychic nature."

Her heart sank. *Oh, boy. No. Just a hard no.* "I'm sorry," she said in a final tone. "I don't work with stuff like that."

"But the article—"

"Yeah, a sensationalist newspaper inventing stuff for readers who like that sort of thing. Listen, whatever you read is just an exaggeration. I'm a graphic designer; if you need something like that, I'm happy to oblige."

"Won't you even listen to what the job is?"

She groaned. *If not a telemarketer, then obviously trained by one.* "Nope. Bye, and don't call again."

She hung up and frowned. Her stomach soured, and the pleasant buzz from the mai tais was fading fast. Did she know a Jason? When? Reeves? Did she know a Reeves family?

Sarah and Finn were getting closer, and she looked down. Finn would get all curious, and she wasn't in the mood for questions.

The smile she offered her friends was overly bright, which made both stop in their tracks.

"What's wrong?" Sarah hurried to Emmie.

"Is it that obvious?" Emmie asked them.

"Something's bothering you. Did you see a ghost?" Finn asked.

"Well, as a matter of fact—" She motioned toward the sea. "—there was one right there. A poor man, drowning for eternity. And I tried to get to him, but then he was gone."

Sarah looked at the sea, shielding her eyes against the glare of the sun shimmering off the water. "Where?"

"He's gone, I said."

Finn frowned down at her, and Sarah turned, a little bewildered.

"What's with the bad mood?" Finn asked.

Emmie shook her head. "Wet my hair for nothing, and now I'm cold." They were still looking at her. "And didn't even help the poor ghost."

"Maybe he'll come back before we leave," Sarah said hopefully, squeezing in beside Emmie on her huge sunbed.

Her friend's bare arm pressed against her own and it warmed her in every way. *I'm a jealous old lunatic,* Emmie told herself.

Finn called out in Spanish to a passing server. The server turned back with a confused and slightly alarmed expression, met Emmie's gaze, then hurried away.

"What was that all about?" Emmie asked.

Finn grinned and translated, *"We need to drink immediately. The lady is very crazy."*

Emmie giggled. "Idiot."

He dropped onto the end of her sunbed, inches from her feet. For a moment, they were together, the three of them. She tried to pause the moment in her mind. *This* is what she'd wanted all along. It was nice, and she hoped the bed would hold up.

"Are you mad that we get a big dose of reality tomorrow?" Sarah asked.

"Yes," Emmie growled.

She leaned her head back to soak up the fading rays of their last golden sunset while Finn squeezed one of her feet absentmindedly and watched the water.

"Though you'll have it worse than me, at the hospital," she told Sarah.

"All fairytales end," Sarah said, placing her chin on her knees.

"They don't have to," Finn said slowly, but he didn't look back at them.

Emmie's phone rang again, and she held it up with a groan. Him.

"Something *is* bothering you." Finn patted her foot.

"Who is it?" Sarah asked.

She muted the call, but this time she went into the phone's settings and blocked that number from calling her.

Bye, whatever Jason you are from my miserable past. "I have no idea, and I don't care. Where's that server?"

❧ 3 ❧

Emmie's phone rang again while she was waiting to pick up her bags from the carousel at the airport in Minneapolis. A different number this time, and she agonized whether or not to answer it. Maybe it was a prospective client offering her a job, something she desperately needed, but she also didn't want to give Jason another chance to speak. Her thumb hovered over the phone's screen until it stopped ringing, and she slipped it back in her pocket. Clients always left a voicemail anyway.

Finn and Sarah had stepped away for a short time to grab a coffee, but she spotted them coming toward her a moment later, sipping their drinks and seemingly lost in their conversation, although Finn was doing all the talking.

Emmie met Sarah's gaze when they arrived and they shared a knowing smile as if reading the other's mind—yes, Finn was never short on words.

The carousel started turning and the exhausted passengers closed in around them as the bags started flowing down the conveyor. After several minutes, there was still no sign of their bags.

Finn led them away from the crowd and staked out a spot along the conveyor's less populated corner, not too far from where the luggage dropped. He sipped his coffee and smiled pleasantly at Emmie as if everything in the world were beautiful. Sarah's expression mirrored his.

Emmie turned her attention back to locating their bags. Dozens of nearly identical suitcases crowded the conveyor now, even as the other passengers pulled them off as fast as they dropped, and after a few false sightings, she considered circling the carousel. Someone else might have lifted them off on the other side.

Before she could step away from her friends, her phone rang again. She groaned. "Just give up already."

"Who is it?" Sarah asked.

Emmie glanced at the screen and silenced it at the same time. Same number, and they had left a voicemail from the previous call.

Sarah approached her. "Could it be a job?"

"It's some Jason guy." Emmie powered off her phone, then slipped it back into her pocket. But whether it was a client, a spammer or Jason, she would sort through the voicemails later. The last thing she wanted now was someone pressuring her.

Finn grinned. "A guy you met in Cabo San Lucas?"

Emmie smirked, although she was in no mood for jokes. "I wish. I don't know him, but he keeps calling."

"Wrong number?" Sarah asked.

"No, he knows who I am."

"What does he want?" Sarah asked.

"He wants to hire me."

"So, what's the problem?" Finn's face lit up. "What's so bad about that?"

"It's for a psychic job."

"Psychic, like what?" Finn asked. "Pick some winning horses at the track? If you've got that skill, please let me know." He sipped his coffee.

"I wish I could pick horses, Finn." Emmie's frown deepened. "I really do. But I'm not going to listen to the message."

"Why not?" Finn asked. "Maybe it's something interesting?"

She met Finn's curious gaze. "Because I'm not interested in making money off tragedies. And I don't even know who this person is. He said his name is Jason Reeves, and that he knows me from a long time ago. Maybe someone I went to high school with?" She turned to Sarah. "Does that name ring a bell?"

Sarah shook her head. "No Jasons in our class."

"Don't you think you should hear what he's got to say, at least?" Finn asked. He took a deeper sip of his coffee.

"What's the point?" Emmie continued searching for their suitcases. "I won't take the job, no matter what it is. That's not the reason I do this. Not for profit or fame. It's the wrong thing to do."

Sarah nodded. "You're probably right, but what if he's desperate for help?"

Emmie frowned and mumbled, "Where did he get my number, anyway?"

"Not too difficult to find your number online." Finn moved up beside Sarah. "And if he says he knew you..."

Their bags finally dropped onto the carousel and they waited in silence as the luggage circled around to them. Emmie and Sarah stepped forward, but Finn rushed ahead at the last second, handed his coffee to Sarah, then scooped all three bags off the conveyor in rapid succession. Grabbing a luggage cart from a rack nearby, he stacked them and pushed the cart toward the exit.

As they headed out into the parking garage, the freezing late afternoon air chilled Emmie's bare face. The vacation in paradise had definitely ended. Back to reality.

Judging by the cloudy breaths that lingered in the air after each exhalation, she guessed the temperature was around twenty degrees. Not the worst Minnesota weather in December, but certainly not Cabo San Lucas. Luckily, there wasn't much snow on the ground. Only scattered pockets thriving where the sun couldn't reach to melt it, and the road salt had left a white powder over the bare asphalt. December was hit or miss for snow anyway. She was definitely *not* dreaming of a white Christmas this year.

Their conversation on the way home was muted, despite the boost of caffeine at the airport, except for an occasional comment on the weather. It was clear that all of them longed for the silence and tranquility of being home.

Driving through her hometown, Emmie had the sense that something was coming to an end. The streets were mostly empty as they were when the weather became so unbearably cold, but a deep unease rose in her chest.

Turning down the street to her house, she spotted fire trucks and flashing red and blue lights surrounding her house. Her heart sank when she saw John's police car parked at an angle out front as if he had rushed to get there.

"Oh no," Sarah moaned. "What did they find in the house now?"

Emmie didn't answer, but instead gasped when her house came into full view. Hanging House was a smoldering skeleton of its former self.

4

E ven before Emmie stepped out of the car, she could smell the smoke. It was strikingly repulsive—the word toxic came to mind—probably the result of all the old materials the builder had used to construct the house.

Seeing the devastation made her stomach drop. She felt a powerful desire to run in there and rescue her possessions from the charred ruins, but deep down she knew it wouldn't do any good.

Climbing out of the car with the others, she hurried toward the house without heeding the calls from the firefighters and John's voice somewhere beside her. Before she reached the stairs, John grabbed her arm and intercepted her. He hadn't let her put her hand on what remained of the door.

He pulled her back. "I'm sorry, Emmie. I asked the station to call you; they tried many times and couldn't reach you."

Emmie's heart sank further, and she mumbled, "I switched off my phone."

John nodded sympathetically. "Not that it would have made much difference. I've been too busy to call you until now. They did their best to put it out, but they weren't able to save much."

Jason hadn't made all those calls after all. "How bad is it?"

"It's all gone, although I did manage to grab a few things from the back of the house before the flames had spread too far. It must've started up near the front. I'm just guessing, though, since that's where your circuit breaker was in the basement."

Emmie shook her head. "How?"

"We might not know what started it for a while, but seeing as though you were gone, it was probably electrical." John gestured toward the firefighters standing near the truck as two of them held one large hose and continued to spray water onto the smoldering wood near the center. "They all need some time to determine the cause, but the Fire Chief did mention that someone left a rear window open, just a crack near the back of the house. Maybe that had something to do with it."

Emmie gasped. "Oh, my God. I left it open after I'd finished painting the inside of the back door. I meant to close it before we left."

"The Fire Chief also said that there were some electrical cables damaged near the circuit breaker. Looked like something had crawled in and got to them. Maybe a squirrel or a cat? Strange how animals are drawn to electrical cables."

Sarah put her arm around Emmie and pulled her in. "I'm so sorry."

Emmie returned her sympathy. "You lost so many things too."

"But your parents' house, your mementos."

Standing behind them, Finn embraced both. "So sorry, girls. Can't replace the mementos, but we'll figure something out for the rest."

The firefighters switched off the hose even though the smoke still billowed from the blackened shell of her home. They'd smashed the windows out along the front and through the windows of her parents' old bedroom, and she could see that the top of the roof had caved in. Emmie's mind went back to the house as it had been before she'd left for her vacation. Most of her sentimental possessions had been upstairs in her bedroom.

She could picture it all in her mind and longed to see her things again just the way she'd left them.

"Is anything salvageable?" she asked as John approached again.

"I couldn't go upstairs," John said. "But maybe after it's safe we can rummage for things. Something always survives."

Probably not all the photos of her family, her clothes, and many of the books on magic, occult artifacts, and some handwritten diaries from Betty's house. Good thing she hadn't brought everything back here. But the truth was undeniable and shocking: the bulk of her life was now up in flames.

"My laptop!" She gasped.

"Where was it?" John asked.

"In the living room."

He shook his head. "Your homeowner's insurance should help you replace it. They'll rebuild everything."

"It had all my freelance contacts on there."

"Maybe the hardware survived?" Finn suggested.

"Not likely." John patted her arm. "But we'll help you get started again. You too, Sarah."

Start again. Emmie repeated the words in her mind as she squeezed Sarah's hand and stepped away from her friends toward the house, moving around the side to get a better view of the damage. Looking through one window near the kitchen, she could see clearly across to the living room on the other side. Everything was black, and they had left nothing untouched. There were the remnants of her furniture like charred skeletons. It wasn't the house itself that weighed on her, but knowing that the connection to her childhood was gone.

The heat from the smoldering wood warmed her face in the freezing air behind her. The flashing lights from the fire truck glowed eerily through the smoky air within the remains.

She walked around to the back, glancing into the backyard at the hanging tree. Of all things, that had survived. But Sarah's area wasn't any better than the front. She walked up the steps and looked inside the shattered door where the firefighters must have rushed in to contain the blaze. Either that or John had smashed in the door while attempting to save Sarah's things. She had also lost everything—though she had left many of her mementos at her mother's house.

The small living area in Sarah's apartment was just as blackened and thick with the nauseating smell of smoke, although across the floor lay a thick layer of ice, smooth and unblemished, almost beautiful as the lights from the fire truck glistened off the surface. Icicles had formed around the windows, and Sarah's piano was also covered in ice, although it wasn't in such bad shape as everything else in the house. Alice's music box sat on the edge of the piano, seemingly untouched in the destruction, and Emmie longed to step inside and grab it. It wasn't more than ten feet inside the door and it would just take a minute, but she turned away and headed back to the front of the house.

Alice was gone now anyway, so what was the point of her preserving that box when Emmie had almost nothing left of her own?

Returning to her friends, she glanced down at her clothes. They were the last things she owned, together with what was in her suitcase, but they were all summer clothes. How much would it cost to purchase a simple winter wardrobe?

Nobody said anything as she walked over and threw her arms around John.

"It's all gone," she moaned.

"You'll be alright, kiddo," he said. "You always seem to land on your feet. Can you stay with you-know-who tonight?"

Emmie nodded and snorted a laugh despite having to swallow tears. "We can stay with Finn, but there's also the other house."

Hearing his name, Finn stepped closer with Sarah hanging from his arm. "Plenty of room for you in my big old museum."

"You go to your other place now," John urged them. "If there is such a thing as destiny, then the old lady leaving you that place is it." He patted Emmie's shoulder, then Sarah's hand, ignoring

Finn. "We've got everything under control here. I'll pull out anything I can."

"Thank you, John," Emmie said.

"We'll keep in touch. You'll recover. At least you're safe. And that's what matters to me." He kissed her forehead.

Emmie nodded and walked away with Finn and Sarah. She was exhausted and mentally drained now too, but she glanced back over her shoulder one final time before getting into the car. Every ghost within the house had moved on, and it was time for her to do the same.

5

The next morning after breakfast, Emmie couldn't find the
strength to do much else except lie on Finn's couch in the
living room with a pillow over her head and try to clear her mind
of everything that had happened. But the images of the previous
night and the anxiety had kept her awake for half the night.

She just couldn't stop thinking about all the things she had
lost and how she would possibly get back on her feet and move
forward from this. There had to be a silver lining to what had
happened, as she'd been told so many times throughout her life:
perhaps that she was finally free to do whatever she wanted
without the burden of having to take care of the house.

It was strange, but what had happened now felt like liberation. Hanging House had been her home for so many years, but
it had been a burden on her life as well.

And it wasn't like she had lost everything. There were still
many books and unsorted boxes to go through in Betty's house,
along with a cache of knowledge within the piles of papers that
she hadn't even begun to understand. She tried to remember
some of the books that Sarah had been studying in Hanging
House for their particular gifts. Thank God they had been too
lazy to move the whole library there and thank God that Finn

had taken his share of books to Caine House to fill his voracious reading appetite.

See, Em. It's not the end of the world.

Her mood lightened until she looked down at her clothes. Just sweatpants and a gray souvenir T-shirt that she had picked up in a Cabo San Lucas tourist shop on the beach. She was embarrassed now that she hadn't bothered to get dressed yet. They were the same clothes she had worn the previous day, although Finn had taken it upon himself to work through a few loads of laundry the previous night so she and Sarah would at least have clean clothes until they restored their wardrobes.

And how much was that going to cost her? She would have to spend some cash just to have something to wear. Sarah had more savings than Emmie, working as a nurse and living with her mother until she had moved into Hanging House a few months earlier, and her friend might still have some winter clothes at her mother's house to fall back on.

Betty had left behind a wardrobe, but Emmie had discarded most of it since the woman had been smaller than her, favoring a style Emmie couldn't relate to—but maybe she could pick out something. A few cardigans? A jacket?

Emmie started using her phone to search for the cheapest clothing stores and sales nearby when Finn walked in. He looked sleek, with his hair still wet after showering, and the vacation tan added a handsome glow. It was odd to see him wearing a black turtleneck and clean blue jeans after spending their previous week wearing next to nothing.

Emmie turned away a little from him on the couch, hugging the pillow tightly while trying to cover her ratty clothes despite having gotten very comfortable with each other in Mexico. He must have sensed her embarrassment because he smiled sympathetically and looked away.

"Did you sleep down here?" he asked. "Wasn't it warm in your room?"

It was nice to hear him call it "her" room.

"Plenty warm, thanks. Slept like a rock. I came down a while ago." She sat up with a moan as he parked himself on the arm of the sofa and leaned sideways against the back cushion.

"Don't you worry about anything," he said. "You're always welcome to stay here any time."

"Thank you."

He gestured to the television across the room. "Want me to turn it on?"

Emmie shook her head. "I'll get up now."

"No hurry." Finn stood and stepped toward the kitchen. "I'm making breakfast."

"Donuts and orange juice?" Emmie grinned.

Finn smirked. "How did you guess? No, really, I wouldn't do that to you under the circumstances. I'm making pancakes. I heard carbs make people feel better, especially for those whose house burned down."

"Where did you read that?"

"On the Internet, so it must be true."

Emmie looked around. She hadn't heard Sarah's voice all morning, an odd thing for that girl. "Where's Sarah?"

"She slept in late too. I guess we're all still in vacation mode."

"How do you know?" she asked quickly.

"Um... just assuming, I guess." His eyes widened a little and a knowing smile spread across his face, but a knock on the door wiped it off.

"Who could that be?" Emmie asked.

Finn stepped toward it. "Maybe John stopped by to check on you?"

"That would be just like him. Maybe he brought some of my stuff?"

She climbed off the couch and stepped toward Finn, although she couldn't see who'd come as the door blocked her view. It wasn't John, judging by Finn's tone—which tended toward the wary with the police officer—but it was a man's voice. She stopped at the edge of the living room.

Finn peeked around the corner and grinned at Emmie. "Someone here to see you." He glanced down at her pajamas. "Probably should change your clothes."

"Who is it?" she asked.

"For you to find out," Finn said.

An insurance adjuster or someone from the fire department? *I should have known I wouldn't get the day off. Vacation's over, troubles are back.*

While Finn kept the visitor engaged in a lighthearted conversation on the steps to the house, Emmie ran upstairs as fast as she could and changed before hurrying back down to greet whoever it was.

Arriving downstairs a few minutes later, she was confronted by a tall young man wearing dark pants and a full-sized wool coat standing in the entryway engaged in a jovial conversation with Finn. The man's coat was open, revealing an embroidered vest over a white shirt with a mile collar. There were brown beads around what she could see of his neck, and he sported a thin red string around his wrist. He was both exotic and handsome in a rugged way, with prominent cheekbones and a nose that might have been broken at some point but didn't detract from his good looks. His longish black hair and intense almond-shaped eyes seemed Asian, but he could have been from any number of places. He couldn't have been over thirty years old, and his focused stare and tanned skin looked oddly familiar.

"Emmie Rose?" the man asked. As soon as he spoke, she recognized his voice from the phone.

"Jason." She lost her smile. "What are you doing here?"

He wrinkled his nose. "I guess you're not happy to see me."

"Not really. I was pretty clear on the phone that I wasn't interested in your offer."

"I got that, but do you even remember me?"

Emmie studied him for a moment. Someone from her past? High school? California? "Should I?"

"You know Betty Chan, right? Her house is right down the

road. She set up those sessions in Minneapolis, if you remember, with Dr. Albright? The guy who tried to teach us about the exciting world of the supernatural? Turned out it was a lot different than they led us to believe, right?"

He gave a shy smile that was somehow not shy. "My nickname was Joker back then."

Joker! Of course.

Now she remembered him, but he'd been so different back then. Not so... stylish. Ages ago, he'd worn simple t-shirts and blue jeans, and his hair had been short.

His parents were a mixed-race couple. The father was American and the mother Vietnamese. His nationality had stuck with Emmie because she had boldly asked about the woman's hand-embroidered purse. The colorful, flowery designs had caught her eye, and the woman had been all too happy to talk about her heritage.

"My American boy," his mother had said proudly to Emmie while patting his leg as they waited outside Dr. Albright's office.

During that brief visit, she'd learned that his father was a University of Minnesota history professor and his mother was a scholar of Buddhism. Both had shared stories of Southeast Asian culture, and tried to get their son engaged in the conversation, although he couldn't be bothered to look up from the thick, oversized book he was reading.

The conversation with his parents had ended abruptly when Dr. Albright had called them into his office. Behind his parents' back, while leaving the room, Jason had tossed the book at Emmie, hitting her chest with a hard thump. It had knocked her back in her chair, and it had hurt. A lot. And then he'd laughed at her pain, even after Dr. Albright's office door closed between them.

Such a nice American boy. Everything about him stirred her anxiety. Oh, she remembered him, all right.

"I know I was a bit of a bully back then." He held up a hand as if to soothe her. "I know it's not an excuse, but I was in a very bad place at that time, and I wasn't very nice to you, or anyone, for that matter."

More memories flooded back. She hadn't wanted to be scrutinized by any doctor about her gift anyway but he hadn't hesitated to tease her incessantly during any private moments during those visits, pointing out every little awkward thing about her: her ill-fitting clothes, the hairstyle that she had loved at that age because it hung low over her face and she could hide behind it, the black nail polish that she had painted on, mistakenly believing she might control the spirits if she seemed more of a badass.

"Joker, with the card tricks."

"What sort of tricks?" Finn asked.

Jason opened his mouth to answer, so Emmie cut him off. "Cheap mind games, like what I did with Tarot cards when I had that skill as a child. He'd trick gullible kids out of their lunch money by guessing the card in their hand. He *bragged* about it." She nodded. "I remember you. You were an a—"

"Whoa!" He laughed. "No need to go there. Let me explain."

"And I see you're still pushy, *Joker*."

He grimaced. "No one calls me that anymore. Look, Emmie, I know I was a horrible kid back then and I'm very sorry. I hope you don't remember a lot of what happened."

"Only the bad stuff."

"Again, I'm so sorry, but can you just give me five minutes of your time?"

Emmie folded her arms over her chest and frowned. "I'm not doing psychic stuff for money, Joker—Jason."

He pressed his hands together and pleaded, "Five minutes?"

Emmie was a moment away from shutting the door on him when Finn looked at her and gave a subtle motion with his head as if to say, *give the guy a chance.* It *was* Finn's house, after all.

She sighed. "Five minutes."

"That's enough."

Finn led him in and they sat down in the living room. Finn

and Jason sat on the two chairs opposite the coffee table and Emmie sat on the couch, pushing aside the blanket that had warmed and comforted her only minutes earlier.

Emmie still had her arms folded over her chest. "All right. I'm listening."

Jason nodded. "I completely understand your skepticism, but just hear me out. There's a lot of people, families out there, who are hurting after the loss of a loved one when something unexplained happens. They're just looking for answers. These are good people. I'm sure you've run into many people over the years asking for help."

He paused as if waiting for Emmie to respond, but she kept quiet. *He tried appealing to my greed and it didn't work, so now he's appealing to my heart.*

"These are the people I meet all the time because of my occupation. Desperate families seeking help to find someone or just understand what happened after a murder or suicide."

"What *is* your occupation?" Finn asked before Emmie could.

"I spent a lot of time traveling after I got out of college, but I had learned so many things about the world from my parents. They had taught me all about religions, history, languages and cultures, so after I drifted for a few years, I discovered I could act as an interpreter, mostly for Vietnamese, although it isn't called for much, but that led me to find work as a collector of artifacts. I acted as a sort of middleman dealing in occult trade throughout the world. There's a lot of money in it, if you know where to look, but you need to have an eye for it."

The room was silent as he looked from Finn, then to Emmie.

"All of this is... legal?" Finn asked.

"Absolutely. I take meticulous records, pay all my taxes, and get all the proper permits. Nothing hiding in the shadows." He grinned. "Well, except for the occasional ghost."

Emmie didn't smile. "So why would anyone ask you for help with a ghost?"

Jason's face brightened. "That's the interesting part. I meet so many people, some who'll pay good money to acquire relics for museums or for scholarly purposes, or they believe these objects might give them good luck or make them powerful. People with deep pockets. And in the process of connecting these objects with the people who want them, I come across a lot of other people in mourning, desperately seeking answers. They don't know where to turn. They can't go to the police because, as you know, the subject matter of ghosts and possessions is completely ridiculous in most of the world's eyes, but I listen and, if I can, I try to help these people."

"So how do you help them?" Finn asked. "Are you still psychic?"

Jason rolled his head a little. "No... not really. I was throughout my childhood, but not anymore. I think it has mostly faded away now."

"You see ghosts too?"

"No ghosts," he said sharply. "Thank God. My gift was clairvoyance."

"You mean like seeing the future?"

"Not like that. Just great at guessing stuff—a casino's worst nightmare, if I'd developed it." He grinned. "Sometimes I could push my thoughts to someone else. ESP stuff."

"Never worked on me," Emmie said.

Jason looked into her eyes. "Which is why I'm here, really. Your gift is strong. Dr. Albright even said so, and he demanded the same of me. He wanted to study me like a bug under a microscope, like he did with all of us. It's what these people did and do."

"What people?" Finn asked.

Jason shrugged. "That group he's involved with."

Emmie pictured Dr. Albright in her mind. He'd been a fragile, gray-haired old man during her visits with him long ago. His hands shook while transcribing Emmie's words into a notepad he carried around. She couldn't imagine his condition now. "He *is* involved with? He's still alive?"

"So I hear." Jason turned back to Emmie. "But I understand what you went through as a kid."

Emmie groaned. "You don't have a clue what I went through as a kid."

He nodded sympathetically. "If you mean that I added to your misery, I can truly say only that I'm sorry again. My parents were pressuring me, bullying me, to be something more than I was. You were the real deal. They were always comparing us."

Emmie shifted in her seat on the couch and leaned forward as if to stand. "And here you are pressuring me now."

"It's not my intention to pressure anyone. I can get these people the help they need. I understand the occult world and how to go about it. And then I read the story online about you, and I knew it could all come together."

"*Come together,* meaning knowing a psychic who can help people for a hefty check?" Emmie frowned. "Again, we don't solve murders for profit."

"Hear me out. Have you heard of Whisper House?"

"Can't say I have."

"It's a supposedly haunted house in southern Minnesota that goes for short-term rentals. There has been paranormal activity there—like the name says, ghosts whispering and all. And some people like the thrill of staying in it. So a bunch of rich kids decided to throw a Halloween party in Whisper House—a few young couples—and you know how it is; people drink, things get out of hand, and then stuff happens... Except that on this night something really bad happened." He looked from Finn to Emmie and back. "A girl allegedly killed her boyfriend out of nowhere."

"Whoa," Finn said with wide eyes.

Emmie shook her head. "How is that paranormal?"

"And depending on the boyfriend, it might even be justified," Finn said.

"That's the thing." Jason nodded at them. "The girl swears she was possessed by a spirit."

"An evil spirit?" Finn asked curiously. "Let me guess, they used a Ouija board before it happened?"

"Of course." Jason nodded wryly. "But here's where you come in. The owner of the house is devastated by what happened. She believes in spirits, which is why she bought the house, she says. Because she felt good ones there. She certainly doesn't want some sort of devil lurking around."

"Tell her to get a priest," Emmie said.

"Doesn't work that way. Unless you do believe in the devil?" Jason tilted his head at Emmie, and she shook hers. "Anyway, the owner wants the bad spirit out after what happened. She also stays there with her family sometimes, and she's determined that the house should be safe. And, ironically, nobody wants to rent a haunted house with a brand-new ghost tenant."

"She wants to clean house, so to speak," Finn said with a wave of his hand.

Emmie scoffed.

"She just wants you to communicate with the spirits and guide them away," Jason continued, and softened his tone. "Yes, she's wealthy and she'll pay quite a large sum of money for that. Easily what you might earn in several months, and it would be pocket change to her. But most of all, she feels the death is her fault, in a way—and now a house she loved has become sinister to her. She needs to know what happened."

Emmie was silent because she couldn't help thinking about the money. She had lost everything, and even replacing her laptop to do freelance design work was going to mean debt in the short term. And she couldn't rely on Finn's generosity for too long, even knowing that he didn't mind.

"What would I have to do?" she asked. "We don't give clean house certificates. I doubt she'll be able to rent it again."

"Doesn't matter anymore. She wants it for her family again, for her. But she's scared now." Jason scooted forward in his chair. "Just stay in Whisper House for maybe a couple of days, however long it takes, and observe things. Try to communicate with any spirits. If there is anything in the house, you'll feel it. And you'll be able to drive it away. That's it."

"That's it?" Emmie gave a short laugh. "You think it's that easy, do you? Have you got any idea what an evil spirit, as you call it, can do to a psychic? Oh, I guess not. You aren't one."

"Come on," Jason urged. "You've been dealing with them your whole life. You can't get hurt, right?"

"Oh yes, I can."

A heaviness passed through her. Jason didn't know anything. He never had, and the eagerness on his face proved it. He just wanted the middleman's fee, and he knew or cared nothing about what they might go through. She stood.

"Your five minutes are up."

Jason seemed confused.

Of course, you thought you won, didn't you, Joker? Emmie stepped toward the door.

Finn frowned at her, as if asking her not to dismiss the situation so fast; that only irritated her more.

"Not everything is money." She clenched her fists and turned her back on them, leaving the room.

Finn can show him to the door. I want nothing to do with Joker. Not ever.

❧ 6 ❧

S arah had heard a stranger's voice in the house, but by the time she finished getting ready and headed down to see who it was, she'd only found Finn sitting in front of his laptop at the kitchen table with a few books stacked up beside him.

Finn's face almost seemed to glow in the laptop's light, and his eyes sparkled.

So lovely.

He had intense, intelligent eyes. Something she'd noticed soon after meeting him, but now they stirred her on a deeper level as if she were peering into a forbidden level of his being. She paused a moment to watch him and studied the contours of his cheeks and jaw and mouth...

... and how she longed to kiss those lips. The thoughts warmed her face.

The increasing intimacy they'd shared during the vacation hadn't faded, and she hoped it would never fade. Her chest fluttered while stepping toward him.

Would he look over and catch her staring at him? Before he had the chance, she broke the silence.

"Where's Emmie?" she asked.

He glanced up from his laptop with a warm smile, then

gestured toward the door without looking away. "She stepped out for a walk." His gaze locked onto hers for a few thrillingly awkward seconds.

Sorry, Finn, I can't help myself!

Her heart beat faster and she forced herself to look toward the door. "For a walk? It can't be more than thirty degrees out there."

Finn raised his eyebrows with a slight grin. "You didn't hear anything from up there?"

She stepped toward him and her legs weakened. "No, what happened?"

Finn pushed away his laptop and stood. "You want some coffee while we talk about it?"

"Yes, please."

He gestured to the seat next to his laptop. "Me too. I feel like indulging myself at the moment."

She sat in the open chair beside his seat and watched him prepare the coffee in the kitchen. He glanced over at her a couple of times. Each time, her face warmed, even as she tried not to stare.

What's gotten into you, Sarah? You're acting like a teen on a first date. He's going to talk serious now. Don't get all googly-eyed on him.

After serving the coffee and sitting beside her at the table, Finn briefed her on their encounter with Jason Reeves and Emmie's reaction. "I guess she needed to cool down after Jason left. She was pretty upset with him."

Sarah stood and stepped over to the window. Emmie's car was still in the driveway, but there was no sign of her. "How long ago?"

"Ten, fifteen minutes. She couldn't have gotten far. Probably walked over to Betty's house... Oh, I guess I should just call it *her* house now."

Sarah considered calling her friend, but it would be better to talk in person if she was upset. Accepting Jason's offer might be the best option under the circumstances. She put on her jacket and headed out the door.

The winter chill struck her face and bare hands until she climbed into her car. Emmie's house was only a short distance away, but... that wind! *You're not in Cabo San Lucas anymore.*

She drove to Emmie's—and her own—new permanent residence before the car had even warmed up, found the door open and hurried inside.

"I'm in here, Sarah," Emmie answered from one of the bedrooms in the back.

Emmie was sitting alone on the floor in one of the rooms that she had been using to sort through the mountain of books and documents. The stacks of books had filled every corner only a month earlier, but now the bare, scuffed white wall was visible. They had all made a lot of progress since she had inherited everything. Still a lot to do, but at least now it was a lot more organized.

"Did Finn send you over to talk to me?"

"No."

Emmie smiled warmly. "Thank you for coming over."

"Of course." Sarah dropped next to her. "What are you going through today?"

"Pulling up some not-so-great memories." Emmie glanced over the mounds surrounding them, then picked up a photo album and opened it in front of Sarah. She pointed to a photo inside. "Who's this?"

Sarah grinned. The photo was like a school class picture, but with only seven students. They ranged in age from about ten to seventeen. None of them were smiling, but she instantly recognized Emmie's somber face. "My best friend."

Emmie reached over and they hugged for a moment. "You're my best friend too."

They gazed at the photo album again together.

"So who are all those kids?" Sarah asked.

"Most of them I barely remember. One kid... Jason..."

Emmie's finger stopped on a frowning boy. "Can't seem to forget him."

"Is he the guy making that psychics-for-hire offer? Finn told me about it."

Emmie turned to Sarah. "We only knew each other a short time, but... we didn't get along so well."

"You don't think it's a good idea?"

"You do?"

Sarah nodded. "I think it'd be okay. It *would* help us out."

"It just doesn't seem right. Do you think it's right?"

"What we do is so *personal*. But from what I heard, that owner isn't looking to exploit us or anything. She needs our help, and we all have to make a living somehow. It's not like you're cheating her or doing anything unethical."

Emmie was silent for a moment, pushing the photo album aside and picking up another book beside her. She opened it and flipped through several pages before stopping on one page with the headline *Possession*. "I came over here to find this."

Sarah leaned toward it. "A book on spirit possession?"

"All that stuff about the young woman who killed her boyfriend got me thinking. Something doesn't seem right."

"About what?"

"What that girl is saying. The whole possession idea. If that were true, spirits would be possessing us 'mere mortals' all the time. Josephine possessed you for a time."

"Yes."

"But she couldn't control Finn. Had to get to him through seduction. Why not just possess him like she did with you?"

Sarah grinned. "She couldn't penetrate his thick skull?"

"Besides that." Emmie chuckled, then pointed to a page in the book. "Because spirits can't. It makes sense that only psychics can be possessed. After Jason brought up the 'devil made me do it' defense, I remembered I'd read something about possession a while back, and I had to read it again just to make sure I understood it correctly. It's right here. '*No person who isn't psychic can be possessed by a spirit or influenced to engage in actions outside the person's current moral standards.'"*

"So your friend Jason—"

"He's not my friend." Emmie looked into Sarah's eyes for a moment. "Sorry. Not good memories of him. Not one."

"Sorry." Sarah smiled warmly. "Sounds like this guy's return opened an old wound."

"At the worst time, too."

"But maybe his offer is a blessing in disguise? If it was up to me, I'd be fine accepting something like that. We are still helping people, after all, and we can still do the pro bono stuff too. I'm just saying maybe think about it."

"Apparently it's a lot of money." Emmie pointed at the page in the book. "And it got me thinking, that's for sure. If a spirit was possessing that young woman when she killed her boyfriend like they are suggesting, then she'd have some psychic abilities, right?"

"Finn said that Ja—" Sarah paused. "—the *intruder*..."

Emmie grinned.

"... mentioned they were playing with a Ouija board. Wouldn't that open the person to the spiritual world?"

"If they're psychic, I'm almost sure. Ordinary people, no."

"Maybe the girl is psychic. I guess we would need to meet her in person to know that."

Someone knocked at the door and a moment later someone entered the house. Finn's voice called out, "Come out, come out, wherever you are."

"We're in here, Finn." Sarah called out.

Finn stepped into the doorway a moment later and leaned against the frame. "What are you girls up to?"

Emmie gestured at the book in her hand. "Just trying to make sense of what Jason said."

Finn nodded. "Good. I've been doing a little research on him myself. He seems legit, if that helps at all. Stuff checks out. He does have an actual trading business."

Emmie grunted. "I still don't trust him."

"Then maybe we just take a cautious approach with him, but give him the benefit of the doubt? I'm sure you two will be better off after the check clears."

"We?" Emmie asked. "Why, are you sitting this one out?"

"No way, but I'll go as the unpaid intern."

"Absolutely not—" Emmie stopped short and turned toward Sarah. "We'll split the money three ways. That's the only fair way to do it."

Sarah smiled and Finn lifted a hand. "I accept your offer of employment, but you can't argue when I spend the money any way I want, like on another vacation for just the three of us."

"I get the subtle impression that one of us is rich." Emmie nodded and gazed down at the book in her lap. "But like Sarah said, we need to have a conversation with the murderer first. What's her name?"

Without a pause, Finn blurted it out. "Michelle Anderson."

The Minnesota correctional facility where Michelle Anderson was being held had an outer metal fencing around the perimeter of the yard. It was intimidating as they passed through the gated entrance, surrounded by armed security guards who thoroughly searched their car before allowing them to park in the visitor's area.

Finn grumbled, "This isn't really the sort of place I like to visit under any circumstance. Guards always make me feel like I've got something to hide."

"Do you?" Sarah asked with a wry grin.

"Not today. Left it all at home."

"Too late to back out now." Emmie chuckled.

Passing through the metal detectors inside the main door, they entered a small waiting room a little further down. There were several families huddled with solemn expressions. But one face immediately caught Emmie's eye.

Jason.

Emmie's heart skipped a beat. They had agreed to meet him there, so it wasn't a surprise, but she hadn't gotten used to his presence yet either.

Jason stood and stepped toward them with a polite, modest smile. "I'm looking forward to working with all of you."

Emmie met his gaze. "We'll see how it goes."

Finn stepped over and shook Jason's hand. "You're still welcome to join us at the house."

"Like I said, I can't." Jason smoothed his leather jacket. "Though I'll be in the area for a few days."

"To keep an eye on us?" Emmie asked pointedly. "Make sure we do our job?"

Jason laughed. "I'm just the deal's facilitator. I have no doubt you'll do a great job whether I'm here or not. Your reputation precedes you. It's just some business matters I have to take care of, some transactions."

Sarah gestured to the main desk at the far side of the room. "We should get checked in."

Jason stepped toward Sarah, eyeing her face and clothes. He held out his hand. "We haven't met."

They shook hands. Sarah was polite as always. "I'm Sarah."

"Jason Reeves. And what's your skill?" Jason grinned with a hint of audacity, while holding Sarah's hand a little too long.

"Empath," Sarah answered, pulling her hand away.

"Nice to meet you. I already put your names on the list. They'll call us when we're allowed into the visiting area." Jason looked at Emmie, then at Sarah. "It's just the two of you going in to see Michelle, right? Like I told Finn earlier, they limit the number of friends who can enter."

Finn nodded. "Just them."

Emmie eyed Jason's outfit. A more rustic style today: faded blue jeans and a deep red sweatshirt beneath a black leather jacket. A stark contrast to his previous outfit. Nothing that stood out from everyone else, except for his gold necklace strung through a hole in the center of a small gold coin. There was a Chinese symbol etched into its face.

Finn gestured to the coin. "Is that Taoist?"

Jason removed it and handed it to Finn. "You know your stuff. Buddhist talisman to protect me from evil spirits. Got it in China. Ever been there?"

"Twice. I'd love to go back someday."

"I'll let you know when I plan my next trip there. My mom's sister has a place right outside Beijing. With your occult knowledge, you'd do well with the crowd I hang with."

Finn's face lit up. "We should talk about that." He studied the necklace for a few more seconds, then handed it back to Jason. "Exquisite."

"Over a thousand years old."

Finn nodded slowly. "Can you stick around for a bit? I'd like to talk more about your experiences overseas. I travel occasionally too."

Sarah scoffed. "All the time."

Jason glanced at Sarah, then back to Finn while grinning knowingly. "I'm sure it's not beaches and palm trees you want to talk about, judging by what you've told me about your background. I've got *lots* of stories to tell—the occult attracts all sorts of wild characters—and I'm just getting started. Sure, I can chat for a while."

A guard walked over a moment later with his hands resting on his belt. He glanced at each of them, his face stern and cold. "Which two of you are here to see Michelle Anderson?"

Emmie stepped forward and gestured to Sarah. "I am, and my friend."

"Follow me."

Another guard checked their identification while leading them into a larger room with dozens of circular white tables with four white stools attached to the table with one seat on each side. The drab, cold environment resembled a school cafeteria except for the barred windows and a few guards standing near the doors. Cameras looked down on them from every angle, no doubt to make sure that visitors and inmates didn't pass anything along to each other.

Only a few seconds after sitting down at one of the tables, a young woman stepped toward them from across the room. With her matted brown hair, blue eyes and a ponytail, she looked as if she belonged in a college classroom rather than an orange jumpsuit. She met Emmie's gaze, although there was no happiness at the moment of recognition.

She stood at the edge of the table and put on a brave face while she introduced herself. "I'm Michelle Anderson. Are you the psychics?"

Emmie shot a glance at Sarah, then back to Michelle. "How did you know that?"

Michelle sat down, glancing over her shoulder in both directions. "Your friend, Jason, told me you were. Isn't that true?"

So that's why Michelle had so readily agreed to talk about the case with complete strangers. Jason had schmoozed her.

"Yes," Sarah said. "It's true. I'm Sarah and this is Emmie."

Michelle looked relieved. "Oh, thank God. I wasn't sure I should accept the invitation at first—I mean, you're not the first *concerned* person to request an interview—but he said you were the best. I need to talk to someone who *understands*."

Emmie nodded sympathetically. "I'm not sure there's much we can do. We want to hear your story..."

"That's all I ask." Her eyes watered a little as she threw a glance toward one of the guards nearby who was watching them. She twirled her hair as she spoke. "My parents won't speak to me, my friends are gone, and I'm all alone in here. But first, listen, I know this is all about what happened at the house, but I swear, I love Sterling with all my heart, even to this day. I wouldn't have wanted anything to happen to him. I need you to believe that."

Emmie nodded. "We do believe you."

"And I could never do anything like that to him..." Michelle stared into empty space. "Never."

"But you did, right?"

Her expression saddened. "Yes. Everyone knows it, even me,

but it's crazy because I would never do such a thing. We were so much in love, and then I kind of lost it for a minute. Like I became a completely different person. I know that sounds crazy."

Sarah shook her head. "Not to us, it doesn't."

She glanced at each of their faces. "I'm not crazy. Well, I felt like I was after it was over. What could've caused me to do that?" The pain erupted on her face and she held back tears before continuing. "The doctors say I don't have any personality disorders. But it was a haunted house, so maybe something evil possessed me. Is that possible? Can you explain how something like this can happen to me?"

"We'll try." Emmie wanted to reach out and comfort the girl, but held back with all the cameras watching them. "What happened before the murder?"

She nodded and took a deep breath. "I don't know. I really don't know. It was all just so strange and everything was going fine because we were goofing around on Halloween night, you know, and we wanted to do something really fun, so we were trying to stir things up with a Ouija board. It was Diego's idea. Maybe we conjured up a demon or something. We didn't think it would actually work."

"You tried to talk with spirits?" Emmie asked.

She nodded. "It's a haunted house. That was the whole reason we were there. So after messing with the Ouija board for a while, we started hearing noises from upstairs."

"Did you see any ghosts?" Emmie asked.

She shook her head. "No. But Sterling went to check on it. He didn't come back."

"And then you went up there to check on him?" Sarah asked.

"Yes. I called to him, but he didn't answer, so I went up there thinking he might be playing around. It scared me a little, but we were having a lot of fun and I thought he might want a little alone time with me, if you know what I mean. I loved my

boyfriend. He was everything to me. I would have married him."
Her eyes watered.

"Were you angry with him?" Emmie asked.

"About what?"

"Anything."

She shook her head vehemently. "No, not at all. We were
having so much fun."

"Did you sense that there might be a spirit in the room with
you?" Sarah asked. "Any shadows moving or anything that resembled a figure?"

She shook her head again. "Nothing like that, but Diego was
trying to do something like that. He was really pushing the
whole Whisper House story to get us freaked out."

"I'm assuming you had alcohol at the party?" Sarah asked.

"We weren't drunk." Michelle frowned. "No drugs either, if
that's what you're thinking. Just friends goofing around, having
fun and getting along just fine, and nobody was mad at nobody.
But I think Diego and Jennifer really wanted to see ghosts that
day. Real ghosts. Maybe they did something to cause this."

"What sort of noise did you hear upstairs earlier before this?"
Emmie asked.

"Just like a thump or someone bumping into something."

"Did your friends hear these noises too?"

Michelle nodded. "Yeah, we all heard that..." Her voice
trailed off, and her eyes glazed over. "So strange."

"Do you believe in ghosts?" Sarah asked.

Michelle shuddered, almost as if awaken from a brief nap.
"What? Yes. I suppose so."

"What did the noises sound like?"

"Like whispering. I guess that's where the house got its
name."

Emmie leaned forward. "These whispering noises—did they
sound like they were trying to tell you anything in particular?"

Michelle furrowed her brows and stared down at the table.
"It was so soft, like someone whispering secrets about you from

across the room. It wasn't like they were right next to me or anything, but I didn't get the feeling that I was safe. Whether it was a demon or a ghost, I don't know, but I didn't want to stay there anymore after that."

"What did you do?"

"What was I *supposed* to do? It was Halloween, so we got freaked out and laughed about it. The house was creepy the whole time, but it wasn't until Sterling got up and went to check out the noises..."

Emmie nodded solemnly. "What was he doing when you saw him?"

Michelle's eyes fixed on one spot on the table as she pulled on a lock of her hair. "I went over all that with my lawyer. Sterling wasn't trying to hurt me or anything. He was just looking through the closets for the source of the noise we'd heard, and when he turned around I..." She cringed and tears streamed down her cheeks. "I don't know why—I really don't. But something came over me. I couldn't stop it, not at all, and it was like someone else had taken over, as crazy as that might sound."

"Did you hear anyone telling you to do it at that time?" Sarah asked. "Voices inside your head?"

"No, nothing like that. I was drinking, but not *that* drunk, just like I get after a couple of beers, except..." She closed her mouth, wiped away her tears, and glanced back at the guard nearest the table.

They waited for her to continue.

Michelle wiped away another tear with the back of her hand and sniffed. "We should have never ever visited that house. Something's going on in there, I'm sure of it, and I know whatever did that to me is still in there."

Sarah took the young woman's hand. "We'll do everything we can to help you."

"Maybe none of what I said makes sense, but I'll tell you one thing." Michelle stared into Emmie's eyes. "The ghost in that house is *you*."

❧ 8 ❧

Sarah drove the rest of the way to Whisper House. Emmie took the break to enjoy the scenery of St. Lombard from the passenger seat. They hadn't escaped the city yet, but the heavy traffic was behind them.

Emmie glanced over her shoulder at Finn, who'd been silent for several minutes with his gaze locked on his laptop screen. No doubt he was deep into his research.

"Anything yet?" Emmie asked.

"I'm still looking. Not all that much information that might be useful on Audrey's site. No talk of the murder. Of course she wouldn't exactly mention a murder. There is the usual short spiel about the house and its history. I guess she wants to have a presence online but not get too many guests, as Jason said. Just people rich enough to leave a big deposit in case they spoil anything."

The silence lasted for almost a minute. "That's all you're going to tell us?"

Finn paused to look up. "You could probably look it up on your phone, you know."

Emmie held up her hand defensively. "You usually love to do

the briefing. Just trying to find out about this place before we get there."

"You'll have the information if you let me read." He went silent again, his eyes scanning the screen.

Sarah glanced over at Emmie and whispered in a loud, comical voice, "He hasn't had his daily fix of information yet."

Emmie laughed.

Finn looked up at Sarah. "What is this? A mutiny against me?"

She grinned with her eyes still on the road. "We're just getting started, Captain."

Finn groaned and took a deep breath as if to reset the conversation. "There's a lot of stuff here, but not so much of it is relevant. It's more of a step-by-step of all the renovations she did on the house to bring it back to its former glory. And along the way, mixed in, are all little nuggets of information that might turn out useful."

"I guess not enough to help us deal with whatever is out there..." Emmie said.

Finn gasped. "Good thing she's paying us instead of vice versa. The place would set us back twelve hundred bucks per night."

"For the whole house?"

"Per person."

"What?" Sarah looked back at Finn suddenly and the car lurched to the side.

Emmie grabbed the steering wheel, but Sarah took over again, laughing.

"I got it. Sorry about that." She glanced at Finn in the rearview mirror. "That's more than our stay in Mexico, right Finn?"

"A gentleman doesn't speak of money," Finn said with a grin, "but it looks like Whisper House is strictly for rich people looking for thrills. Doesn't sound like she has the intention of opening it to the general public. The thing is, the reviews for the house all talk about the delightful frights, adrenaline, a lovely time by Lake Baldwin in the summer with your own pure, true Victorian ambience—but no one wrote anything like, *and it was fun when my friend went berserk and killed someone.*"

"So it doesn't sound like anyone else had a bad experience," Emmie said.

"Not at all. Just typical vacation jargon in most of the reviews."

"What does it say about the history of the house?" Sarah asked. "The origin of the ghost stories?"

"Looks like a rich widow named Joan Carter built it in 1889. Some stuff on her being an artistic free spirit, liked to paint and sculpt and whatnot. Seems to have dabbled in a bit of everything. She invited artists into her home and held séances there, according to this. I just looked up Joan through my usual channels, but there is next to no information going back that far. At least nothing that was digitized. If Audrey doesn't enlighten us, there might be handwritten records at city hall here, or at a local church or the library."

"Funny that the site casually mentions her being into séances."

"And strange that she did it all the way out here in the boondocks. I did find a mention of Joan Carter in connection to the *Banner of Light*. That's an old Spiritualist newspaper from Boston. She was credited as a donor and supporter, so she might have been from there originally. I think the Spiritualists started in rural New York, but by Joan's time they were thriving in the big cities, and most of the patrons were rich women."

"What else?" Emmie asked.

Finn grunted. "There's not much history on the website about the spooky aspects of the house. Audrey will probably know a lot more when we talk with her. But it does say that she bought the house fifteen years ago and calls it 'a labor of love.'"

Emmie laughed once. "Yeah, love at twelve hundred bucks per night."

Sarah glanced back again. "I wonder who it belonged to between Joan's death and when Audrey bought it. That's a long time."

"I already looked up a little information on the address," Finn said. "It changed over to a family named Dyer, and a Dyer sold it to Audrey. Don't know anything else about them, though."

Emmie watched out the window as the urban sprawl gave way to forests and fields. Only the pine trees held volume in the barren winter landscape, but most of the trees were seemingly lifeless shells of their summer glory. It was hard to believe that such a drastic transformation occurred every year, and that those dead trees rose from the grave every spring in timeless cycles of birth and death. "Aren't they lovely?"

"I would trade those woods for Cabo San Lucas any day," Sarah mumbled.

Emmie laughed. "Of course. I would too, but there's just something about the forest that draws me in."

"You and Little Red Riding Hood," Finn said.

"And here we are on our way to grandmother's house," Sarah added.

"My, you have such big teeth, Grandma."

"Better to bite off your head after whispering in your ear, my dear," Emmie said.

They laughed until Sarah lost her smile and pointed ahead. "There it is. Whisper House."

9

I t was like a snow palace, white and glistening in the sun: a white Victorian two-story house with a square tower rising to a third level near the center, and black old-style shutters flanking every window. A couple of sprawling oak trees in the front yard shrouded one side of the house, and a thin blanket of snow covered the lawn and roof. Despite the sun beaming down through a clear sky, the frigid temperature had prevented the snow from melting away completely.

The house was *strange*. Emmie had seen many houses of that type over the years, but this one was somehow unique, although it took her a minute to pinpoint exactly what gave her that feeling. It was the details in its construction which provided the odd layers of sophistication. Every corner and facet flowed meaningfully into the other like a work of art. Not a single section of the house resembled a typical two-story home, but instead there was a deeper design, an intellectual level in the architecture that showed the original owner had constructed it for a purpose.

"Now, *that's* a haunted house," Finn said.

"You can tell that by looking at it?" Emmie asked mockingly.

"Sure," Finn said with a facetious grin. "Most Victorian

houses are haunted. It's built into the design. They all come with at least one spirit."

"But *seriously*," Emmie said, "it's true that something about it doesn't feel right to me."

"Ditto." Sarah turned to Emmie with a concerned expression. "Something changed in me just now."

"In what way?" Emmie asked, while Sarah pulled the car into the driveway and parked beside a gold Lexus SUV.

"Just the vibes I'm getting. A distressed spirit inside?"

"We *do* know there's a recent one," Finn said, still looking at Whisper House as if he could see the ghost of the murdered boyfriend.

They climbed out of the car and carried their suitcases to the front door as quickly as possible to avoid standing outside any longer than they had to.

Before Emmie rang the doorbell, she glanced up to discover two odd figurines staring down at them from each side of the doorway. They were like demented cherubs with bodies of children and oversized, distorted facial features. Their mouths gaped wide and their bulbous eyes seemed to come alive as the trio stood there. The arms of the child sculptures were stretched forward unnaturally, as if warping through space and time to longingly embrace them.

"Oh, that's different." Finn reached toward one, but it was just beyond his fingertips. "Not like any gargoyle I've ever seen."

Sarah jabbed him in the side with her elbow. "Be careful."

Finn laughed. "It's not like they're going to come to life or anything."

"We don't know their purpose," Sarah said. "Remember all the voodoo?"

"How could I forget?" Finn leaned to one side then the other while staring into one statue's eyes. "You think they put them there to intimidate the guests?"

"Not at all," a woman's voice said from inside.

All three flinched at once. There'd been no sound of the

woman opening the door right next to them, although she now stood behind the glass storm door. She was grinning at their startled expressions, yet there was nothing frightening about her. She was tall and slim, wearing a dress the color of vanilla and looking as tanned as they were.

Opening the door for them, she stepped out of the way and offered her warm, dry hand to each. "Welcome to Whisper House. I'm Audrey."

They introduced themselves as Finn struggled with the suitcases.

"Let me help you with those." She reached down toward their luggage.

Finn shook his head. "I got it. Just admiring your... art."

Hugging herself, as her arms were bare against the freezing weather, she glanced up at the stone statues. "Everyone comments on them."

"What are they?" Emmie followed the woman's gaze to the statues.

"The first owner of Whisper House sculpted them herself. Straight from her imagination. They weren't hanging up when I bought the house, but I found them in the shed and figured out where they belonged." She grinned. "I *had* to put them back up, despite their *unique* character. Can you imagine hiding those little beauties away in a box?"

Emmie glanced at Sarah. Her friend must have been thinking the same thing. *Yes, I can.*

Audrey beckoned them inside. "Please, come in."

They cleared the snow off their feet before entering the foyer, which was polished to a sheen. The smell of coffee hung in the warm air. The walls, in shades of taupe, gray and white, looked freshly painted, and the chandeliers threw rainbows of light around them.

It was different than Emmie had pictured. Not a typical rental house at all. Audrey had put a lot of time and money into the place, giving it a sophisticated yet comforting atmosphere.

Until the real frights started.

Audrey motioned to a row of antique brass pegs on the wall beside the door where they could hang their coats. "Jason texted me you were about to arrive, so I put on the coffee. You know, you're my first guests since the incident. But I've taken the time to do an extra thorough cleaning. I don't think you'll enjoy your stay under the circumstances, but I wanted you to feel as comfortable as possible."

Emmie nodded. "That's thoughtful of you. Thank you."

Audrey brushed aside a lock of dark hair that hung over her blue eyes, and her gold bracelets jingled. She must have been in her fifties, although her skin was flawless. She motioned to a coffee table in the living room on the left, where the cups were laid out and steam rose from a long-snouted pot.

They walked there and gathered around the table. Audrey poured each of them some coffee into gold-rimmed porcelain cups with hand-painted birds on them.

Emmie accepted her cup and sipped. The coffee warmed her mouth and throat with a delicious blend of flavors she'd never tasted before.

"It's lovely here." Sarah's head was tilted to the side as if listening, but Emmie knew she was just feeling out the place. The bewildered expression on Sarah's face revealed that despite the earlier sensations as they arrived, she now felt nothing.

Neither did Emmie.

Audrey nodded. "It is, you'll see—" She looked from Emmie to Sarah before adding, "I suppose we'd better just talk about it, as there's no sense in pretending there isn't an elephant in the room." She cleared her throat. "The incident... the murder. Jason assured me that you're comfortable dealing with those types of things. I mean, cases related to the paranormal, and that you wouldn't be freaked out."

"Not at all." Emmie smiled, encouraging her to talk.

"I read the article he sent about what happened at Hyde House, with the serial killers. Horrible, horrible stuff, but you found a solution there. I hope you can do the same for me or..."

She gave a deep sigh. "I'm not going to rent it anymore, obviously. People won't come, and I wouldn't be able to, anyway, after what happened. But it is a house I love."

"We understand," Finn said. "On your website, you outlined what you did to renovate it and how much you tried to preserve its character."

"Yes, that's true. But what happened really spooked me... us. My family. After all that, we need to move past the haunted aspect. Please, just clear it all out. Can you do that?"

Sarah seemed to be considering the question and its implications. "We've done it before. But we won't know until we see what we're dealing with."

Still, Audrey seemed relieved by her response. "I believe it's well worth the money for you to even try. Just for me to know more about it."

Finn's gaze wandered around the room, then settled on Audrey. "So you *do* believe in ghosts?"

"Oh yes." Audrey chuckled. "It feels strange to say it out loud, like I have to explain myself even to people who see them like you do."

Finn pressed his lips together as if restraining himself from telling her he didn't see them. It was probably that he just wanted to get the information out of Audrey without diverting the conversation.

"And did you know this house was haunted?" Finn asked. "I mean, did it have a... reputation?"

"Yes," Audrey said. "It had sat empty for almost a hundred years, and it was falling apart. Even the most reasonable, unsuperstitious people wouldn't touch it. But the cost of the renovations might have scared them away faster than any rumors of ghosts."

"How did you come across it?" Finn asked.

"We are originally from California, so when my husband and I decided to buy a holiday property, it had to be as different from our usual life as possible. Having the ocean all the time made us think of lakes and the sort of greenness we don't get to see. When I saw this house..." She turned in her seat as if seeing it for the first time again. "I knew this was it. Even in the state it was in, the house just spoke to me." She motioned to the door. "Those creatures, and the decorations that had survived, paintings and objects that were unique and interesting. The realtor showed us images of the house as it once was, and I just wanted it."

"You thought there might be ghosts and yet you didn't feel afraid?" Emmie asked.

"I felt a wonderful spirit." Again, Audrey laughed, shaking her head. "I know, those goblins there at the door might make anyone think twice about entering, and yet I believed it was just the result of someone's wild imagination—wonderful imagination. When I found out more about Joan Carter, the original owner, I just felt a kinship to her. I can't find another way to put it."

"And when you stayed here, did you hear... the whispering?" Sarah asked.

"Yes, but it was very faint. My husband is a complete nonbeliever, and he always insisted it was just the wind or the leaves or whatever. There's not much that could scare that man. I don't mind being scared next to him, to be honest. It's a strange thrill, but I... like it? Or I used to."

"Did you hear any words?" Emmie asked. "Anything distinct?"

"No. Nothing I could make out or easily explain away."

Finn jumped in. "What do you know about Joan Carter?"

Audrey took another sip of coffee then placed her cup on the table. "Let me show you."

The kitten heels of her leather boots clacked against the polished floor as she moved through the hallway and they followed. After walking past a couple of open doors, she led them to a larger, cozier room with an ornate stone fireplace set against one wall. Two large couches formed the sides of a square conversation area, with two antique chairs and a few tables filling the other sides. Four wall mirrors rose from the floor but stopped short of reflecting someone's full height.

But the centerpiece in the room was the large oil portrait of a woman above the fireplace, against a blood-red wall. The woman had strong dark eyebrows, a squarish chin and a stern expression, yet she was handsome in a melodramatic way. The artist had created a fine portrait by anyone's standards: the painstaking details showed a lace and silk ice-blue dress, a fan with Chinese motifs and good jewels at her ears, throat and wrist. Diamond stars kept her glossy curls in place.

Emmie doubted anyone could have had piercing eyes like that in real life. *Eyes like x-rays.*

"Isn't she something?" Audrey stepped in front of the painting and faced them. "I was able to piece some of her story together because of the books and documents my family found here during the renovations."

Joan's stare seemed to mesmerize Finn. He moved closer as he asked, "What did you find out?"

"She and her husband were from good families in Boston. He was an industrialist who died in some sort of accident, leaving her with a fortune, and she got another one from her father—so she was very wealthy.

"Carter was her maiden name, and she went back to using it after her husband died. It seems she *was* very independent, from what I've read. Way ahead of her time.

"But she moved to Minneapolis with her boys soon after her husband died and lived there for a short time before building this house. Apparently, she loved the Minnesota cold, if you can believe that, and the fact this was not a large urban center. She seemed to thrive here and entered a burst of creativity through painting and sculpting and other sorts of artistic endeavors around the house. She even designed the place herself."

"It's definitely a unique house." Finn still scanned the walls where other paintings hung.

"Unique is an understatement. But there was plenty of tragedy here in Joan's time. She had two boys when she arrived, but one of them died of a fever soon after and she turned to Spiritualism for comfort, which was very popular in those days. Being heartbroken, she frequented séances and even ended up hosting some of them in her house. She redesigned a room for just that purpose. Would you like to have a look?"

Finn's face brightened. "Yes, please."

Audrey led them back toward one of the open doors they had passed earlier, and they entered a circular room with no windows. The walls were covered in hand-carved square tiles, meticulously painted in striking shades of deep reds and earthy tones. The paint had faded in some areas and the wood had chipped away, yet the colors were still vibrant even after a century. Each tile showed intricate details down to the width of a fingernail. The common theme between them reminded Emmie of a mandala, with circles within circles and squares within squares. The carved element added depth, a breathtaking third dimension.

His face full of anticipation, Finn looked toward Sarah. She shrugged. His gaze turned to Emmie, and he raised his eyebrows when he realized she was watching him.

No, Finn, nothing yet.

Emmie followed the contours of the curving walls and realized they were standing in a perfect circle. A thick oak circular table was centered beneath a brilliant antique chandelier. Each light fixture held the same intricate mandala theme in its design, although the room was lit by smaller, modern light fixtures evenly spaced around the walls near the ceiling.

"This room is on your website." Finn threw Audrey a clever look. "You didn't mind playing this up a bit, did you?"

Audrey bit her lip and looked charmingly ashamed. "True. But as nothing ever happened while we lived here, I thought other people might find the ghostly atmosphere fascinating. The whole story of the woman as an heiress and also an artist who fell into the séance craze of her day—"

"Oh God," Sarah said suddenly, cutting Audrey short. She had moved to the wall and was peering at the photographs on it. "What is this?"

Finn stepped behind her and leaned forward to look. He laughed and held her shoulders as if to soothe her. "Old-time spirit photography."

Emmie also approached. The old images showed men and women in Victorian dress sitting in front of a neutral background, and behind them hovered semitransparent faces and bodies, some sharper than others.

"People would pay photographers back then for this kind of photo," Audrey said, "where their loved ones were supposed to show up to say they were fine."

"They're fake." Emmie shook her head in disapproval. She had manipulated hundreds, if not thousands, of images as part of her graphic design career, and these photographs were crude. "They're obviously using superimposed plates."

"Photography was so new back then," Finn said. "They didn't know the difference. Like Audrey said, this helped the family get the sense that their loved one was still around or at peace."

Audrey had moved toward another photo a few feet away. "She died in the house, you know."

In that larger photo, Joan was sitting in a chair like the others, with a faint shape hovering behind her that seemed to touch her shoulder.

Emmie pointed out the shape. "Was that supposed to be her dead child?"

"We have to assume so," Audrey said.

"A lot of people died at home back then," Sarah said. "Do you know how she died?"

"Food poisoning," Audrey replied. "She was found here with her other boy."

"Where did you read that about Joan?" Finn asked.

"It's in her obituary, and in some other papers I ran across while renovating."

Sarah stepped back, still staring at the manipulated photographs. "Even if they are fake, they're creepy."

"The Victorians were a morbid bunch," Finn said, moving with her. "Took pictures of the dead and proudly displayed them, along with locks of hair and teeth of the deceased. Have you guys seen the death masks?"

"Only in pictures," Emmie answered.

"Those are creepy, along with the casts of the hands of children who died, and there are even some stories of people embalming their babies."

Audrey shuddered and smiled nervously. "Now you're even scaring me! But I suppose it serves me right for encouraging this sort of atmosphere."

She led them away from the photos over to one of the more intricate mandala tiles. Her fingers caressed the details. Time had worn down the carvings a little, but they were still beautiful.

"The renovation was done with the utmost care to preserve the things Joan left behind," Audrey said. "I'm certain that she created all of these, but maybe there was a purpose to it all. To call on the spirits?"

"How much do you know about her connection to Spiritualism?" Finn asked.

"Only what I've discovered in the house. She was connected to a group, but in her time there were so many. Her passion for the whole movement is evident in her paintings and sculptures. They're in almost every room, and it takes a while to appreciate her talent and skills."

Emmie had leaned down to get a closer look at some tiles near the floor, but now she stood straight. "How did the idea of renting this house come about?"

"We don't use the house all year long, although we started to come even in the winter because it gets so beautiful here, and my children loved the snow. Then they went off to college, and we used it a bit less. And when a house like this isn't used, the pipes freeze, the doors and windows get stuck, even the light fixtures suffer. It needs life, so we started to rent to a few chosen people who would appreciate a harmless, scary tale and could afford substantial deposits to cover any damages." With a sigh, she faced them again. "So I did play up this whole haunted thing; I mean, those photos—" She motioned back toward the séance room. "—get put away when we come, and then it's just our house. But there's a closet stuffed with Ouija boards, crystal balls, and all those sorts of things for the guests to *discover*." She shook her head at them. "But we never thought anything could lead to murder."

"Can we see...?" Emmie glanced toward the ceiling.

Audrey formed a solemn expression, looking at each of them, then nodded. "This way."

10

Finn let Emmie go first and walked behind Sarah with his hand still on her shoulder as if trying to protect her from the malevolent spirits. Emmie held back a laugh. He just couldn't stop caressing her.

Audrey led them over to a corkscrew staircase that made one complete rotation to the floor above and they climbed after her. On the way up, Emmie spotted several more paintings and artistic designs embedded in the walls that she hadn't noticed from below. But that had been the whole point of the winding staircase, hadn't it? To direct the eye of the curious guest.

They passed a few rooms whose doors were slightly ajar. A peek inside showed that the original character of the materials and mood were still there, but mixed with other antique furniture and more modern lamps and fabrics.

Audrey paused at the last door along the hallway and took a deep breath before opening it.

Emmie also held her breath for a moment, expecting to see the young man Michelle had murdered, and she even took her time focusing into the empty space around every corner. No spirits in the room, as far as she could see.

It was a clean room, full of light. The open blinds allowed the sunshine to beam across the wood floors. An antique dresser beside the queen-sized bed was covered with a white doily, although there was nothing on it. Another taller dresser held several framed black and white photos crowded beside a lamp with a flowery shade.

Emmie looked at Sarah's expression for guidance. Sarah glanced back, reflecting her own confusion. If the murder had happened in that room, they should see or sense *something*. But instead, there was *nothing*. Not even a rumored whisper passed through the air.

"I haven't had time to put everything back where it was before the..." Audrey's voice trailed off as she glanced down at a section of the rug near the bed.

Emmie followed her gaze. The thick, deep red and blue rug covered most of the highly trafficked areas, but it was misaligned with the furniture, as if someone had thrown it down.

Audrey lifted the edge of the rug with the toe of her boot. "You can still see a stain. The poor boy just bled out here. The blood—"

"Go on," Finn said. "We don't scare easily."

"The blood even seeped between the boards and dripped downstairs a little."

She removed her foot fast and let the rug drop.

"I assume the rug is new?" Emmie asked.

Their hostess nodded, but her face was pale.

Sarah stepped forward and touched Audrey's arm. "Such a horrible thing to happen in such a lovely place."

Audrey met Sarah's gaze and her expression lightened. "Yes. Exactly."

Finn was again watching Emmie with raised eyebrows as she scanned the room. *No, Finn. No ghosts.*

Audrey stepped to the door with Sarah comforting her along the way. "I don't like to spend much time in here."

"I'm sure nobody blames you," Sarah said.

Moving closer to Emmie, Finn whispered. "Really? Nothing?"

Emmie shrugged. "Give it some time."

Audrey led them out into the hallway with Sarah still moving beside her. "Feel free to grab any bedroom you like. They're all freshly made up."

Not this one. Emmie closed the door to the murder room on the way out. No sense in upsetting Audrey any more than necessary.

Audrey paused in front of two large windows near the top of the stairs and opened the curtains, allowing more sunlight to flood in.

Finn stepped over and stared out. He pointed. "What's that?"

Emmie joined them, looking to where Finn had pointed. A small house sat at the back of the property, surrounded by a few large trees with the lake beyond it.

"That's Joan's lake house," Audrey said. "In the summer, you can't see the lake at all from this window because the trees obscure the view, but now it's visible, except for the layer of snow over the ice. It's the place where she used to paint and sculpt and write. I store many of her things out there."

She led them downstairs to the back of the house and entered a room that extended into the yard. It was like a sunroom, with windows covering three sides and the back row boasting a full view of the lake. To the right of the lake sat the smaller house having the same Victorian design.

"Of course, the lake house is more fun in the summer. It doesn't have bedrooms or even a bathroom, just one large library and studio with a beautiful view. In this weather, it's for the true Minnesotans—or people who loved the cold like Joan."

"Are we allowed there?" Emmie asked.

"Sure, but there's no heat. Well, there is just a fireplace we haven't used in a long while and an electric heater. The walls of that place aren't well insulated. To be honest, I worried about guests getting hurt there in the winter. You know, kids on a lark getting drunk and falling in the ice or something. People come from other states and don't understand how it is here. So I made it very cozy for summer, not so cozy for winter."

"I see." Emmie still looked at the lake house.

"The keys are hanging here." Audrey pointed to a set of keys on a hook next to the door. "Just please be careful out there."

"We will be," Finn assured her.

Emmie threw him a mischievous look, and he held back a smile, pretending not to see it.

"I should be going now," Audrey said, looking at the sky. "I'm only off to LA in a few hours, but I don't like driving to the airport in the dark in this weather. By the way, the pantry is fully stocked since you are also here as my guests."

The unease Emmie had previously held at the thought of contacting spirits for money had faded a little at Audrey's story. Now it didn't feel so much like she was selling her skills. "The payment is enough," she said, "but we appreciate it."

Back in the living room, Audrey wrapped a thick white scarf around her neck. "This house sat empty for a century after Joan died, with cousins fighting for her inheritance, then not wanting to live here, then not being able to sell it until I fell in love with it. I'm still in love with it. I don't want to sell it to people who will raze it to the ground and build some awful hotel or apartment complex here. That's the only kind of people who would buy it now." She paused as she looked at them, as if to make her point clear. "But if there is an evil spirit here... a malignant thing, then I won't expose myself and certainly not my children or my husband to it."

"I understand," Emmie said a little sadly. "More than you know."

"Jason gave me his word that you were the best," Audrey continued. "And seeing you, I somehow believe it."

"Still..." Emmie said thoughtfully, "it's not as if we can offer any guarantee..."

"Understood." Audrey's bracelets jingled as they shook hands. "I just want to know what is here. What the bad thing is. And I think you might be able to find out." Her eyes scanned their faces. "I saw you feeling for it. You haven't found it yet, but I think you will. I think you'll be able to tell me whether it's gone, too."

They moved with Audrey through the foyer as she took her coat and put it on.

"Again," Audrey said, "please be careful. I don't want to feel any guiltier than I do now."

"We can handle things." Finn swallowed hard.

Thankfully, Audrey didn't seem to notice his reaction as she stepped outside. They stayed behind the threshold as the cold breeze flowed in around them.

"How's the cell signal here?" Finn asked suddenly.

"It's relatively good," Audrey said. "Most of the time. Unless there's a storm. Then all bets are off. There's WiFi, but the cable company has a spotty record in this area, being so far from town. Is that important to you?"

Finn forced a smile. "Kind of."

"You should be fine. There are no forecasts of a storm for the duration of your stay. But for the best signal, make calls in the driveway."

On her way out to the car, Audrey glanced back and waved. Her eyes traveled up the house as if she'd spotted something unnerving above them. A minute later, she was gone.

After Emmie closed the door, Finn raced to the kitchen. Sarah followed him.

"What's going on?" Emmie went to see what they were doing.

"Starving." Finn was going through the large refrigerator, pulling out drawers and moving things aside. "A bottle of champagne, smoked salmon, ham, turkey, cheeses." He looked over his shoulder at them. "I think this job of yours is pretty good, girls."

"Job of *ours*. Are we going to go through all of it?" Sarah asked.

"We can only try!"

"Maybe not in the first day, though?" Sarah said.

Finn grinned as he scoured through the pantry and came out with breadsticks and a bottle of red wine. He found a wine opener in a drawer and proceeded to uncork it. He stuffed a bread stick between his teeth, took the bottle and some snacks and motioned with his head toward the red room with the portrait.

Giving up pretending she wanted to stop him, Emmie found three wineglasses in a cupboard and followed eagerly. Sarah threw up her hands and joined them.

They gathered around the circular Art Deco table in the red room. Removing the breadstick from his mouth, Finn poured them each a glass of wine while studying the mirrors around them.

"Why do you suppose someone installed so many mirrors?" he asked.

Sarah stared at the one in front of her. "They seem old, so it was probably not Audrey. That's what happens when you mix wealth with vanity, I guess."

Emmie stepped over and stared at herself in one of the mirrors beside Finn and Sarah. It had a gilded frame with serpents rising on either side to meet and entwine on the top. The reflection was clear, although foggy in some areas. "To think Joan stared at herself in the same mirrors..."

Glancing around at the other mirrors, she spotted only the lower two thirds of her body in the reflections. How short had Joan been anyway? Or had the woman hunkered down in the center of the room to observe herself from all sides?

Getting between them, Finn pulled them closer as if posing for a selfie while staring into the reflection. For a moment, they grinned as if they hadn't seen each other for a while.

But just as quickly, they separated and spread out across the room to study some of the other antiques, mirrors, paintings, and statues.

Joan's style of painting was reminiscent of modern art despite her being a 19th-century woman living in the Minnesota countryside. Maybe her early education as a wealthy heiress in Boston had exposed her to art, and she must have traveled to Europe at some time. Emmie was drawn to a painting depicting a Victorian house at night. The brushstrokes were bold, almost impressionistic, but there was no mistaking the façade of Whisper House and the trees surrounding it. In the work, three rooms upstairs were lit.

A similar painting hung next to that one; the two were companion pieces, one showing the house in winter and the other in spring, with the trees in full bloom. Joan had painted the scene at dusk, and there were only two lights in the upper bedrooms in that one.

"The child who died," Sarah whispered by her side.

Emmie shuddered, then laughed at herself. "I didn't hear you there."

"Lots of emotions in those paintings. I get the feeling Joan grieved a lot for her son, even as the other survived."

Lots of emotions. Emmie was drawn to the overall heartbreaking mood of the painting. "What a way to express it. So subtle and yet so..."

Emmie turned to get Finn's reaction, but he had stepped away and now stood facing the open doorway.

"Disturbing." Finn sipped his wine. "I told you about those Victorians and their morbid fascinations."

Emmie exchanged a solemn glance with Sarah. Had the painting struck a nerve with him? Maybe the talk of a brother dying had reminded Finn of his own brother's death. "I don't get the feeling that it's focused on anything morbid. Nothing really haunted about it."

"I suppose this is one of those things that Audrey played up to her guests." Sarah moved toward Finn. "You okay?"

He turned toward them suddenly and raised his wineglass. His eyes watered. "Of course I am, and one thing is clear. There should be at least one ghost in this house, and I swear we'll find him just as soon as we finish off this wine."

After the wine warmed Emmie and soothed her mood, they decided to get their bearings without the benefit of Audrey's guidance and explore the entire house, starting with the upstairs bedrooms. Gripping her glass of wine, Emmie shuffled behind Sarah, trying to focus on the task at hand, although the wine blurred her vision a bit.

They took advantage of the tour to choose where they would sleep. Sarah and Emmie decided to stay together in a room with twin beds and Finn took one with a king-sized mattress. None of the rooms had an ensuite bathroom.

Finn groaned. "Twelve hundred bucks a night and I have to go out into the hallway to get to the john?"

"They were built like that back then," Emmie said. "Just be glad you don't need to make a trek to an outhouse."

"Plenty of bathrooms, though," Sarah pointed out. "Two on each floor. It looks like she renovated an old closet into a bathroom up here to accommodate the second one rather than change the layout of the original rooms."

"You'll have your own *john,* Finn," Emmie said. "It's not going to be like Caine House when we are there and you accuse us of taking hours in front of the mirror when *you* take just as much time."

"Thank God," Finn mumbled.

Returning to the main floor, they circled through a large reception room, the red room with the portrait, a large dining room, two bathrooms, the same pantry Finn had scavenged through only a little earlier, the sunroom facing the lake house, and the séance room. They even made a quick visit to the cramped, musty basement, which was only a little larger than the furnace room. They still hadn't encountered any signs of spirits. Nothing at all.

So Emmie threw in the towel and opened another bottle of wine for herself and Sarah while Finn switched fully into paranormal investigator mode.

Out of the six suitcases they'd packed in the car, three were full of Finn's electronic devices and cables. And after he had installed most of them, Emmie found, standing at the door with her wineglass in hand, that the séance room looked more like a production studio than anything else.

"You're kind of putting all your eggs in one basket by setting up all your cameras in one room," Emmie said as he adjusted the controls on a camera.

"Got to start somewhere, and this has the best chance of ghosts per capita. If there's nothing here, I'll just pick it up and move it."

"Why not up in the room where the murder occurred?"

"I'm guessing you guys can solve that issue soon enough—as soon as Sterling decides to show up. I'm chasing all those stories of whispers. Despite what you said, there's got to be spirits here somewhere, right? Maybe you don't see them because they've been here a really long time. Ever consider that you can only see more recent ghosts?"

Emmie smirked. "Don't think ghosts have an expiration date. Once they're here, they stay until they've resolved their issues. The house isn't *that* old anyway."

"Well, if someone held seances here, it should prove interesting." Finn glanced around the room. "Maybe we'll run into someone from the distant past this time, back when talking to ghosts was something the cool kids did. You know, around the Victorian age."

"That was back when talking to *fake* ghosts was cool. Most Spiritualists were fakes."

"You're a psychic, so you should admit some were real."

"No doubt, *some* were real. But I think a lot of them just wanted money for bullshit." She glanced toward the living room. "Where did Sarah go?"

"I think she went to the sunroom."

"You *think* that's where she is?" Emmie said with a sly grin. "I think you *know* she's back there."

"I forget you can read minds." Finn paused and fluttered his eyelashes at her. "What am I thinking about now?"

She smirked. "It doesn't take a psychic in this case..." Emmie walked away.

She found Sarah in the sunroom lounging in a burgundy chaise longue beside a bright brass lamp with a lacey beige antique lampshade. The fading blue light from the setting sun filled the glass ceiling. "What's your sense about this place?"

"It's weird, but I have zero sense."

"I'm glad you're saying that because I think it's a bust too, and that *is* weird. I mean, so many things happened here. A *murder* not even two months ago, and nothing."

"They do take their sweet time sometimes." Sarah opened and closed her eyes slowly, softly in the sunlight.

"I guess there are worse places to be." Emmie swirled the excellent wine she was drinking, "but I do feel like this is a job now. That we have to deliver, you know?"

"We will," Sarah said. "We'll find out something, but it might not make everyone happy. It's just so hard to believe that the young woman we met in the prison could do something so awful. She didn't seem like the type."

"Is there a *type*?"

Sarah shook her head slowly. "I suppose not."

"She doesn't deny it, as much as they may try to argue temporary madness. Is it possible she didn't tell us everything?"

"Anything is possible..." Sarah said. "But what motive could there be to just stab someone in the heart?"

Through the forest of bare trees, Emmie could make out the faint outline of the lake house. The moon had risen over the edge of the horizon and its ghostly glow grew brighter as the darkness moved in. It wasn't a surprise to see the daylight end so soon, as they were approaching the shortest day of the year.

"Sarah?" Finn called from down the hall. "Can you come here a minute?"

Sarah glanced at Emmie. "Not sure what he needs me for?"

"To cheer him on?" Emmie laughed.

Sarah set her empty glass down and hurried away, leaving Emmie standing alone by the window.

Maybe they couldn't feel anything because they were selling their gifts. She reminded herself that the money from staying there would help pay her bills. Every job was like that, though, including her graphic design job in California. In any job, you sold that talent to stay alive, and that's just the way it was.

What the hell am I even saying? Am I drunk on the job?

She sat down in the chaise longue and closed her eyes for a moment, leaned her head back, and then opened them again to a fresh view of the ceiling and a small but ornate chandelier hanging above her. The ceiling tiles were unusual, like what she had seen in the rest of the house. Each tile looked made of tin, with embossed concentric designs, one within the other, growing smaller toward the center. A similar strange design to the other tiles, and this, too, must be Joan Carter's imagination.

Finn's and Sarah's voices echoed toward her as their footsteps got louder. She didn't bother to eavesdrop on their conversation but instead finished her glass of wine just as they entered the room.

"Any luck?" Finn asked.

She was about to laugh at him for asking at every turn when she spotted something odd in the corner of the room. A section of the wall didn't quite match everything else around it. Tasteful paper covered the walls, but this section had the same concentric designs as the ceiling tiles.

Emmie placed her empty glass on a side table and walked over to it, although the alcohol made her move more slowly. It was a two-foot-wide by four-feet-tall area.

Like a small door.

Emmie pushed it, although it didn't budge. She ran her fingers around the edge of the design, looking for any signs of a handle that might reveal an opening.

"What are we doing?" Finn asked.

Emmie didn't answer but continued pushing and pulling at the section.

"What do you see, Em?" Sarah joined her. A moment later, Finn did the same.

As Emmie's frustration grew, it suddenly popped open. She looked over at Sarah, who had yanked on a wooden handle tied to a rope within a small bookcase beside the section.

Sarah grinned with wide eyes. "Found it. I'm getting good at this."

❧ I 2 ❧

I nside the small doorway, a narrow set of stairs led up into the darkness. A cool draft of air drifted across Emmie's bare arms. She shivered.

"An attic?"

Finn leaned in and peered up at the stairs. "Looks that way, but I can't see much."

"Can you fit in there?" Sarah asked him.

He laughed. "You're smaller than me."

"You scared?" Sarah teased him.

"All the time." He didn't go inside. Instead, he pulled out his cell phone and switched his screen into flashlight mode. Angling up the light into the stairway, he crouched with them to try to see into the darkness.

Emmie grabbed his phone and squeezed through the doorway. The spiraling stairs ascended two stories, but there was an opening halfway up, although the light from the phone didn't reach beyond that. "There's a room up there. I'm going to check it out."

The staircase was more vertical than typical stairs, with shallow steps, and it was not more than two feet wide. Emmie's footsteps creaked against the old wood as she pushed herself up and entered the narrow space over the hole. She paused at the top of the stairs with her chest and head rising above the floor of a small room. It was empty, looking like it had once had a use but had sat undiscovered through all the renovations. Had Audrey not seen the hidden door? Or had she left it alone on purpose? Emmie held her arms close to her chest as the cool air flooded in around her.

"What do you see?" Sarah asked from below.

"Lots of dust and a few old metal toys. It's sort of like an attic but maybe a little more like a playroom. If there was a child living here originally, that would explain it. The coast is clear. If you want to come up here with me, you should bring your jackets. It's not insulated—like being outside." She shivered again.

Finn was coming up behind her, so she continued her climb into the small space, kneeling on the dusty surface as her friends joined her.

Taking back his phone, Finn stood, although hunched forward. The ceiling couldn't have been more than five feet from the floor, and it slanted. Finn leaned sideways to avoid hitting his head, but also pointed out that the underside of the roof had nails poking through like spikes.

"Careful here."

"If this was a playroom," Sarah said, "she didn't leave them much room."

Emmie tapped her foot around on the wood. "Do you think the floor will hold all three of us?"

Finn focused the light on the worn wooden planks beneath their feet. "We're probably good. They built old houses to last." He scanned the walls with the light and stopped on a ladder against a different wall. That one led up to another small opening.

"Another room?" Sarah asked.

Walking over, Finn peered into the hole. "I can see a little light."

They joined him at the bottom of the ladder.

"That must go up to the tower we saw from outside," Emmie said.

Peering through the opening at the top of the ladder, she could see four windows—one on each side, like a lookout tower. A great place for an imaginative child to hide away from the world. She couldn't help but think of the old treehouse behind Hanging House, where Frankie had played. What was the allure of climbing to these heights? The seclusion? The fresh perspective of the world as the children saw farther than anyone else in the house?

Finn shifted his weight onto a rung in the ladder and the wood cracked and splintered beneath him. "I guess I won't be going up there." He now shined the light on horizontal scratches in the wood against a wall. The numbers next to the scratches showed that someone had marked a child's height at random intervals. "This is definitely a place where a kid hung out. Probably Joan's kids. Or at least the kid who survived."

Emmie gestured to another object a couple of feet away. Judging by the design of the rectangular shape, it was obviously another mirror, although its surface was covered in a thick layer of dust. She stepped over and wiped it, revealing the dark reflections of the room.

"A mirror?" Sarah said. "How many is too many?"

"Maybe the mother made the kid obsessed with grooming?"

"He must've been just like you, then," Sarah teased him.

"My mother certainly tried." Finn smoothed his hair with wide, exaggerated gestures.

Only a sheet of wood separated the rafters on the wall from the freezing outdoors. "He couldn't have been up here too often. It's too cold," Emmie said.

"His summer retreat then?" Finn suggested.

Emmie glanced around, but this time focusing her mind a little more on any possible spirits in the room. She turned to Sarah. "What is your sense of this place?"

Sarah paused and looked up again toward the tower. "If

there's anything here, I don't feel strongly that it involved violence."

Finn shined the light into the corner, then across the ceiling again. "I'll put a camera up here tonight, just in case. Maybe it's a good place to keep an eye on."

"Good enough for me." Emmie shivered again. "You would think that after living in Minnesota most of my life, I would've gotten used to the cold, but... Let's go warm up."

Emmie turned to exit, then glanced back. "You guys coming?"

Sarah smiled. "I'll stick around a little while longer to help Finn set up all his toys. You going to sleep already?"

"I'm tired, but maybe that's just the alcohol talking."

"It's been a stressful day. I don't blame you."

Their eyes met for a moment. Emmie's mouth cracked open to say something, but she held back. *Yes, it has been stressful. For both of us—but you have a shoulder to cry on, I guess.*

"All right, then." Emmie turned away. "See you later."

"Good night."

Returning to the sunroom, Emmie paused beneath the blackened ceiling glass and stared out the window. The forest's beauty that had captivated her earlier now became like a cage of shadows, and they wouldn't release her until she finished her task.

She glanced around the room and wavered as the effects of the alcohol surged. "You can come out now. I'm a big girl. I can handle it."

She held her breath for a moment to listen and focus. Only the muffled voices of Finn and Sarah came through the walls like... a whisper.

13

It was still early, but the wine was in full effect and Emmie was more than ready to go to her room and crawl under the sheets, to sink as far away as she could from any more talk of ghosts. She removed her socks before detouring into the bathroom. Slick marble tiles cooled her feet—no doubt Audrey had installed them recently. They served as a reminder of the Cabo San Lucas luxury she had left behind days earlier.

She washed her hands on the way out, looking at her tired reflection with curiosity. Her lightly tanned skin would soon fade, just as would the memories of their vacation to Mexico, and that was fine with her. The woman staring back at her wasn't even the same person she'd known only a year earlier. Things had changed so much. And where was it all headed?

The question hung in her mind as she got lost in her own eyes. The wind pushed against a small window beside the bathtub, whistling between the cracks in three gentle, steady bursts like someone's breath over her shoulder.

Whoooosh, whoooosh, whoooosh.

Who are you?

The gusts of air had formed the words, but she had no answer.

Emmie Rose Fisher.

"Emmie Rose Fisher," she said out loud. Her voice startled her. "You're drunk, girl."

She rubbed her forehead and headed back to her room. Sarah and Finn's conversation echoed from downstairs. How long would they stay up?

Closing the door behind her, she made sure the latch clicked to give her as much peace and quiet as possible.

The room's charm lightened her mood. The pink and white flowery bedspread and the lavender curtains held a warm, feminine appeal that was unlike her, which was maybe why they made her feel good. There was a small white makeup table and mirror in the corner and an ornate dresser with glass knobs on the drawers. The flowery beige and white textured wallpaper added to the Victorian theme, and despite what Finn had said, that the Victorians were a morbid bunch, she felt safe in that space.

You're fooling yourself, girl.

She wasn't there to get away from ghosts but to face them.

Do that later.

Leaving the lights on, she lumbered across the room to the twin bed with a dark wood frame that was meant for her.

Sarah had claimed the twin bed near the door, and they'd agreed to sleep in the same room for practical purposes—it was easier to get help during an encounter if the other was nearby.

At least, Emmie *hoped* Sarah would come in later.

She changed into her pajama bottoms, but left her top on, not wanting the cool air to strip away the little warmth around her chest.

The air shifted through the room as if someone had opened a door downstairs, and the wind pushed against the window and shuddered the frame at the same time. She hurried under the blankets, pulling them up to her chin like a child hiding from the monster beneath her bed, and closed her eyes.

Within a few minutes, her mind swirled with a thousand

ideas, all crying out for attention. Then the world went dark and she slept.

A short time later, she awoke noticing her breathing. Harsh, drawn-out breaths, as if she were struggling to take in enough air to make it until the next gasp. She cracked her eyes open and saw that Sarah's bed was empty.

Something was wrong with her breathing. It sounded strange and foreign, as if someone had placed a wet rag in her mouth—but her mouth was closed, and by shifting her tongue around she found nothing unusual.

She shifted her position and turned over to her other side so that she faced the wall. The familiar sound of her usual breath came back but the other melodic sound was still there, hovering somewhere behind her.

Emmie paused for breath for a moment. Instead of the silence of the house, or Sarah and Finn laughing, the breathing moved closer and continued from only inches above the back of her head. The tiny hairs against her cheek tingled, but she resisted lifting her hand to brush them.

If there was a spirit in the room, she was prepared to turn around and face it, but the strange, soft breaths formed words, soothing whispers, as when one of her parents used to wake her up gently.

Instead of turning over and looking at whatever, whoever, was causing the disturbance, she remained still and tried to make out the words.

They sounded distant and pleasant, almost cheerful. Several words filled her ear before a pattern emerged. It wasn't something she understood, but maybe she wasn't meant to understand it. This was something above her understanding. Something for Finn to decipher. A repetition, like a chant.

Despite her best efforts to pick out the words, she could only grasp the sounds. Slowly she moved out of her sleep and opened her eyes, yet still avoided turning around to face the intruder.

Not that she feared for her safety, but it wouldn't help to scare the spirit away.

"Who are you?" Emmie echoed the question she'd heard in the bathroom.

The whispers continued. At least she hadn't scared away the intruder. Better talk to it on the first night and get rid of the suspense, anyway.

"What's your name?" Emmie's heart beat faster. Her voice almost drowned out the whispers.

Both the rhythm and the tone of the sounds changed.

They're trying to communicate.

The whispering grew louder. And the sounds became a little clearer.

What language is that? Latin? Arabic? Nothing like she'd ever heard before. A Gregorian chant was the closest thing she could compare it to, although the sounds were less lyrical and again more like a mother whispering her child to sleep.

Emmie turned slightly as the source moved closer. She couldn't tell if it was a man or woman. Maybe a little more feminine because of the softer tones.

OO EE HH AAAA RR NN SS AAA LL MM...

Emmie formed the words in her mind, although none of it made any sense. She was still a little drunk. The alcohol must be interfering with the communication.

OO EE HH AAAA RR NN SS AAA LL MM UU WW OO FF HH EE VV BAA KO...

She jumped when Sarah threw the door open and appeared in the doorway laughing. Sarah quickly went silent.

Emmie flipped over and reached out toward the empty space from which the whispering had come, as if trying to pull the spirits closer.

Sarah moaned. "Sorry, Em. Didn't mean to wake you."

The whispering had stopped. And nobody else stood in their room.

Emmie dropped her arm and let it dangle against the side of the bed, while closing her eyes again. "We'll talk tomorrow," she said, both to Sarah and the spirit.

14

E mmie awoke to a quiet house. A little too quiet. Her head throbbed, and she hesitated to even move a little for fear that it might get worse. She knew before she turned that Sarah wasn't there, but the echoing laughter from her friends goofing around downstairs was gone, which was somehow good. It was nearly eight o'clock and maybe Finn was still asleep, although he wasn't the type of person to waste any time getting to work.

The morning sun streamed in through the openings around the window blinds. Not enough to make her squint, but it still hurt her eyes. A soft whistling noise came in through a crack around the window somewhere, reminding her of the whispering voice she had heard the previous night. What did it sound like again? She couldn't remember now—and how much wine had she consumed the previous evening? Too many glasses.

The leaky window whistled again.

Did I imagine the whole thing? I was pretty out of it. She couldn't be sure of anything now.

Emmie swallowed. Her throat was dry, and she longed to get up and pour herself a glass of water, but her muscles weren't cooperating. She shifted in her bed and glanced across the room at two more paintings by Joan—at least, she assumed them to be hers, as they had the same style as the paintings of the day before, and also matched their theme. One showed the exterior of the house from the back; a clothesline in the foreground was draped with two sets of clothes for boys. Small jackets, short trousers, and shirts. The other painting showed a variation of the first, although from a different angle and a different season, judging by the environment. Just one set of clothes, and the trousers were longer now. Somehow Joan had managed to make the clothes in the second painting hang *sadly.*

Her head throbbed as she sat up in bed and then steadied herself into a standing position.

Definitely had too much to drink.

But in a way, she felt *better.* Her mind had cleared and despite the pain in her head, she hurried through her morning routine in the bathroom and stepped out into the hallway listening for her friends.

In the bright morning light, some old framed photographs along the walls between the rooms caught her attention. In the one next to her room, a woman was wearing an oversized lacy hat with a veil, her corseted form hunched forward as she stood beside an older man with a long white beard. Emmie was certain that the woman was Joan, though her face was not visible. The man was wearing a top hat and held a cane. Neither was smiling as the lake outlined their forms.

There was something else in the old man's right hand, something dangling at his side. Emmie leaned forward and focused on the object.

It didn't help that it was out of focus. "What the hell is that?"

Old aviator goggles, or maybe motorcycle goggles? Hadn't the 1890s been too early for all that? Would welder's goggles have existed at that time? Something to ask Finn—if she remembered. She'd prefer to know whether that was Joan's father.

Audrey hadn't mentioned the father being here, but there seemed to be a complicity of some sort between them, with Joan almost swaying toward a man who would have been much feebler than her.

Emmie picked the frame off the wall and held it closer. Despite the image being in black and white, the landscape was picturesque and ideal. What would life have been like back then without the distractions of personal electronics and the incessant demand for faster and smarter?

Along the far right of the photo was the corner of a small white structure. Emmie reminded herself they needed to visit the lake house today.

She returned the photo to the wall and headed downstairs, expecting to find Finn working with his gadgets or at his laptop somewhere in the corner and Sarah keeping him company, but the downstairs was just as quiet as the upstairs.

"Finn? Sarah?" Emmie's voice echoed through the house. A quick glance at the car out in the driveway showed that they hadn't gone anywhere, but Finn's coat and Sarah's jacket were gone from their place next to the door.

The sky was gray and the bare trees swayed in the gusting wind. Out for a stroll in this weather?

Calling out their names a few times, Emmie walked through the lower level before arriving in the sunroom at the back of the house. The key to the lake house, which Audrey had pointed out during the tour, was gone. *That's where they went.*

She looked out the large clear windows across the backyard. In the morning light, the lake house stood out, with several large trees surrounding it.

Emmie's face burned. They had gone out exploring that place without taking her along. They had left her alone in the house.

I guess we aren't a team of three anymore.

Something brushed against the back of her shirt as if the air conditioning or heating had kicked in and a puff of air had passed over her. She wouldn't have thought twice about it although the sensation was accompanied by a soft, whispering voice. The same one she had heard the previous night. And the same sounds.

OO EE HH AAAA RR NN SS AAA LL MM...

❧ 15 ❧

The whispers faded as soon as they came. Emmie glanced around, though there wasn't any sign of the spirit who had made them. Even with a clear mind, she still couldn't make sense of what the spirit might be trying to say. It sounded vaguely English, but the sounds didn't connect as a complete sentence or even a word.

She would need to tell her friends that there was definitely a spirit in the house. Maybe if Sarah had been there, they might have communicated with it and gotten some answers.

Staring out into the backyard, she spotted her reflection in the window's glass. Her face was strained. *And for good reason.* Partly from drinking too much the previous night, but even as she stood there in silence, her body tensed as a warmth spread through her. They should have waited for her to wake up. Her eyes focused on the lake house again. "What is it that couldn't wait?"

. She wasn't going to just sit around and wait for them to come back. Hurrying to the front of the house, she put on her jacket, hat, and gloves and headed out the door.

Light flakes of snow drifted down from the dull sky and swirled around her in the icy breeze.

Emmie walked around to the back toward the lake house. The yard sloped gently toward the lakeshore with dozens of scattered pine trees surrounding the property. It wasn't heated, according to what Audrey had said, so there had to be a very good reason to go out there without her. The brown frozen grass was matted where Finn and Sarah had trudged.

The house was about the size of a single bedroom with a little chimney off to the side and the door facing toward the main house. The only window she saw from that angle was a small one set into the main door, and a storm door half obscuring it. Approaching the entrance, she stared at an intricate design carved into the door. Hand-carved, like the other designs on the ceiling and small door. Joan had spent a lot of time and energy creating an environment of her own within the house. Nobody went through that much trouble without a very good purpose—but what?

The lake was a flat sheet of white. Another house sat on the opposite shore, barely visible behind a row of trees surrounding it. With no open water in sight, ice had no doubt formed across the surface over the past month, as it took weeks for a lake to freeze. The area was serene and beautiful.

Serene because everything's dead.

Emmie stepped up to the entrance, pulled the storm door, and pushed open the main door without knocking. Finn and Sarah were sitting in chairs beside each other with open books across their laps. They were still in their outerwear, and both looked up at her with wide eyes and startled expressions.

"Hey, Em," Finn said. "Decided to come back to the land of the living?"

"What's going on?" Emmie asked, trying to hold back her irritation.

"Just exploring, as usual," Finn said.

"Without me?"

Sarah's expression switched to surprise. "Well, you were sleeping."

"You could have woken me up."

"We're not that cruel," Finn said. "You had quite a few glasses of vino last night. Better to let you sleep it off."

Emmie shook her head in strong denial. "I'm not hung over."

"All right." Finn looked down at the book again, as if the conversation about last night or this morning had ended.

Emmie didn't think it had, but they were not meeting her eyes.

"Finn found some really interesting stuff about this place," Sarah said.

The air was only a little warmer inside the house, far from warm enough for Emmie to face without her jacket. She spotted the small electric heater Audrey had mentioned during the tour. The coils within the heater glowed bright orange, although she didn't know how much good it was really doing.

Sarah pointed at a daybed across the room. "You can sit there. We'll turn our chairs to face you."

Again, Emmie shook her head, trying to suppress an irritation that kept bubbling up. "That's okay. Don't want to sit. I've been lying down far too long."

She decided to concentrate on the room rather than on the indifferent back of Finn's head. It resembled a library and a studio, as Audrey had said. The lake houses Emmie had come across in her life around Green Hills were usually full of fishing equipment, beach toys, and landscaping tools useful once summer arrived. Here the bookcases were stacked to the ceiling, although not with just books. There were many decorative items like pottery, small metal sculptures, painted miniatures, flowers pressed in glass cases. If Audrey was right, these might all be the work of Joan. Centered in the room was a thick oak table with ornate flowery designs carved into the corners, and Emmie leaned against it to glance up at the ceiling, where she spotted the same concentric design as before. She agreed with Audrey that, considering Joan's artistic nature, she must have created them. She had been rich enough to have tiles and carvings made of them for the entire house.

"Something wrong?" Sarah asked her.

Emmie flinched at being watched and didn't answer, instead asking, "So you found the documents Audrey mentioned?"

"Not just that," Sarah said eagerly. "Looking through the shelves, we found lots of goodies. Books of sketches and annotations."

"Funny that Audrey just dumped it all out here," Emmie remarked. "Probably get more spoiled here than in the main house."

"The papers were kept in containers, so maybe she intended to preserve everything."

Sarah motioned to a solid oak desk in the corner beside the shelves and in front of the window. The surface was covered in items one might associate with an artist at that time: small busts made of clay, a tray with implements for sculpting like a hammer, chisels—many of them had signs of rust—and measuring tools, along with a stack of old-fashioned scrapbooks that might be filled with sketches. On another tray, thick glass bottles were lined up which might have once contained anything from paint to medication. Books were in piles on the floor around her friends. Probably the result of Finn's rummaging.

As if reading her mind, he looked up from his book. "Get this: I found this stash of old letters bundled together in a drawer of that desk and read through a few of them."

"Love letters?" Emmie asked.

"In a way." He flipped through a few of the pages. "It's a bunch of rich women discussing a certain guy named Owl Cromwell. They talk about him a lot, as if he were some sort of demigod. In the letters, they refer to themselves as Owl's Ladies."

"Sounds like something kinky." Sarah chuckled.

Finn grimaced, holding up a photograph of the same old, bearded man Emmie had seen inside. "This *would* be kinky."

Sarah wrinkled her nose.

"Right?" Finn laughed. "You would think by reading some of these letters that it was something like that, but they talk about him very highly. Lots of spiritual respect there."

"I saw that guy's picture in the house, next to our room," Emmie said. "What a strange name for someone commanding respect. Owl."

"Wise old owl?" Sarah said. "What if he was psychic? And had something to do with the séances."

"Could be." Finn set the photo of the old man aside. "But he was also leading some sort of group effort to instruct them in his philosophical beliefs. Ideas based on energy and light."

"Like a cult?"

"I'm not sure if it went that far, but as you said yesterday about those photos we saw, a lot of people were taken advantage of by fraudulent mediums back then. There was a sort of hysteria happening and the vulnerable got pulled in hook, line, and sinker."

"So this guy would have taken a bunch of Joan's money, and the other women's too, I assume," Emmie said.

"For the good of Owl's odd philosophy. Many people are taken in by the idealistic allure to change the world for the better, only to be led astray."

Sarah raised her hand. "And something else we discovered..."

"You *have* been busy this morning." Emmie forced a smile.

Sarah nodded enthusiastically, but hadn't seemed to notice the tension in Emmie's voice. "Remember how Audrey said that Joan died of food poisoning? Well, it turns out that, according to this—" She held up an old, yellowed newspaper. "—there was a rash of food poisonings in town. Several other women died."

"On the same day as Joan?" Emmie asked.

Finn reached down into a box and pulled out a newspaper, scanning through the articles until stopping on one near the bottom of the last page. Tapping the paper, he held it out to Emmie. "Here's an obituary for a woman named Gertrude

Smith. The same day as Joan. I've got more somewhere, including one for Owl Cromwell. All of them died on the same day and, I'm assuming, in the same way."

Sifting through a small pile of papers, Sarah took one with typed text and some parts in handwriting. "Joan's death certificate. And also one for her son, Edgar. Twelve years old. Poor kid. Still the same day."

Finn folded his arms over his chest and leaned back as if he had won a contest. "Coincidence? Not a chance."

"What's your theory?" Emmie asked. "If the ladies and Owl all met here, they might have eaten bad fish, uncooked meat, contaminated water, and gone on to feel sick and die elsewhere."

"Under normal circumstances," Finn said. "But this group doesn't seem like your typical Women's Saturday Night Book Club, does it? This Owl guy led them to something. That's just how cults work."

"Then you *do* think it was like a murder-suicide pact?"

Finn tilted his head with a slight grin.

It irritated Emmie, that smugness; she lowered her eyes and glanced at the sorted piles around them. "Why is this stuff here? It makes sense we'd find letters between the women and Owl. Joan would have kept them. But stuff about their death?"

"We found some documents from lawyers too. The Dyer family tried to have Cousin Joan committed to a loony bin before her death."

"To stop her from giving money to Owl?"

Finn nodded. "And there are papers related to inheritance, angry letters between family members, although I've only read a few."

"You went through all this just now?"

Finn shrugged. "It's been at least a couple of hours, right? I read fast."

Emmie stared at him, then met Sarah's gaze. "You too?"

"I skimmed over some of it," Sarah said.

"All right." Emmie folded her arms over her chest. "You've

concluded that some Dyer family member holed up here and gathered all the papers needed to claim the inheritance?"

Sarah nodded. "We assumed."

"And the person who gathered the information must have known something connected all the deaths in some way. But if it was a murder-suicide cult thing, wouldn't the police have found them together? That would have made a bigger splash in the news, even back then."

"Not necessarily. The families of the women could have easily put the bodies in different houses to hide what happened. They had the money and motivation to keep things quiet. It would have been an embarrassment for the families—a sin—for the women to be connected with a radical man like Owl, and a suicide would have prevented a burial on church grounds, a very important thing back then. Scandals spread like wildfire now, but in those days there were a lot of big stories that got pushed under the rug... for the right price."

"Something like that today would be all over social media," Sarah said.

"Exactly."

"But if Joan participated in mass suicide in the house," Sarah said, "why haven't we seen her?"

Emmie remembered the whispering from the previous night. "I heard something before I fell asleep yesterday."

Finn and Sarah sharply turned their heads toward Emmie.

"A spirit?" Sarah asked.

Emmie nodded. "A voice, or voices, and I think it was trying to tell me something, but frankly I was too out of it to focus. I don't even remember what they were saying."

"And I'll bet anything the voices are related to Owl and his philosophy, whatever that is. I've sorted those books here." Finn gestured to a nearby stack and tapped his hand on the volumes. "If we're to understand what's happening in this house, I've got a lot more reading to do."

Emmie gestured at the design on the ceiling. "Have you guys

found any mention of the designs? I've seen variations of it everywhere." Emmie followed the flow of the intricate patterns with fascination.

"Some of these notebooks are full of drawings, equations, notes on margins. I'll look for those shapes too. I left my phone in the house. Would you take pictures of these?"

Deciding to cooperate, Emmie fished out her phone and zoomed in on the detail of the ceiling, taking a photo. She went ahead and photographed the shelves, the things on the table, and the very table she had been leaning on.

"Well, since you're so talented at reading fast..." Emmie gave Finn a wide, flat smile. "I'm sure you'll let us know what you find in Owl's philosophy."

"Not so much a talent, but I *am* relentless." Finn folded some papers and picked up others. "I'll get to work."

Sarah stood, took a blanket that was folded over the cot and returned to the chairs, telling Finn, "I can spread this over us to keep warm and I'll skim stuff. If I find something good—"

"Shouldn't we try to summon Sterling?" Emmie cut in.

Sarah's gaze jumped to Finn. He stared back at her. "He needs help... don't you?"

Before Finn could answer, Emmie said, "He needs to focus. And the spirits are stubborn, so I could totally use your help. As always."

The electric heater buzzed for a few seconds and the lights dimmed then popped back on.

Finn glanced over at a lamp, then at Emmie. "Look at that. You mention spirits and the obligatory electrical problems start."

As Emmie stepped toward the door, Sarah's gaze was locked on Finn. "You coming?"

Finn kept quiet but watched Sarah with a mournful smile.

He's reeling her in like a fish on a hook.

"Sarah," Emmie said, more sharply than she'd meant to, "I really need your help."

As if broken out of a daze, Sarah looked over at Emmie again with a startled expression and stood up, resting her hand on Finn's shoulder for balance. "We'll come back in a bit."

Emmie reached out and tugged on her friend's hand. *Sarah, you're making a fool of yourself.*

"See you soon." Finn picked up a book again.

Emmie opened the door, letting out the little warmth the electric heater had produced. She opened it even wider as Sarah stepped outside, and a rush of cold air swept in and filled the room. A strong wind mixed with light snow whipped across Emmie's face as she shut the door. The low clouds overhead were growing gray and thick.

Sarah hurried down the steps first, but Emmie lost her balance for a moment and the wind knocked her foot into an aluminum snow shovel sitting beside the door. The shovel twisted sideways and crashed down, catching on the handrail and coming to a stop at an angle over the door. The handrails on either side of the stairs weren't flush with the house, leaving a small gap into which the shovel had slipped.

Sarah didn't seem to notice. She hurried ahead and screamed, "It's too cold!"

Emmie hesitated, glancing up at the lake house. No sign that Finn had noticed the commotion outside.

Serves you right.

Before she knew it, Emmie was racing with Sarah back to the warmth of Whisper House.

At the door, Sarah looked toward the little house. No doubt with her mind still on Finn.

16

A few minutes later, they had made coffee and walked through the house to the sunroom with their cups.

Emmie led Sarah to two oversized leather chairs sitting against the far wall away from the windows and made herself comfortable in one. Sarah took the other.

"I'm not sure we should leave Finn alone out there." Sarah held her coffee, but didn't drink it.

"Why not?"

"He's reading so much about the first boy's death. We both know that Finn's not great at expressing his feelings, but I know it's affecting him, making him sad. I'm sure he relates to the surviving brother on a deeper level, comparing it with his own brother's death."

Emmie scoffed. "Sure you didn't imagine that?"

Sarah's eyes widened. "But losing a brother, Em. It must be traumatizing. We are the only children in our families, so it's more difficult to relate, but Finn lost his brother to—" Sarah cleared her throat. "—something he probably feels was preventable."

The snow was coming down faster now, and the wind pressed against the glass around the room as the window frames squeaked. *Finn ought to be feeling the cold by now.* A smile slipped across her face, although she forced it away, then glanced toward Sarah. "Don't worry, he'll be fine."

Sarah nodded, her face full of concern. A silence hung between them as they each took a sip of coffee.

Emmie gestured toward the hidden door leading up into the tower. "We should probably get started there."

Sarah looked over with a confused expression. "Not in Sterling's room?"

"We'll get there soon, but the whispers didn't come from Sterling, I'm sure of that. Something doesn't feel right about that space."

"I won't argue with your intuition. Lead the way."

After grabbing their jackets from the front door, they returned and climbed through the small, hidden door, continuing up onto the first level that had been like a playroom. But Emmie stepped to the spiraling staircase and started moving up toward the tower, which they hadn't reached last time.

"Emmie? Why are we going up there?"

A sullen stubbornness drove Emmie to keep climbing without answering, despite the cold air around her. She moved to the top of the ladder and stood on a platform in the tower. Gray, hazy light came in through the four windows around her. The view must have been spectacular in the summertime, although now, with snow coating everything, it was impossible to get a good sense of distance. The wind whistled through the cracks in the walls on every side.

Sarah came up a moment later, panting and still shivering. Her fingers dug in along the windowsill, her face only inches from the glass. She turned and stepped over to the opposite side of the tower facing out over the backyard. "It looks like Finn turned off the lights in the lake house," Sarah said. "Why would he do that?"

"Really?"

Would Finn know she had left the shovel there? *No chance. How could he know?* But he was smart...

"He can take care of himself. We've got our thing to do." Emmie sat down and extended her hand to Sarah. "Time to communicate."

Sarah glanced out the window one more time before sitting next to Emmie. She wouldn't stop shivering. "Right. Psychics R Us." She made a fist and curled forward with her arms over her stomach. "But let's do the *express* version of communicate this time, okay?"

Emmie grinned and nodded once before closing her eyes and focusing.

Within the darkness of her closed eyelids, Emmie watched twisting rays of light move across her third eye as she had called it as a child. She'd found that the initial shapes didn't mean anything except that she was entering that space where she became a radio beacon for spirits.

Any second now.

Yet sometimes it just took a little longer and sometimes they never appeared at all and sometimes only the spirits from a distance approached her open signal.

She waited. Taking in slow deep breaths in the same process her mother had taught her.

Communicate and meditate.

She had gotten stronger lately... right? But after a few minutes, there was still nothing except the same swirling designs in her mind. No sign of any spirits anywhere.

But her psychic vision had connected with something fresh and unfamiliar within the blackness of her concentration. An energy field surrounded her, made from that same design she'd seen around the house. Concentric mandalas, except now they pulsed, moving and flowing toward the center. She focused on its vibrant energy, and it pulled at her. Just a little, but enough to make her lean back, as if to minimize its pull.

Something banged against the ladder to the tower. Wood

repeatedly creaking as someone made their way up the ladder. If it had been Finn, he would have called out to them.

Finn's locked in. He can't get out.

Was Sarah hearing the creaking? If she was, she wasn't reacting to it.

Emmie couldn't see anyone in her third eye, although she knew someone had entered the room. The spirit was standing behind them, and the hair on the back of her neck tingled.

If I turn around, I will see it. But she didn't look. Not yet. It was better to remain still and focused, and allow the spirit to adjust to their presence.

A whisper began as a soft, distant chant, but it grew louder and clearer. The source came from the spirit in the room, and its presence moved down beside her left ear. There was no breath and no physical contact, but it couldn't have been more than an inch away.

OO EE HH AAAA RR NN SS AAA LL MM UU WW OO FF HH EE VV BAA KO...

The sounds repeated over and over, like a recording set on a loop.

"Who are you?" Emmie asked.

No answer.

Can't let you slip away again. She cracked her eyes open and turned her head toward the presence. Nothing there. The sound stopped, but then it rose again—this time near Sarah.

Still seated and with her eyes closed, Sarah shuddered, then she coughed and gagged.

"Are you okay?" Emmie watched her friend's face.

Sarah's eyes snapped wide open and bulged in their sockets as she threw her hands up across her throat. Her mouth dropped open and saliva dripped down over her clothes.

"Sarah!" Emmie crawled to Sarah's side, grabbing her arm and glancing around for the source of the whispers. The sounds stopped a moment later, and whoever had been in the room with them was now gone.

But Sarah continued choking as her muscles tensed and her face strained, turning a morbid shade of blue.

"Should I call for help?" Emmie asked.

Sarah didn't respond. Instead, she fell forward on her hands and knees, shaking like a terrified animal, then turned her face away and vomited on the floor, gasping for breath after she had cleared her stomach.

Her mind hyper-alert, Emmie wrapped her arm over her friend's back. She had seen Sarah react strongly to ghosts before, but nothing like this. She dug into her pocket to grab her phone, but before she could pull it out and dial, Sarah inhaled normally again between brief bouts of coughing.

She held out her hands toward Emmie's phone. "No." Sarah moaned and took in a few deep breaths.

"Are you sure?" Emmie asked. "I haven't seen you this bad before."

"I... think I'm okay now." Her breathing slowed. "Did you hear anything?"

"Yes. You?"

"No. Did you see anyone?"

"No, did you?"

"No." Sarah sat up and wiped her mouth with the edge of her shirt. She smiled weakly. "Sorry."

She's concerned that I'm *inconvenienced by what happened.*

Emmie smiled warmly and waited, relieved that color was returning to her friend's cheeks.

After a few more breaths, Sarah looked at the clear green fluid she had thrown up. "Odd. As if I hadn't eaten or drunk anything."

"I'll clean it up, but I'd rather we went down now."

Sarah frowned. "I'm the nurse here." She touched her neck. "I've never felt that... strange before."

"Were they choking you?"

"No."

"But you felt their presence, right?"

"Yes. They were standing here right next to us."

"More than one?"

"I don't know."

Emmie could see in Sarah's eyes that the encounter had weakened her. The questions could wait. She helped Sarah up and toward the ladder. "We're done for now."

Before stepping down, Sarah turned back to Emmie with tired eyes. "At first, it was just nausea like what happens with some spirits, feeling their pain, but then it got a lot worse all of a sudden."

"Like they were attacking you?"

Sarah shook her head. "No, like all of my insides were pushing to get out."

"Oh God. Do you think that could actually happen?"

A sparkle of humor filled Sarah's eyes. "Geez, I hope not. Don't worry." She glanced down at her shirt. "I better get cleaned up before Finn gets back."

"A little vomit won't put him off."

Sarah's subtle smile faded as she paused for a moment. "The weird thing is that when everything inside of me was pushing to come out, it felt like the right thing to do."

17

Finn cranked up the electric heater to the warmest setting, but it didn't warm him enough—not enough for him to get comfortable, anyway. Dropping back into his chair, he eyed the stack of hardcover books. He really could have used Sarah's help. And her warmth.

Within moments, the power went out.

Oh shit.

Probably just a tripped circuit or, judging by the age of the house, a blown fuse. He got up and searched behind bookcases and in the closets for a circuit breaker but concluded that it must be inside the main house.

A nuisance, but not a big deal.

It would surprise the girls to see him return so quickly. And maybe he'd make another attempt to bring Sarah back with him, although Emmie wasn't making it easy for him to get some alone time with Sarah. Was all his attention on her making Emmie jealous?

Not trying to rock the friendship boat, Emmie.

But Sarah was giving him clear signs to move forward. All the flirting, the eye contact, the intimacy. Still, it would be awful if he misinterpreted her signals and caused awkwardness between them. He needed alone time with her to make absolutely sure they were on the same page, but Emmie was standing in the way.

He put on his jacket and went to the door. The window had frosted up a bit, but it couldn't hide the heavy snowfall coming down outside. Bracing himself for the wind and freezing temperatures, he opened the main door and pushed on the storm door. It cracked open half an inch before it slammed against a hard object and refused to budge. Something blocked it from the outside.

Dammit!

He pressed his forehead against the icy glass, trying to spot the obstruction. Nothing he could see from that angle. He peeked out through the crack and saw the gray handle of a snow shovel lying in front of the door. It must have fallen when Sarah and Emmie left.

Finn pushed harder, hearing the wood crack beneath his weight. If he had to break the door down, he would, although the door and glass had the same intricate designs as the rest of the house. Original, and impossible to replace. Paying for the damage wouldn't bother him too much, but he would rather avoid destroying part of Audrey's cherished renovation project.

And Joan's ghost might get mad at him as well; ghosts didn't seem to like him much.

A sinking sensation washed through him when he patted his pocket. As he'd just told Emmie, he'd left his phone charging in the house.

All right, another way out? No back door and no other windows except for the large, picturesque ones looking out over the lake. Also irreplaceable, he suspected.

Turning back to the storm door, he spotted four small latches around the glass window. It was meant to come off in the springtime and be replaced by a screen window. He managed to turn the latches, but years of paint over the wood frame and the door had sealed them together. Without assistance from the outside, it wouldn't come off.

A shiver traveled up his back. Panic already, or just a little cold air? A mix of both?

The electric heater's skimpy warmth had already escaped through the open door, and he took a deep breath as the cool air crept under his jacket. Nothing *little* about it; this was an arctic blast. He was sheltered, out of the wind, yes, but the temperature couldn't have been more than twenty degrees. For all practical purposes, he was *outside*.

Okay, Finn, time to use that brain you flaunt so often.

Instead, he pushed against the storm door again, this time without holding back a barrage of curses at himself for not bringing his phone. The shovel didn't budge.

What are the odds? He *had* heard something strike the door when the girls left, but at the time he hadn't thought twice about it. Too absorbed in those damn books. Sarah or Emmie must have inadvertently knocked over the shovel on the way out. But hadn't they heard it fall? Either way, the temperature was dropping fast. The chill had penetrated the thin layers of clothing beneath his jacket.

He hurried over to the large windows overlooking the lake and found the same type of latches as on the storm door but didn't bother with them since they were painted over too.

I'm trapped.

His face and hands numbed, and his legs shivered. His heart beat faster at the realization that it would take a liberal dose of luck to escape without breaking anything. And maybe some brawn for good measure—but only if necessary.

He pushed the door open as far as it would go. Enough space to get *something* out there, something narrow to push or pull the shovel out of the way.

Now you're thinking.

An old metal clothes hanger would probably work the best, but there was nothing like that in the house as far as he could see.

Digging through a box of papers, he discovered a foot-long

metal ruler. Not ideal, but maybe it would work. The shovel wasn't that far outside the door. He got down on his knees and pushed against the storm door while jabbing the ruler as far as it would go through the crack. The handle stopped it from going more than a few inches out and it tapped the edge of the shovel but made no difference. Too small.

He cupped his hands and blew into them. His bare fingers were growing numb and ached when he tried to bend them. Even stuffing his hands under his armpits didn't help much.

My kingdom for a pair of gloves!

His legs shivered almost uncontrollably while standing in front of the door with the wind whistling through the crack. He spotted the back side of Whisper House and wondered how long Sarah would wait before coming out to look for him.

Finn closed his eyes for a moment and pictured her. Maybe there was some little speck of psychic ability buried beneath all that hubris. He focused on her and called, "Sarah, get out here."

His voice died in the silence. Of course, she wouldn't hear him.

Because you're not psychic. Not even a little.

Doesn't hurt to try.

But Sarah would come back soon on her own, wouldn't she?

She would feel his distress and rescue him. Because they had a connection between them now, and it had grown stronger lately. A deep, wonderful bond even stronger than her friendship with Emmie.

She likes me, she likes me not...

The desk caught his eye. He stepped over and saw an assortment of sculptor's tools, some of them rusted. And there was a black hammer. The metal head was flat on one side and sharp on the other, and the wood handle was still solid after so many years.

Looks like the only way out is blunt force.

He held it up with a grin, as if it were Thor's hammer.

Moving back to the doorway, he paused for a moment and took aim at the door. "Sorry, Joan and Audrey."

He hurled it through the glass as hard as he could. The impact sprayed the antique glass out across the cement steps, and some shards scattered inside near the bottom of the door. The hammer thumped onto the steps outside. Razor-sharp glass teeth remained around the edges of the window.

Taking up a thick paintbrush, he used the wooden shaft to clear away as much of the glass around the frame as possible. He opened a space large enough for his head to peek out, although he had to be careful with the edges. Now he could see the shovel lying across the door. The opening was too narrow to fit through, otherwise he would simply reach down and pull it out of the way. But it wouldn't take him long now to free himself.

He could already hear Audrey's gasps of distress at what he'd done to her house, but he was more intent on finding something to reach out and hook the shovel. The item didn't need to be so small this time.

Digging into a closet, he found an antique mahogany painter's easel and an old black cane with an ornate pearl handle. A name was inscribed into it: Mr. Owen Cromwell.

Owl.

Finn's gaze stopped on something painted on the wall behind the cane. He pushed aside the objects obscuring it, and even partly frozen he paused to contemplate the bleak mural of a boy standing beside a tree while looking out over the lake. No doubt Joan had painted it. These colors were faded and sad, and the scene was reminiscent of early Impressionist painters of the early 1900s with an extra dose of drab thrown in. Only a section a few feet across was visible. The rest of the painting was blocked by larger items in the closet and... wallpaper. Someone had covered it. Not Audrey, judging by the age and style of the paper.

He was tempted to remove it, to reveal more of the clue, but the sad scene of a boy would have to wait.

Right now, Owl's cane was the answer, and he hurried back to the door and extended it through the shattered opening until it was hooked under the shovel. He was careful to avoid the shards of glass protruding from the door's wooden frame and lifted the cane carefully until the shovel was high enough for him to grab with his other hand. As he tossed it away from the door, the aluminum shovel clanked down the cement steps and lodged itself in the thin layer of snow that had accumulated since the girls had left.

The storm door opened. Relief swept through him; he would clean up the glass before the snow covered it, but his body ached in the freezing air. His face and hands were numb, and he needed to get back inside Whisper House as quickly as possible.

Despite his numb limbs, he refused to leave behind the handful of books and notebooks he'd discovered, as they held precious information he had to share with Sarah and Emmie. He grabbed them and hurried outside, picking up the hammer at the bottom of the steps along the way. Cradling the books with both hands, he hung the hammer by its claw from his pocket. No sense in leaving it there for someone to trip on.

On his way to the house, the snow came down in light flakes the size of small white feathers, although the gusts of wind blasted it somewhat painfully into his face. The dark gray skies hung overhead despite the weather reports predicting only a couple inches of snow, at most, for that area. The bulk of the winter storm was supposed to pass through a couple of hours north of their location. They would miss the worst of it, thank God.

Bursting into the house and stomping his feet to clear his shoes, he called out to Sarah and Emmie through lips that had gone stiff, although there was no reply.

Leaving the books on the kitchen table, he removed his coat and absorbed the warmth slowly and painfully as it thawed his skin. A noise came from down the hallway near the sunroom; a creak in the floorboards, as if someone had taken a step.

Finn walked toward the noise, expecting the girls to come out from one of the rooms at any moment.

"Sarah? Emmie? Anyone care that I almost froze to death?"

He was being dramatic, of course, but the whole thing had stressed him out, although he would never admit to that. Still, he would welcome a little sympathy. Especially from Sarah.

Moving into the hallway, where the noise had come from, he found no sign of them, but as he walked to the doorway of the séance room, someone's voice filled his right ear.

OO EE HH AAAA RR NN SS AAA LL MM UU WW OO...

❧ 18 ❧

The front door opened and closed, and Emmie's heart beat faster. Her bedroom door rattled a little with the change in air pressure, although Sarah seemed not to notice.

But Emmie had heard it. Finn had gotten out.

Of course he got out. What did you expect?

Emmie raised her voice to mask the noises from downstairs. She continued reminiscing about the old days in high school without a pause as they sat facing each other on the bed.

But the wind whistling in through the cracks around the window frame caught Sarah's attention. Her friend climbed off the bed and stood at the window, peeking out through the blinds with a concerned expression.

"He isn't back yet." Sarah spoke without turning around.

"I wouldn't worry." Emmie forced a laugh. "Remember when Mrs. Hansen yelled at us in the eighth grade?"

Sarah nodded once and glanced back, although her expression hadn't changed. "I wonder if he needs our help."

Emmie couldn't stop herself from grinning. *Not anymore.*

And it wasn't like she expected him to freeze to death out there. He was too smart for that. It was just a simple shovel blocking the doorway, after all. Nothing more than a practical joke. But her breathing shallowed while listening for sounds of how Finn might react to what she'd done.

He wasn't shouting, at least. And maybe he'd simply pushed the shovel out of the way—not an inconvenience at all. Her little *practical joke* had been a dud.

But when she heard footsteps approaching in the hallway, her body tensed and her pulse thumped in her ears. She turned to face the door. No sense in cowering for what she had done. She would face his rage head on.

When he knocked on the door, Emmie shuddered.

I shouldn't have done it. Bad choice, Em.

He didn't wait for an answer before opening the door and stepping inside. He stumbled in, holding his hand while shivering. His hair was wet and disheveled, although his expression was nothing like she expected. No rage, no anger. Just a beaten-down man putting on a brave face for them.

Sarah lurched over to him. She was dressed in her bathrobe after having gotten out of the shower only minutes earlier. "Are you okay?"

"Not really. It was an adventure, that's for sure." He stepped toward them glancing down at Sarah's robe.

"What happened?" she asked.

Finn held out his hand and uncovered it, revealing a small amount of blood around his palm. "Cut myself, I guess. Didn't even realize it until after I got into the house and started warming up."

"What did you cut yourself on?"

He glanced up at them. "I had to break the glass on the storm door to get out. The shovel must've fallen over and jammed the door after you left."

Emmie stared at the wound and was filled with deep remorse for not having gone back and moved the shovel out of the way. Why had she let him stay imprisoned in there? She would never have wished for him to get hurt or even feel that cold. What had she been thinking?

Did he know that it was her fault? His eyes didn't show it.

"Why didn't you just call us?" Sarah asked, still inspecting the wound and slowly leading him out the door.

"I ran my phone down yesterday taking photos and looking up info on the web, and I left it charging in the house. The one time I forget to charge up my phone before bed..."

"You need to clean that," she said. "Was it just glass that cut you? Not anything metal, like rusty nails?"

"Not that I know."

Emmie stood and followed them to the bathroom, where Sarah directed Finn to wash the wound while she retrieved some bandages from her suitcase. Standing beside Finn, Emmie put her arm on his upper back. His body was cold. Dead cold. "My God, how did you get like this?"

"The power went out after I cranked up the heat."

Her heart sank. It had been worse for him than she had imagined. "We should have checked on you."

"Yeah, but... no big deal. I should have known better than to push my luck in an old house like this. Probably still the old wiring out there."

Returning, Sarah put the Band-Aid on Finn as if he were a patient of hers. She wiped his face and moved his damp hair off his forehead. "Good as new."

Again he glanced down at her robe. "Why are you wearing that?"

Sarah looked at Emmie then back at Finn. "We had a little accident while trying to communicate with spirits."

"What sort of accident? Get one of those exorcist demons that pukes on you?"

"Something like that."

Finn must have realized his mistake and put his arm around her, pulling her closer. "Sorry. You okay?"

Sarah nodded while smiling, then looked up into his eyes. "Nothing major. Did you find anything while you were out there?"

"Lots of stuff, although my research was cut short by the power outage." Finn let Sarah go. "I brought some of the books inside with me. Whoever this Owl Cromwell guy was, he was into some whacked-out ideas. Sort of a combination between Nikola Tesla and Gurdjieff."

Finn inched toward the door. The gears behind his eyes had gone into overdrive.

He's itching to tell us about what he found. "Let's hear about it," Emmie said.

Losing no time, he led them downstairs to the kitchen table, where a stack of three thick leather-bound books and a larger, thinner book sat in the center of the table. They crowded around it.

Finn opened one of them before they sat down. He flipped through the pages. "All this in here is handwritten. It must've been a personal journal, something to capture Owl's ideas while he was trying to figure things out." He closed that book and opened the larger one. "This one was published." Opening it to the inside front page, Finn pointed to the photograph of a man in a suit sitting with his hand on a table.

The man was younger than the white-bearded version Emmie had seen in the photo next to her room, but unmistakably the same. A regal posture, thick, wise brows, and a laser-sharp stare. "No mistaking a mug like that. The old guy with Joan in the photo is Owl Cromwell."

"Absolutely. And you see here..." He pointed at the information at the bottom of the page: Printed in Boston, Massachusetts. "So a younger version of the cult master lived or went through Boston at one time. Which means either he came to Minnesota and Joan followed or the opposite. She may have encountered him there and then come to live here for the freezing cold, as Audrey said, then lost her child and—"

"Got into Spiritualism," Sarah said, "along with so many other women who were misled."

"Correct," Finn said. "And she was rich, so she might have

financed his coming here and then started getting other women to buy into his wonky ideas."

He opened one of the thicker hardcover books. Emmie caught a glimpse of what was in it: handwritten text like a diary, except there were lots of drawings, mathematical equations and strange symbols scribbled in the margins and along the edges.

Emmie pointed to it. "You understand all that, Finn?"

He stared at it without answering as if he were trying to digest all the information. "Kind of."

Sarah leaned forward to peer at the notes. "That looks like someone heavy into math, but also seems like a masculine handwriting."

"Don't be sexist." Finn grinned.

Emmie had pulled a thinner scrapbook her way and flipped through it. She found dozens of small colorful drawings pasted in it. They were intricate mandalas, and of the same designs she had seen around the house.

"I was right." Emmie pointed to one of them. "The hidden door has this design on it, and the ceiling of the séance room, and in the lake house. Joan created them all, but are they connected to the math and equations?"

Sarah also looked, flipping pages. "Were they trying to, like, open a portal into another world?"

Finn laughed. "Stargate!"

"Hey, it's not a far-fetched idea." At Finn's skeptical stare, Emmie explained, "Well, not such a crazy idea, considering."

"Considering what?" Finn asked.

Emmie struggled to find the right words. "The mandalas. Couldn't they be like doors to get to the other side? If they were obsessed with talking to spirits and Joan had lost a child, and the other ladies were also grieving for someone, they must have believed there was a way into the realm of death and back. Or just one way?"

Sitting down as if finally admitting to exhaustion, Finn pondered her words as he again looked at the notes and equations. "It was as if he wanted to marry mysticism and science." He motioned over the page. "All these notes relate to repetition and some drawings—" He tapped one that showed waves. "—indicate that he was working with the principle of vibration too. Have you heard of the Hermetic Teachings?"

"Oh God," Emmie said. "This sounds like the stuff I flunked in school."

"Doubt it was this stuff," Finn said. "But to cut a long story short, the idea is that the form of anything at all, this table, you, the wine, anything, is determined by the frequency of the vibration of its atoms and molecules. Well, more or less that. So that would apply, in theory, even to spirit. Quantum mysticism nowadays also embraces this idea and says that what we think, or whether positively or negatively, will create a motion and manifest physically." He turned the notebook toward them and put his finger over a line, reading it: "Energy follows thought."

"That would be a séance, wouldn't it? Calling spirits?" Sarah frowned while considering the concept. "Holding hands would be a way of sharing and creating heat, therefore, energy."

Finn leaned back. "Absolutely. They would have thought so. And yes, the mandalas could be like doors—portals—so it's not surprising they cover the hidden doors Joan created in this house. The house has an inner maze that she reproduces in the mandalas. They must always have been playing with this type of idea..."

An image came to Emmie's head. A photograph. "You know, Owl was holding some sort of goggles in one of the pictures around here. I thought they were like aviator goggles, but at that time, they didn't exist."

Finn's eyes lit up, and he leafed through the book of annotations. "Look at this, then." A drawing showed diagrams of a pair of goggles. The drawing and notes were like schematics, broken down into the various parts of the goggles' construction, with details about what each component was made of.

"He made those?" Emmie said.

"It says right here he did. His notes go on to talk about energy, combining it, withholding it and neutralizing it, and other more complex ideas of the universal laws of physics and the circular nature of time. Albert Einstein only published his general theory of relativity in 1916, so it looks like this guy was ahead of his time and way more eccentric than any physicist."

"But what would he use those for?" Sarah studied the sketches with a puzzled expression.

"All the letters and some other stuff I read in the lake house showed it was much more than just a scientific interest. They were philosophical and spiritual writings showing that he was proposing another nature to reality."

Emmie felt a little less bad now about leaving Finn out in the lake house. Despite his trouble and injury, he had discovered new information. Her actions hadn't dampened his drive for knowledge to their advantage. She still hoped he never realized what she had done, even as she tried to rationalize it.

"'The path to a man's soul is found in his Truth,'" he read on the page across from the sketch. "Truth with a capital T, no less. But those people capitalized every other word. Looks like he was big on getting to the source of reality." He tapped some words: "The Truth in all things."

"Doesn't sound like science," Emmie said. "It sounds like he wanted to start a religion."

"A cult," Sarah said. "They always end in death."

"Which they consider a sort of twisted liberation."

"So it must be Owl Cromwell whispering to us," Sarah said. "That makes sense after I got so sick earlier. He's trying to poison us."

"If it's him," Emmie said, "I haven't seen him yet, but someone is definitely here. We should focus on contacting him instead of Sterling or Joan."

Sarah formed a worried expression. "I have to admit, I'm a little scared. If he's the same spirit we encountered earlier up in the tower, I'd rather not go through that again."

Finn met Sarah's eyes. "What happened? Is that why you were in a robe?" He leaned over, putting his hand on Sarah's shoulder. "Sarah, did anything hurt you?"

"No," she said quickly. "No, it wasn't like that. I felt like maybe there—" She stopped short and looked at Emmie. "Those pictures you took of the lake house. Do you have them?"

"Yes..." Emmie pulled her phone from her back pocket while trying to remember what photos she'd taken there that might have suddenly interested Sarah so much. She brought the photos onto the screen and handed the phone to her friend.

Sarah swiped through the photos and stopped on one. She zoomed in on an object in the background and turned the screen toward them. "Do either of you recognize this?"

Emmie shook her head. The image showed a glass case displaying small, lacey white flowers with five petals.

Finn studied it for a moment, then burst out with a single laugh. "Socrates!"

"The philosopher?" Emmie asked. "How does he fit into this?"

"He doesn't." Finn grinned. "Not really. But they used that same stuff to silence him. It's hemlock. Poison."

F inn stared into Sarah's eyes. Her eyelids drooped and her movements were slow. Not quite herself lately, although she had mentioned feeling sick.

"Hemlock has plenty of medical uses too," Sarah said. "Like treating epilepsy, insomnia, even breast cancer. Of course, back in those days, it was celebrated as an ornamental plant since they didn't fully understand the dangers."

Emmie groaned. "But they must've known it was poisonous."

"To an extent, I'm sure they did, but the average person didn't always get accurate information back then. It was common to get advice on health from a barber or a clergyman. But hemlock is a beautiful, flowery plant, perfect for decorations, and I'm sure someone made a lot of money selling it as an essential part of anyone's home decor."

Emmie cringed. "That's messed up."

"Very messed up, and a lot of people died from it." Sarah touched her stomach and glanced away as she winced. "The pain would've been horrible. Something like what I felt."

Finn looked into Sarah's eyes. "Are you... feeling the poisonings?"

Sarah touched her stomach. "It comes and goes."

His body tensed as he looked toward the kitchen counter, where he'd left his phone charging earlier. "We should get you out of here. It's not safe." He turned to Emmie as his face warmed. "Why didn't you tell me she was going through *this?*"

Emmie crossed her arms defensively. "You know she gets sick."

"Not *poisoning* sick."

"She's not in any *real* danger."

Finn's eyes widened. "Isn't she?" He gestured to Sarah's face. "I knew it was something more than just the weather. She can't stay here."

"Finn," Sarah spoke softly while touching his arm, "you're overreacting."

"But you're feeling the effects of hemlock. The *poison.* You need a doctor."

Sarah shook her head. "I haven't consumed it physically. How would I explain this to a doctor?"

"But *they* died from it."

"I'm fine now."

Finn stared into her eyes for a few seconds without speaking, then glanced over at Emmie who looked back at him quietly. He clenched his teeth. Something had gotten into that girl recently. Jealousy, for sure, but it was more than that. Her demeanor toward him had completely changed since the vacation, and that expression... Contempt?

What are you so afraid of, Em? That I'll run off with your best friend and leave you all alone?

Maybe if you keep up that *attitude.*

But it wasn't just her attitude getting in the way, now she was keeping secrets from him too.

"Don't be angry at Em," Sarah said, breaking into his thoughts as if she could read them. "She's not forcing me to stay here. Nobody is. It's just all a part of my gift anyway."

Sarah put on a brave face, although Finn saw through the

mask to the pain in her eyes. He stroked her back as Sarah's smile soothed his panic. She had that power over him. She could connect with strong emotions, but she could affect them as well. The gift went both ways. "Just say the word, and I'll call the doctor."

"No need. Doctors can't help in my case. It's just part of the job." She turned back to Emmie. "But we shouldn't get sidetracked by how I'm feeling. Worse things happened in this house. These people all died together, and their families probably covered it up. I am almost sure that they died of poisoning. Not food—hemlock, judging by what Joan preserved behind glass."

The books caught Finn's attention again. He paused to open a notebook and paged through to find something he'd seen earlier: a drawing of the hemlock plant broken down into its parts with handwritten notes scribbled beside each part. The leaves were noted: 'In moderation, little harm, but use no more than six.' The stem, seeds and roots were noted: 'Beware of these.'

"You see here?" Finn tapped his finger on the page. "She knew they were dangerous. This wasn't just a woman seeking a home decoration. She'd cultivated a lot of knowledge by then, and I'm sure she was depressed."

Emmie leaned forward. "Losing her first son might already have set her mind on suicide. Being here with Owl Cromwell and other women who were searching for loved ones beyond death could have turned her mind completely."

"There's an obsessive nature to the mandalas and decorations, even to the paintings. But are we sure that *she* did it?" Sarah asked. "Could she have really poisoned all of them? So depressed and desperate she killed her other little boy as well?"

"The only way to know that for sure is to locate her." Emmie looked around. "If she died here along with everyone else, then they all have to be here. The truth is in this house somewhere."

Sarah nodded. "Just a matter of time before we find it."

Finn turned his focus to Sarah again. She was a nurse, but he'd discovered she could be stubborn sometimes. "Maybe you should lie down for a while?"

Sarah let go of him and his body chilled again.

"You're concerned about me," Sarah said. "It's sweet. But I'll let you know when things get to be too much. You know that I'm tougher than I look."

Finn nodded slowly. Maybe it was better to reel in his feelings for a while, at least while Emmie was around. "Yeah. I forgot."

Emmie grabbed Sarah's arm and laughed while meeting her friend's gaze. "Tougher than me in a lot of ways."

Ugh. Emmie was almost begging for her friend's attention.

Time to step aside. Emmie, she's all yours.

Finn picked up the book containing the diagrams for Owl's goggles. No sense in wasting time trying to unravel Emmie's insecurities.

They watched him.

"Something wrong?" Emmie asked.

With you.

Finn shrugged. "Maybe I'm not feeling so good either. Still need to warm up." He stepped over to the counter and grabbed his phone. "I better get back to work looking up some of this stuff."

He left the kitchen without looking at them and headed upstairs to his room. He *did* need to warm up after escaping from the lake house, and he could do some of the research from his bed. And probably get more done with a little privacy too.

Passing the door to the girls' room, he spotted the photo that Emmie had mentioned, showing Owl holding the goggles. Yes, they were the same ones as shown in the diagram; the mad professor had built them—but where were they, if they had lasted at all? He snapped a photo of the picture and went to his room.

Crawling under the thick comforter over his bed to keep

warm, he opened the book across his lap and stopped at the diagram of Owl's goggles. He took a photo of that page too. If the goggles still existed, he could enlist a little help from a new friend with knowledge of such things to find them. He texted the two photos and a brief description of what he was looking for to Jason Reeves.

But no immediate response.

Sarah stopped by his room to let him know she was taking Emmie into town.

"Emmie thinks the shops here might be cheaper than closer to home. We do need warmer sweaters, and socks," she said.

"*You* could borrow mine," he said. "I have clean, fluffy ones."

She blushed, laughed, then shut the door in a hurry. He smiled. *She likes me...*

Emmie... likes me not. He tilted his head from one side to the other, then shook it as if shaking off a creature perching there. *I'm just so tired.*

It was good for them to leave for a while. Maybe getting away from the house would help with Sarah's sickness—that made sense. He would miss her company, but he accomplished a lot more when isolating himself with an intriguing book—and the books he'd found so far were growing more fascinating by the minute.

For the rest of the evening, he did exactly that—immerse himself with all the strange knowledge he'd discovered, and he relished the solitude. Diagrams and philosophical ideas demanded all his concentration and challenged him to consider things far beyond anything he'd ever encountered. The intelligence and depth in the books and notes were mind-boggling, and he occasionally found himself scratching his head.

The two women returned in the evening, with Sarah looking healthier, which he was glad and relieved to see. After they'd all said goodnight and settled into bed, his phone alerted him to a text.

Jason had responded with a brief message and directions to an address somewhere north of St. Lombard.

Found them. Meet me at this address at 10 a.m. tomorrow morning. Don't be late.

❦ 20 ❧

"What did you tell the girls?" Jason asked the next morning while shaking Finn's hand on the sidewalk outside Billy's Occult Museum.

"The truth. That I was going to see you."

Jason grinned. "Emmie must have loved hearing that. Why not just tell them you were heading out to the library or something? Might have saved you a little stress."

"I thrive under stress. And they're psychics, remember? They'll get it out of me one way or another."

"But they can't read minds, right?"

Finn thought about it. "God, I hope not." He rubbed his eyes.

"Didn't sleep well?" Jason asked.

"Kept... waking up. Too many damn noises."

Jason's eyes widened. "What? You heard something?"

"No... no, nothing like that."

It was too cold to stand outside and talk. The snow was coming down a little faster now. The weather reports had showed they'd receive some accumulation over the next twenty-four hours. A typical December snowfall.

Finn gestured toward the museum. "Let's get inside."

Jason didn't argue. They hurried along the cement walkway toward the front entrance of the museum. "Were they upset at you leaving them in that place alone?"

"Not upset at all. Emmie seemed very happy, actually—maybe a little *too* happy. Neither of them was feeling good. Sarah, physically, and Emmie... She's got issues lately."

"Because you came with me?"

"More than that. *Much* more than that."

A large wooden skull hung over the door of the museum, surrounded by dozens of smaller items and signs warning visitors of the horrors inside. The building was a repurposed gas station, judging by the layout, with occult-themed signs hanging from the metal poles where the gas pumps had existed. "Are you sure we'll find the goggles in this place?"

Jason didn't slow down. "I'm sure."

"Doesn't seem like the right home for something owned by an obscure cult leader. I thought nobody had heard of Owl Cromwell outside of St. Lombard."

"It's here."

Finn narrowed his eyes. "So, how did you find it?"

"You want me to reveal my sources?"

"I don't think your sources are spies in danger of execution."

"How do you know?" Jason actually seemed to mean it for a second, then shrugged. "Just following the breadcrumbs."

"Let me guess. You discovered the Dyer family held some sort of estate sale down the line and a bunch of Joan's Spiritualist stuff ended up in collectors' hands or in weird little museums not too far from Whisper House."

"Something like that."

"Bet you find a lot of stuff this way. Grandmother's crystal balls and devil figurines. What if this place doesn't want to sell it?"

"I already talked with the owner. He's expecting us and is willing to talk cash." Jason paused before opening the door and leaned closer. "You're supposed to be the target here that we're going to fleece."

"Oh? Maybe give me a heads-up next time so I can get into character."

Jason scoffed, looking Finn up and down. "You'll do fine. Let me do the talking, or just follow my lead."

This guy's a pro. Finn followed Jason into the museum.

Inside, they kicked the freshly fallen snow off their shoes. A musty antique smell filled the air. It was like that in every small museum Finn had ever visited—the same old wood scent mixed with accumulated dust that smelled almost sweet—and it was comforting in a way; it was the smell of *history*, a veritable time capsule around them.

"I've done business with Billy many times," Jason said, "but he tends to think he's smarter than he is, and he can get stubborn. So watch out."

Finn nodded once.

A gaunt elderly man with a stern glare stepped out of the darkness wearing a flannel shirt and blue jeans held up by a thick brown belt. His gray beard contrasted with his bald head. The old man adjusted his square-rimmed glasses. He spoke only to Jason, as if Finn weren't even there. "I knew you'd come back."

Jason gestured to Finn. "Hello, Billy. This is the friend I told you about."

Billy glanced at Finn for a moment, then back at Jason and then at Finn again. "I heard you want some old Spiritualist goggles?"

"Yeah," Finn said. "Fascinating stuff."

"Why?" Billy narrowed his eyes at him.

"I found some old—"

"He wants to see ghosts," Jason said, cutting Finn short.

Finn held back a cringe. Did he almost give away something important and let the price rise? He smiled awkwardly instead. "Who *doesn't* like spooky stuff?"

"... spooky stuff," Billy repeated.

The lights were low and some of them were colored, no doubt to help play up the ambience for visitors. Finn had visited dozens of occult museums around the world since he'd started investigating the paranormal. This place was less than impressive, but he wasn't there to be impressed. *Just get the goggles and get back to Whisper House to figure out how they work.*

"How about giving my friend the grand tour?" Jason asked Billy, widening his eyes at the man meaningfully. "It's his first time here."

"Yeah, sure. Plenty of *spooky stuff* in this place."

Billy seemed to have that small-town unflappable quality, like he'd seen everything and believed nothing and no one. But he didn't seem to care enough to even make a spectacle to a man he was supposedly cheating. Nevertheless, he led them into the showroom, which consisted of dark dioramas and antique paranormal objects, creepy murals and a slew of framed photos filling every gap. Everything was divided and grouped into walled-off sections. Many of the items near the front were the oldest, dating back to the Civil War, and they moved up in time while weaving through the aisles.

The man motioned toward a strange diorama. It was obviously intended to resemble a séance room such as the one in Whisper House, with plenty of objects traditionally connected with Spiritualism scattered around. A Ouija board and several candles sat on the table, along with a crystal ball and a lamp in the corner. A small antique brass chandelier above the table flickered while the table itself seemed to hover above the ground beneath the fingertips of the mannequins seated around it.

A thin rope separated the visitors from the scene and a handwritten wooden sign hanging in front of them read, "Do NOT touch the displays."

"I'm assuming that you're familiar with all the stories of Spiritualists that thrived around the turn of the nineteenth century." Billy walked beside them with his hands in his pockets.

Finn nodded once. "Yes, I am fascinated by that stuff. My great-great-aunt Linnea—"

Billy cut him short even as Jason threw Finn a pained look that asked him not to overdo it. "So this one is representative of what it might've looked like back then with the medium surrounding himself with his clients, which consisted mostly of lonely rich women back then."

"Like Linnea," Finn said stubbornly.

"It was especially popular among that particular group," Billy continued with his spiel, "since they tended to be drawn in by the more emotional aspects, like contacting their dead loved ones. I suppose it's a little like that even now."

Billy's movements were slow and drawn out. Every once in a while he glanced at Jason with a blank stare, as if asking whether he could stop. His voice rose and fell while rattling off the descriptions of some of the items in the diorama with a minimal amount of enthusiasm. It was obvious he didn't believe any of it. He was just in it for the money. Good.

While Billy's back was turned, Finn stepped to the next diorama, which seemed to go back a little further in time as they moved through the winding path through the museum. It was a dramatic séance with a male mannequin sitting at the head of a small circular table, surrounded by three female mannequins in Victorian dresses. They'd posed the women as if the man had just delivered shocking news, and there was nothing unique about it except for the goggles over the man's eyes—the same goggles Finn had seen in the diagram and in the photo at Whisper House. No doubt, this was Owl.

"Are these my goggles?" Finn didn't have to feign his enthusiasm.

Jason joined him and turned to Billy. "Are those what I asked you about on the phone?"

"Those are it." Billy also joined them in front of the display. "Built by a guy named Owl Cromwell, from Boston, I think, who traveled around giving lectures on Spiritualist theories to anyone who would listen." Billy pointed at an old pamphlet announcing a lecture by Owl to be held in that very town, a hundred and thirty years ago, and continued, "But his cheerleading among the ladies for his movement ended in tragedy in a big house somewhere south of here."

Whisper House.

Here was the actual relic that Owl had conceived and built, and Billy didn't have a clue about Joan or the house they probably still haunted. *You don't know what you don't know.* Finn focused on the intricate design of the goggles from that distance. A thousand questions jumped into his mind, but Jason elbowed him before he could speak.

"Mind if I take a closer look at those?" Jason asked Billy.

Billy gave a dramatic sigh. "They aren't fake, and they're not damaged." He looked from one to the other. "We've been through this before, Jason. What are they worth? Really?"

Jason looked at Finn. "What do you say, my friend?" His reflection in the glass winked at him as he continued, "At least a couple of hundred, right?"

Acting a bit shocked, Finn allowed his gaze to drift to the goggles. "I haven't even held them—"

Billy paused, still gazing into Jason's eyes as if searching for any signs of deceit, then unlatched the rope separating them from the diorama. "Go have a look."

Jason stepped in and slipped the goggles off the mannequin. He studied them for a minute, putting them on and holding them up to the light at various angles until turning to Finn with a small, solemn nod. "This is the good stuff."

The look in Jason's eyes was meant to tell target-Finn these were the real deal, while the subtle smile to Billy said, "He'll fall for it."

A further look at Finn as he handed him the goggles said, "Make sure they really are what you are looking for."

Finn slipped them on with real anticipation and saw exactly nothing. He looked around in every direction, with Jason holding him by the arm, probably so he didn't fall through a glass display, and still saw nothing.

But he was sure these were an antique, and who else but Owl would build such a thing? He let his mouth hang open. "These are incredible! They totally shut us off from the world."

Billy snorted, which was just the reaction Finn had hoped for. *Good, he thinks I'm an idiot.* Finn raised the goggles to his forehead and grinned.

"Worth a couple of hundred?" Jason asked.

"Well..." Finn balked, then took out his wallet, looking through it. "I really thought..."

Billy folded his arms over his chest. "You want them or not?" He peeked into Finn's wallet, which Finn wanted him to do, as Finn made calculations under his breath.

"Need to pay for gas..."

"Credit card?" Jason asked.

Finn ran a finger over one of them. "Not sure how much room I've got..."

"Two hundred," Billy said with finality. "Cash only."

Jason turned to Finn and met his gaze. There was a gleam in his eyes and a hint of a grin. "Take it or leave it, my friend. You never know when someone else might walk in."

"I've got three sets," Billy said suddenly. "Two in the back. I need to keep one for the display, but you can take two of them for four hundred."

The man was licking his lips. Finn now removed cash from his wallet and started counting and making more calculations. "Gas... Lunch..."

Watching Finn count out the money, Jason turned to Billy with a smile. "You can swing three fifty, Finn."

Jason didn't wait for him to reply before snatching that amount from Finn's hand and handing it over to Billy, who fingered the notes and broke into a wide grin. "I'll grab the other one." He hurried away.

Jason stepped closer to Finn and whispered, "I need to get my commission, or he won't believe the deal."

Billy disappeared into a back room for about ten minutes and returned with a paper bag and a smug smile. He handed the bag to Finn, then patted his stomach as if he'd just eaten some delicious treat.

Finn glanced inside. Two sets of goggles. He held back a wave of excitement sweeping through him. "That's it?"

"That's it." Billy ushered them across the room and almost pushed Finn toward the door. "Goodbye, then."

Finn followed Jason outside. "Thank you! If I see anything through these, I'll let you—" The door snapped shut behind them.

Finn held back a wild laugh until they rounded the corner, and Jason held up a wad of cash.

"That your cut from Billy?" Finn asked, a little outraged.

"No. You're not seeing that money again. Just business, nothing personal."

"I didn't really even need two sets of goggles..." Finn gestured to the cash. "How much?"

"A hundred and seventy-five."

"Half?" Finn frowned. "I—"

"This," Jason went on, stuffing the money into Finn's coat pocket, "is for *my* goggles."

"Ah. One is yours, is it?"

"Too right."

"You don't even know if it'll do anything."

"Don't worry about me. And if you and the girls discover anything—*anything*—about how they work, you let me know right away. Deal?"

"Would I scam you?" Finn said with a devious grin.

"No." Jason patted his arm. "The girls may not be able to read minds, but I can."

Another wink, and he walked away in the whistling wind.

21

Finn stepped inside and kicked the snow from his shoes while taking them off. It was a little past noon, but gray clouds hovered low and darkened the sky, made even darker by the thick snow falling in a steady torrent. The wind had kicked up, and he hadn't checked the weather reports lately, but there was no mistake about it. This was a full-on Minnesota blizzard.

Sarah greeted him at the door with a pained expression. "We were worried about you."

Finn smiled warmly at her. "I was worried about me too. The weather reports said it wouldn't be too bad, but I almost didn't make it back to the house. The plows haven't gone through, and I'm not sure they will make it out this far for a while either."

"Haven't you learned long ago never to trust Minnesota weather reports?" Sarah teased him.

He removed his jacket and left his wet shoes by the door on the rug. Sarah was inspecting the cuts on his hand when Emmie came around the corner without more than a brief glance at him.

"Find anything interesting with Joker?" Emmie asked.

Finn stretched out a brown paper bag and Emmie accepted it. "We found the goggles. The real ones that Owl used."

Emmie looked at the bag, then opened it and dug them out. "How did he find them?"

"Jason wouldn't say."

Emmie rolled her eyes while holding up the goggles to the light. "I wouldn't trust too much of what he says."

"I'm sure they're authentic."

Emmie handed the goggles back to Finn. "How do you know?"

"They match the diagram." Finn walked to the kitchen with Sarah at his side and sat down at the table. Emmie stood across from them while Finn inspected the goggles beneath the overhead light. He pulled at the straps and twisted the stones.

"The lenses are rocks, and the frames could be modified welder's goggles." He turned them over in his hands, moving part of the strap up to his eye and examining it while squinting.

"How much did they cost?"

"Not much." They'd laugh at him forever if he told them he'd paid three hundred and fifty dollars for something that made one effectively blind.

"Why get two sets? Let me guess, Jason talked you into getting the second set as a *deal*."

Finn laughed. "It wasn't like a deal with the devil. He gets one, and I get one."

"That's not the whole story." Emmie stared at him.

Finn shrugged. "We just agreed that I'd try them out here at the house. I wanted to do that anyway."

"So what do they do?" Sarah stared at the goggles.

"I'll figure it out." Finn lowered the goggles and turned to Sarah. "I'm thinking we should have a good old-fashioned séance. Try to contact spirits again, like Owl did. There's got to be a reason Owl used these stones in the goggles where the lenses should be. This isn't normal. None of this is normal, really, but the man intrigues me. A geeky guy after my own heart."

"Maybe there's no purpose to them," Emmie said. "Just a prop in his scheme to grift old rich women."

"Yeah, maybe. But the stones are very unusual, and..." He held them out and sensed the uncommon weight as he shifted them in his hands. "Heavy. Not anything manufactured—not around here, anyway."

"But what's the point if you can't see through them?"

"The question is why was Owl and his gang using them? Assuming he had psychic powers, they must do *something*."

"Maybe there's an answer in what you brought in that can explain it." Emmie gestured to the books on the table.

Finn didn't seem to hear her. Instead, he pulled out a pocketknife and scraped the edge of the stone lenses. His blade didn't leave a scratch. "Definitely not normal."

"Some sort of sensory-deprivation device? I wonder if Owl's ladies covered their ears and noses too while trying to communicate with spirits."

"Wait," Finn said while looking at the object through one of his small handheld devices. "Do you know what this is? Obsidian. Volcanic rock. No wonder it weighs so much and almost looks... alien."

Sarah reached out and rubbed her fingers against the stone. "I hope you didn't pay a lot for this..."

"I got a good deal. A *great* deal. If they don't work, all is not lost. Obsidian stone is rare, so I'm sure they're worth more than what we paid. But I don't think that's why Jason wanted them."

Emmie shook her head. "That's what I'm afraid of here. That we're part of some bigger stealthy plot. We can't trust that guy."

Finn scoffed and pulled one of the books on the table closer. "He's an entrepreneur. He probably knows he can sell them at a premium if they turn out to do something." He turned to Sarah. "You ready for a séance?"

Sarah nodded, and after a moment Emmie did too. They rose together and moved to the séance room.

"I'll be right there." Finn tinkered with the goggles for a few more minutes, comparing the physical lenses to those shown in the diagram. Not many details revealing how they worked, at least not in that book, but plenty of information regarding the properties of the obsidian glasses and the craftsmanship in constructing them.

Finn stood and headed toward the séance room, where the girls had already gone quiet. They'd be trying to pull in whatever spirits might be hanging around nearby, and his mind was still on the construction of the goggles when he entered and slipped them over his eyes.

He expected nothing in the darkness of the impossibly black obsidian stone, but what he saw was anything but nothing.

They were all there. A window into the past: Owl, and all his Victorian ladies, huddled around the same table where Emmie and Sarah had sat a moment earlier, although the girls were gone now.

Owl and the ladies were wearing the same goggles as Finn, holding hands with their heads down, engaged in a séance that hadn't happened, but *was happening* in that moment. Not ghosts. These people were solid and more real than reality, more real than him or Sarah or Emmie, if that was even possible.

This was like a miraculous dream or an incredibly vivid computer simulation.

His legs weakened at the sight of the spirits, and his jaw dropped open. He became aware that he might just collapse, but there was nothing he could do except steady himself as a chill swept through him. Everything he'd known a moment earlier was gone. He wasn't just in Whisper House anymore, but instead in Joan Carter's home, as it had looked and felt and smelled like back then, and the gathering was happening *now* as he stood there staring down at them.

Emmie's voice called to him from somewhere far off, as in a whisper, but he couldn't answer. He couldn't form the words to express what he was seeing.

He reached out toward them instinctively, trying to connect with the new reality around him, and spotted his hand in their world.

He gasped. His hand, arm, body... all a cloudy gray ghostly form.

A scream welled up in his throat and he let it out.

22

Emmie shuddered. Finn's scream had sent a chill up her spine, and now he stood only a few feet in front of them staring into the empty space around the table with his mouth wide open and the goggles covering his eyes. Voices filled the room, but they were whispers from somewhere far away.

"What is it?" Emmie asked, her heart beating faster.

Finn pointed toward the seance table. "They are right there." He adjusted the goggles and slipped them above his eyes for a moment to glance over at the girls before putting them back on.

"Where?" Emmie asked.

"I can't believe this." He turned his head from side to side.

"What are you looking at?" Sarah asked.

"Don't you see them?"

Emmie didn't see them. It was just the room as it had been before, but now the whispering was a little louder. She turned to Sarah. "Do you?"

Sarah shook her head. "I don't, but I know they're here. I hear the whispers."

Finn stepped forward and cautiously stretched his hand toward one of the chairs.

"Stop, Finn." Emmie jumped forward and yanked at his shirt.

"Wait, don't get too close. We aren't sure yet what this is all about."

Finn moved back, but he didn't remove the goggles. "This is the most amazing thing I've ever seen," he said in the tone of someone who took acid and is tripping. Extending his hands to touch the back of the chairs, he crept around the table leaning in toward each chair at the invisible occupants. "I have no idea how these things work, but I can see the room just fine. And..." He turned and looked at Emmie and Sarah, then recoiled. "Both of you look so... strange."

"What do you mean strange?"

"You look like... one of them."

"One of whom?" Sarah asked.

"A ghost. And the ghosts are nothing like you described them. These are flesh and blood. Solid."

"They're not solid to us," Sarah said. "We don't see them."

"This thing." Finn adjusted the goggles against his face. "This is mind-boggling."

"Maybe you should take them off," Emmie suggested, getting anxious.

Finn ignored her.

Sarah ran out of the room and came back with the other set of goggles on her face. She had the same reaction as Finn, turning her head toward each chair. "Em, you have to see this."

"Who's in the room?" Emmie asked.

"They're all here. Owl and all the women. Six spirits total, including a young boy." Sarah held up her hand in front of her face, turning it over as if she had never seen her hand before. "Oh my God."

Emmie took a deep breath and tried to clear her mind in the hopes that she would see them without needing the goggles, yet she still saw nothing. The whisperings grew louder and faded like waves crashing on the shore.

Sarah slipped off her goggles and handed them to Emmie. "Your turn."

145

Emmie accepted them, sliding them onto her face. She gasped at the results. Not only were all the spirits there in the room with them, just as they had said, but the environment had changed, appearing as it must have been a hundred years earlier. Owl was sitting at the head of the table while the five women sat around him. They all held hands in a circle, just like she had seen in old Spiritualist seance photos.

Joan sat across from Owl while a young boy stood next to her watching everything with wide eyes. It was the same boy she had seen in the pictures around the house. And just like Finn had said, all of them were solid, appearing as anyone else they might have seen on the street that day.

Emmie glanced down at her feet. She was nothing more than a shifting gray puff of smoke hovering above the ground, but her form resembled the semi-transparent figure of a superimposed photo.

Owl's group was praying and chanting, with each of them wearing the same goggles that Emmie and Finn were wearing now, except for the boy. Owl raised his hands while guiding them through the whispering words that filled the room. His followers did the same, and the young boy watched his mother to mimic their rituals and words, although his voice was drowned out by the others.

"Let me have your goggles, Finn," Sarah said.

"Can't you see them with your own eyes?"

"We can't. Let me have your goggles, please."

Finn removed them a little hesitantly.

A few seconds after putting them on and looking around the table, Sarah gasped. "Oh, that poor boy. They are exposing him to all this strange Spiritualist stuff."

"Sarah," Emmie said, "this seems so real, like it is happening right now."

"I can feel their fear," Sarah said.

"What kind of technology is this?" Finn asked. "That guy wasn't a fake. He was a genius!"

The whispers within the group grew louder as Owl guided them through some sort of ceremony. The young boy's voice rose above the others for a moment, occasionally calling out the name "William."

"Stay focused, my ladies," Owl said in a soothing voice. "Don't be afraid. The spirits are bound by my guidance and skills. They will be here shortly, but keep your eyes closed until I allow you to open them."

Emmie moved around the table toward Owl, and the details of what he was whispering became clearer. It wasn't English they were chanting, but instead some odd language or a string of words like a mantra, as some religions sang during prayers. She moved up to the man within an arm's length and watched him perform until he snapped his head toward her, staring directly into her eyes.

"They... are here!" Owl shouted.

Emmie's heart raced as she stumbled backwards. Her mouth dropped open, and she let out a loud gasp.

Owl faced his followers. "Now! Open your eyes and witness the spirits who will give us the answers we are seeking. They are here with us now. Do you all see them?"

The women shrieked and gasped. One screamed as she pushed back in her chair, the legs scraping against the floor. The women on either side of her pulled her back down.

"Don't stop the mantra, my ladies." Owl leaned forward and raised his chin. "Continue the vibration, even as the spirits hover around you. It is all as it should be. Our worlds have joined and we must hold on."

The women continued chanting, but the sounds were broken by the whimpering and shrieks from some of them. They were watching Emmie and Sarah with wide eyes, and most of them were terrified, except for the woman sitting beside Owl. Even behind the goggles, the woman's face was immediately recognizable. It was Joan, and her expression was full of both wonder and desperation.

The young boy Sarah had noticed sat beside her, imitating the other participants and chanting, although he kept his head lowered.

Owl held up his hands, still holding on to the women beside him. "You will give us the answers we seek. These women wish to communicate with their loved ones."

Finn tapped Emmie's shoulder. "Maybe we can take turns with those?"

"Not now. We might need to do something."

"Please ask them about my little Nellie," one woman pleaded, her eyes watering.

"Elizabeth, we will surely discuss your daughter." Owl straightened in his chair. "There will be plenty of time for answers."

"Oh, this is too much!" another woman cried out in a panicked voice. She tried to stand, but fell back down.

"Don't be afraid, Abby. They are only here because we called them."

"You called us?" Emmie asked Owl, though she wasn't sure they could even hear her.

Sarah stepped over to Joan, leaning down to the boy who sat next to her and still wouldn't look up. Joan swung her head sharply toward the empath and yanked the boy into her embrace.

"Can I speak with my William?" Joan pleaded to Sarah.

"We want William," the boy repeated, stretching out his hands and moving them through Sarah's ghostly form. She shuddered and groaned as the boy did that.

"Sarah!" Emmie reached toward her friend.

"They can see us," Sarah said, moving away. "Like we're the ghosts. And I felt his touch!"

"They're dead," Emmie said, "but they don't know it."

"Tell me!" Owl shouted. "Will you give us the answers we seek?"

"Yes," Emmie said. "But tell us first what happened to you?"

Abby crouched forward as if Emmie might attack her. "Please don't hurt me."

"We won't," Sarah said. Her words didn't seem to calm the woman.

"Don't step away!" Owl ordered. "Don't break the circle. We have waited so long for this moment, and you have doubted it." He turned to Emmie. "You must bring us the spirits of their loved ones. Do you understand?"

Emmie tried to make sense of the question. He was telling her to cooperate with their séance, but none of them were alive.

While Emmie hesitated, Sarah answered Owl. "We can hear you. But we want to know what happened in this house."

Joan raised her voice. "Bring my William to me. I beg of you."

"I beg of you," the little boy repeated.

"Do you see all of this, my ladies? All that I have said to you was correct. You can see them around you now, can't you?"

"Yes, yes, oh God, I see them," Elizabeth cried.

Another woman trembled in her seat, seemingly on the verge of panic. She lowered her face. "I'm scared."

"No need to be frightened, my ladies," Owl said in a commanding voice.

Abby nodded several times. "It's true, Professor, it's all true."

The woman sitting next to Owl, across from Joan, turned to him. "This is more than I can take. I wasn't prepared. Please... make them go."

"Patience." Owl commanded, then turned to Emmie with a wide grin. "What's your name, my sweet spirit?"

"Emmie," she answered.

He stared as if stuck in a daydream. "It's just like I imagined. The doorways have finally opened, and the energy flows between our worlds. The vibrations have aligned. All the years of work and sacrifice..."

"You were right all along." Joan nodded.

"And you never doubted me."

Joan squeezed his hand as Owl gazed into the eyes of his followers.

"The Truth has manifested before you all. Nothing is gone. Everything exists still at the same time." Owl's grin widened, and he nodded slowly. "All the portals have manifested here and opened before you. Your loved ones will arrive soon." He began chanting more loudly while tightening the grip on the hands of the women.

But a woman cried out and broke away from the circle, throwing her goggles on the table with tears in her eyes. Another joined her and then two more. Four of the women hurried out of the room, leaving only Joan clutching the boy.

"Don't leave the table! It has just begun, and you cannot falter now. Gather your courage and return, or you'll find no reward." Owl turned to Emmie and Sarah. "I see you both, and this is not the final word between us."

A moment later, Owl's group disappeared.

❧ 23 ❧

The whispering chants faded after Owl's group disappeared. Emmie removed her goggles and tried to catch a glimpse of the spirits. Why could she only see them through the obsidian lenses?

Sarah waved her hand around the space the young boy had occupied only moments earlier. "Where did they go?"

Emmie turned to Finn. "What about your devices?" Emmie gestured to a camera attached to a tripod in the corner of the room. "Maybe you got something on that?"

Finn stepped over to one of the cameras he had set up and watch the screen with intense eyes as he worked with it. A moment later, he glanced back at them. "They're here. Just blurry shapes in the thermal camera, but I got them." He stepped away from the device and gestured to the goggles in Emmie's hand. "But those things are so much better than what I captured here. I had no idea how vivid the other side could be until now. How could a man like Owl make those work?"

Sarah circled to the other side of the table and placed the goggles over her eyes. "Put them on again."

"Why?" Emmie asked. "They're gone, right?"

"Yes, but... try it, then stare back at me."

Emmie lifted the goggles to her eyes. Even from a few inches away she could see through the stone lenses to the room beyond. Sarah appeared as the same wispy figure, even without Owl's presence. "We don't need him here to make these work. It's like another reality, looking through these."

Emmie removed the goggles and Finn was ready to accept them with eager eyes. She extended the goggles to Finn until Sarah spoke.

"Wait. Not yet."

Emmie yanked them back.

Finn frowned at Sarah. "Why not?"

"They can see us, but they can touch us too, at least when we're wearing these. That boy reached out and put his hands through me." Sarah swallowed. "It might not be such a good idea for you to get close to them until we know how to deal with this."

Emmie agreed and held the goggles to her chest. "She is right, Finn. These might be more dangerous than we thought."

"More dangerous than being paralyzed by voodoo and buried alive?" Seeing their surprise at this outburst, Finn seemed to take a deep breath and calm down. "Look, I understand that you are trying to protect me. I appreciate it, I really do, but it means a lot to me to finally get a glimpse into your world."

Emmie looked at Sarah for guidance and her friend nodded once. Emmie offered the goggles to Finn again, and this time he slipped them on without hesitation. "Do you see them?"

He glanced around the room. "No. But the bigger question is: where do you think they went?"

Emmie shrugged. "The ether? It seems we just can't see them except through these. But even then, it seems that Owl had control over that."

Sarah glanced at her goggles, then at Finn, who was staring back at them.

"Finn," Sarah said, "I hate to say this."

"Then don't say it..."

"We need those back."

Finn sighed, took a long look around the room, and removed them with a frown. "Will you give one pair to me when you know it's *safe?*"

"I'm not sure it'll ever be safe. Don't forget a murder happened recently, and one of these spirits is most likely responsible."

"I get it, but I took your word for it when you said you could handle the poisoning. Try and take mine at some point too."

"All right. I promise." Sarah turned back to Emmie. "Owl seemed pleased to see us. Said he had called us there into his séance."

"He's obviously stuck in that final moment before they died, replaying it over and over... until we showed up."

"But it seemed to be happening *now*," Sarah said. "Like a live communication with him."

"That *was* weird." Emmie gestured to the goggles in her hand. "These seem to work in conjunction with his powers. Did you see how he shut us off at the end, like switching off a TV channel?"

"I did. But—"

Finn jumped in. "Wait a minute, wait a minute. What's this about a TV channel?"

Emmie indicated the chair where Owl had sat during their encounter. "The communication ended suddenly when Owl's ladies started freaking out, breaking the handholding circle, and Owl said, 'This is not the final word between us.'"

"Did *he* stop the communication? Or did it end when they stopped the chanting?" Finn asked.

"The chanting. He did mention the vibrations," Sarah said.

"A-ha," Finn said softly. "We were onto something with that."

"At least we know who is in the house," Emmie said. "We finally saw them."

"But no sign of Sterling." Sarah glanced out of the doorway toward the stairs. "Maybe these ghosts can tell us why he died.

It's just a matter of getting them to talk with us without having them run away."

"It shouldn't be too hard to find them, right?" Finn asked. "We can follow the noises. We know they were chanting."

"I haven't felt a lot of emotional trauma since we got here, except for that horrible time up in the tower with you," Sarah told Emmie. "I'm concerned that the goggles might amplify all that too."

"We should be careful," Emmie said. "I haven't dealt with anything like this before. The only real sign of them, aside from what we saw in the goggles, has been the whispers." She asked Finn, "You heard the whispers too, right?"

"Not a thing."

"All right, then we need to go on a hunt." Emmie slipped on her goggles and saw that Sarah had done the same.

Emmie led them out into the main area of the house near the entryway and marveled at everything around them. They were still in Whisper House, interacting with the environment as it had been a hundred years earlier. They were even able to touch and move the objects around them, although with great difficulty.

Everything was new. More ornate designs filled the walls, most of them intricately painted mandalas as Emmie had seen around the house. These must have faded with time, or fallen off old walls, and been replaced by Audrey's coats of paint. Two tapestries hung beside a rocking chair, and the shelves were neatly organized with shiny items she had only seen in antique stores. A massive rug covered the center of the entryway, and she peeked under the goggles for a moment to compare it to the current one. They were the same, although in a different position, but through the goggles the rug still had vivid colors, a perfect example of the quality someone with deep pockets could afford in the late 1800s. Several paintings hung on the walls around them, showing majestic landscapes that would have rivaled anything in a museum.

Emmie walked up to one of the paintings and studied the scene that showed a group of flowers planted next to a lake's shoreline. The water was glistening in the summer sunshine while two young boys played near the shore. The artist had signed it in the lower right corner: Joan Carter.

Sarah approached Emmie.

"What do you see?" Finn asked behind them.

"The painting here has both boys," Emmie said. "The ones in the house nowadays never have them."

"There was a mural in the lake house," Finn said. "I had no time to study it, but maybe two boys were in it."

Gasping, Sarah pointed to the painting. "The boys look the same—and the same age. Oh, Emmie—were they *twins?*"

Footsteps thumped across the floor somewhere out in the hallway. Fast, shallow steps like those of a child running away.

🪬 24 🪬

Emmie hurried to the doorway and slid her goggles back on. Glancing around the area, she didn't see anyone, and the footsteps stopped as soon as her head peeked around the corner. The moment was almost playful, as if they were engaged in a child's game like Red Light, Green Light.

Sarah rushed to her. "It's the boy, isn't it?"

"I didn't see him, but... yes."

Another short burst of footsteps erupted at the end of the hallway near the sunroom. Without waiting for Finn or Sarah to catch up, Emmie hurried toward the sound. Her own footsteps thundered through the house and drowned out everything else, including something Finn commented in a snarky tone as she rushed into the sunroom.

The boy was nowhere in sight, but she didn't waste any time finding him. She ran to the secret door leading to the tower, stepped inside and moved up the ladder. At the top, within the first open section they had mistaken for a playroom, Emmie saw clearly what the space had looked like long ago. A plant nursery, full of potted plants and flowers, most of them huddled beneath the large, slanted glass window from which light streamed in.

The colors were overwhelming, a stark contrast to how the room appeared without the goggles.

But the boy was there. He stood against the back wall with goggles over his face, staring back at her. His hands were behind his back as if he hid something.

Emmie inched up the final rung of the ladder and crouched beside the opening, although Sarah didn't follow her this time. "Hello, Edgar. That's your name, right?"

"Yes," he said in a soft, kind voice.

Emmie looked down the ladder behind her. Sarah stood near the bottom with Finn poking his head into the door.

Sarah told Finn, "This is where I got sick."

He asked Emmie, "Is someone up there?"

"Joan's son, Edgar, is here." Emmie looked at Sarah through her goggles. "Come on up."

"I would, but... I still don't feel good from the last time."

Emmie nodded. "You can hear him, right?"

"Yes," Sarah said.

Emmie moved over and crouched beside Edgar.

"Who are you?" Edgar asked.

His question startled her. "My name is Emmie. Will you talk to me?"

The boy shrugged. "You're scary."

Emmie glanced down at herself, studying her spirit form through the goggles as she must appear to him. "Yes, I can understand why you might think that."

"I won't look at you."

He stared at himself in the mirror without even another glance to the side. Edgar stood expressionless and still until he raised his right hand and extended it to touch his reflection pensively as if it might jump back at him. "Do you see my brother over there?"

Twins. That was why there were so many mirrors. Joan must have accepted and even encouraged the boy to look for his brother in himself. "No. He died, didn't he?"

The boy nodded.

"In this house?"

The boy nodded again. "Mother said not to go swimming, but we went anyway. The water was so cold. William got sick that night, and he wouldn't stop coughing. He couldn't breathe, but my mother wouldn't let me get near him. He wanted to hold my hand, but she thought I could catch what he had." The boy's gaze dropped to the floor. "You're a spirit. Can you get him and bring him here so I can see him again?"

It wasn't possible for Emmie to wrap her arms around the boy and comfort him; it would only frighten him more, even if he felt her touch. "I'm not sure I can. It sounds like he got sick from swimming."

Once again, the boy nodded.

"I'm sorry," Emmie said, "but if he died naturally from being sick, he can never come back."

Edgar erupted into a scowl that wrinkled his small forehead. "Why not? Owl said... He told my mother..."

"Owl must have tried, for your mother's sake."

Edgar turned his head to her, the goggles too big for his face. "He lied, then!"

"I don't think he meant to—"

"He lied to me and my mother!" The boy sneered.

"No, it's not like that. I'm sure he truly believes what he told you, but maybe he doesn't know the full nature of the spirit world. People who die like William move on peacefully to the afterlife; they transform into beings of light and leave us to start a new journey. But that's a good thing."

His attention intensified. "How is that good?"

"I mean that you can be with him again, as a light, but first you need to pass on. I can help you with that."

The boy's face softened, but he looked back at the reflection. "I need to die?"

"Yes," Emmie repeated. "Would you like me to help you with that?"

"Why do people lie so much?" The boy shook his head. "Owl promised my mother we would see William, but he lied. Mother cries every time she looks at me now."

"Maybe we can help her too?"

"You can't help her. Nobody can."

Before Emmie could do anything, Edgar's spirit faded quickly and then disappeared. Emmie looked into the empty space where he had stood only a moment earlier.

A low, rhythmic chant began slowly, like a wave, and broke the silence of the chilly air. It filled her mind so completely that there was no denying someone intended her to hear it. It was the same chant that Owl had led with his group in the séance room.

Emmie slipped off her goggles and looked down at her friends, who were still waiting for her at the bottom of the ladder. "He's gone."

A moment later, a noise boomed from the kitchen. Something metal, probably pots and pans, clanged against the floor, followed by a loud thump as if someone had collapsed, and then a chorus of clattering spread up through the ceiling and walls. The house was alive, but most of the noises came from the kitchen. Sarah and Finn hurried there, and Emmie quickly climbed down to follow.

Storming into the kitchen with her goggles on, Emmie felt her heart drop. One of the ladies from Owl's group, the one the *professor* had called Abby, was leaning over the kitchen sink while water sprayed from the faucet. She was trembling, then convulsing as she gripped the edge of the counter. Vomit dripped down her chin and onto the front of her clothes. Her mouth hung open and her eyes were wide, strained with terror. Her muscles also strained beneath her pale skin. She cringed and opened her mouth wide as if to scream, but nothing came out.

25

E mmie hesitated, but Sarah hurried toward the woman as if to help her. "Wait, Sarah."

Abby had paid no attention to them up to the moment Sarah touched the woman's shoulder. Then she jumped with a choked shriek and stumbled back, throwing her hands into the air like a blind woman fending off an attacker.

"Let me help you," Sarah said.

"I don't think she can hear you," Emmie said.

Sarah reached out again, but the woman convulsed. The goggles slipped off her forehead, where she had been wearing them, cracking against the kitchen floor as she struggled to maintain her balance. A debilitating trauma was spreading through her body.

Emmie instinctually bent to retrieve the woman's goggles, but before she could touch them, they dissipated within a wispy cloud. When Emmie glanced up, the woman had also disappeared.

There was space where the woman had been standing. "This is so strange," Sarah said.

"She's still here, somewhere." Emmie swept her hand through a path of chilly air that still lingered.

"Mind telling me what happened?" Finn asked.

The two of them lowered their goggles to see him.

"One of the women was here, suffering the effects of the poisoning," Sarah told him. "She could sense us, but not see us. I think they need the goggles to see us too. And hear us."

"That might make sense." Finn's mental wheels were obviously spinning as he brushed the hair off his forehead. "Like a two-way device of some sort."

Sarah put the goggles over her eyes again, looking around the kitchen.

"Em, come." Sarah tugged on her shirt and gestured toward a row of glass canning jars that only appeared through the goggles.

One of them was stuffed with green leaves and another filled with hundreds of small white flowers.

Sarah reached for the one containing green leaves and lifted its lid, although she held it out at arm's length. Peeking inside, she cringed and turned to Emmie. "I found it."

"What's it doing in Joan's kitchen?"

"What are you seeing?" Finn asked.

"Something no one should have in their kitchen. The poison hemlock."

"Why would she put this here?" Sarah closed the jar and returned it to the kitchen counter. "Anyone might accidentally ingest that. And maybe they did..."

"Didn't you say it might treat diseases?" Finn asked. "Maybe that's what she was doing? Or do you think it was intentional?"

"I feel as they felt. As if my body wanted desperately to get rid of the poisoning."

"Joan could have done that, or Owl," Emmie said. "It was just like a cult, after all. That's modus operandi for that sort of thing, when the leader gets desperate or has one too many screws loose."

Emmie put her arm around Sarah, seeing her wilt under the burden of what they'd found.

"So sad. And that boy." Sarah shook her head. "Poison in the kitchen he might have eaten, watching all the craziness of the séance. Maybe the family should have committed Joan after all."

"And maybe the genius cult leader is somehow keeping them trapped in the house," Finn said.

A faint whispering arose from every direction. It began as a soft, distant sound, as if someone were adjusting the dials of a radio station to get a better signal. Then it grew louder and filled Emmie's ears like waves crashing against the shore.

"Even I heard that," Finn said. "They are starting the vibration again."

"Michelle said she heard whispers right before she killed her boyfriend," Sarah said. "We saw them chanting."

"Should we be covering our ears now?" Finn asked.

"I'm not sure it would do any good." Emmie turned her head, trying to locate the source of the whispers, but they came from everywhere.

"Do you think it's Owl?" Sarah asked.

Emmie focused on the sound, although it was impossible to tell who it was. So soft and... hypnotic. She stepped out of the kitchen toward the main entrance to the house and circled around the area with her goggles still on. "They can't hide from us forever. We can see into their world."

Finn cleared his throat. A little more loudly than necessary. "I can't," he reminded them. "I don't think it's unsafe—"

As if to contradict him, a loud crash came from upstairs. A thump, as if someone had fallen to the floor.

Sarah hurried to the stairs first and charged up, her footsteps booming through the house. At the top, she turned left, toward the noise. It had come from the same room where Sterling was killed. Emmie and Finn followed her. The bedroom door was wide open, and they rushed inside without hesitation. Through the goggles, the bed was immaculately clean and covered in white lace. A vanity mirror in the corner reflected their ghostly presence.

At first, it looked as if the room were empty, but someone whimpered near the floor, just out of sight.

Emmie circled the bed as the same voice groaned in pain. A woman lay on the floor with her face to the side, gripping the leg of the bed table as she struggled to rise. Her face was white, just like the other woman's. This one had vomited many times, judging by the mess down her clothes and on the floor.

Sarah came around and dropped next to the woman, turning her a few inches before the spirit shuddered and pulled away.

"This is horrible!" Sarah held her stomach.

Emmie avoided looking at the woman directly. It wasn't as gruesome as some of the scenes she had witnessed throughout her life, but it was agonizing. The woman's face reflected a torrent of pain ripping slowly through her. Unless they could break the women away from the illusion that they still lived, they would go through this poisoning forever, and Sarah would keep empathizing.

Sarah tried to grasp the woman's hand, pleading with her spirit to allow them to help her, but something was stopping them from reaching through. "Owl must have control over them somehow."

The woman crumpled to the floor, her arms stretched out and her mouth open wide, draining the last of whatever had filled her throat.

Staring up at the ceiling with dead eyes, she faded and disappeared.

The faint whispering continued around them. It grew louder and Sarah stood, yanking the goggles off. "Get them to stop! I feel sick again."

Finn stepped over and took her by the shoulders. "Let's get away for a minute."

Sarah shook her head, covering her ears. "That won't help. It's coming from everywhere. Owl is behind this, and he's trying to get to us too."

"Did you read anything in those books that might stop him?"

Emmie asked Finn, also removing the goggles. She could still hear the chanting. "There's got to be some rhyme or reason to what's happening."

"Probably is, but too much to read in one night." Finn watched Sarah and winced as if he could feel her pain. "Years of research in all that stuff. But what if we drop to his level and do an old-fashioned séance with the goggles on? You two can bring him to the table, right? Force him to come back?"

"And then what?" Sarah asked between deep breaths.

"You can make him stop the sounds?"

Emmie considered his words. "It won't be so easy. You saw the power that guy had. He didn't look like someone who would react well at being urged to move on. He seemed awfully happy about proving to the women that he was right. Did you hear that they might have been losing their faith in him until we showed up as ghosts? He's stuck in that moment."

"They still ran off," Sarah said. "All but Joan."

"If he knew they were too scared or had their doubts," Finn said, "he might have been angry enough to poison them all?"

Sarah glanced at Emmie. "Could he have influenced Michelle to kill her boyfriend?"

"I don't think he's psychic." Emmie glanced around the room. "Though he might be doing all this from the spirit world. Finn is right. We need to get him to the table. We weren't ready for him before, but we are now."

Sarah nodded. "It's two powerful psychics against a brainy guy."

"I can relate to that," Finn said dryly.

Sarah laughed, her eyes shining at him although her face was pale. "You're cuter than he was."

"Maybe I should start my own cult, then. Definitely something kinky."

"Just not with me in it," Emmie said.

The whispering chants filled Emmie's ears. There was no ignoring them. Owl wouldn't stop until he had their undivided attention. Had that been the same incessant whisper Michelle had heard before killing Sterling? Had it driven her mad?

But the words she'd read in the book on possession came back to Emmie as she hurried downstairs to the séance room with Finn and Sarah. *No person who isn't psychic can be possessed by a spirit or influenced to engage in actions outside the person's current moral standards.*

A chill swept through her.

But psychics are fair game?

Her eyes met Sarah's and she nodded. "I know what we should do."

26

Emmie looked from Sarah to Finn.

"Okay, so maybe instead of playing this hide and seek all night, we feed his ego. He seems to value the adoration of women, so we'll give him what he wants. Praise. Lots of it. If we can get him to see that he doesn't need the ladies anymore, that he's succeeded in whatever nutty objectives he was trying to accomplish, then maybe he will release them from the loop."

"And what if he doesn't buy it?" Finn said.

"Then we'll try and force him to move on. One way or another, he's going to stop with the whispering and the chanting. For our own sakes, we can't let it continue."

"I'll look in the book with all the writings and sketches. There's got to be something in there I can use to lure him back to us," Finn said.

He walked out and headed downstairs.

They followed him; Finn split off after they reached the bottom of the stairs.

Emmie walked into the séance room and took one of the spots that had been occupied by the ladies earlier.

Sarah sat beside her, but she had lost her smile. "Maybe we should give Finn more time to read what Owl himself wrote."

"We don't need a lot from him. Just something to get Owl out of his shell."

They left the seat where Owl had sat earlier open. It was better that way. If Owl showed up, they would want him to feel in charge and not threatened by their appearance.

A few minutes later, Finn walked in with the book and sat across from them, opening it to a page where lines were written in a steady hand.

"You said it sounded like chanting," Finn told Emmie. "One line that repeated several times?"

He turned the book toward her; Owl had written it out like song lyrics over the page.

... *AAA LL MM UU WW OO YAA MEE LLL MM FEE WOE SSS...*

The same sounds she'd heard upstairs. "That's it. I don't know what it means, but we can chant the lines just like the ladies did. I think that would get his attention, especially if we got it right."

Finn's expression changed to worry. He took back the book, and his eyes scanned through the text. Pulling out his phone, he took a picture of the page, then pushed the book back to Emmie. "Someone once told me to never read from a book out loud..."

"That was yesterday," Emmie said uncertainly. "And it might be different again tomorrow."

"If a portal opens, I'm throwing you inside," he told Emmie with a lopsided grin.

Something in his eyes made Emmie's smile freeze on her face. It was as if he were looking through her. But she had no time to wonder if he had figured out what she'd done to him at the lake house. She concentrated on the lines, running them over in her mind a few times before slipping her goggles back on. They weren't too difficult to memorize, but what if they were in a foreign language? What if it wasn't an empty chant, but actual words: a spell?

No time to wonder about that either. They held hands and started, saying each sound as a loud whisper.

OO EE HH AAAA RR NN SS AAA LL MM UU WW OO...

The three of them spoke in unison, finding a simple rhythm and correcting each other's mistakes until they had all mastered the chant. The words took on the same melodic tone she had heard the ladies repeat over and over again. Their voices blended seamlessly. There was no noticeable difference between their tones—Finn's deep ones and Sarah's soft voice or her own low-pitched sounds.

A whisper is a whisper.

They repeated the lines for several minutes, and Emmie sensed Finn's exasperation. The frustration a blind man might feel.

Just a few more minutes.

Strange sounds rose in the empty air above Owl's seat. A thump and then a rustling noise, like a body dragging itself across the floor.

She turned toward the source and looked down. Owl Cromwell lay there with his mouth open, the goggles turned up at them. His authoritative posture was gone, and saliva dripped down his chin as he struggled to climb up into his chair.

"It seems... that I've lost my way," he said.

$$\text{❧}\quad 2\,7\quad \text{❧}$$

T he man's posture now reflected defeat as he reached a
hand toward Emmie, taking deep breaths. "They don't
believe me."

"Who doesn't believe you?" she asked.

"My ladies, but they saw it with their own eyes. I called upon
the spirits, and they manifested right before them. Yet none but
my dear Joan believe it."

"They saw it. And they don't believe you're a psychic?"

Owl nodded. "They believe the naysayers now. Yet I've tested
my own beliefs. My power exists. I am connected to the other
side! To something so much greater." Owl made a weak fist. "All
the energy in the universe is within our grasp, and just as I have
written in my books and taught in my classes, it can belong to
each one of them, if they would only follow the path to Truth."

"We believe you." Emmie watched as Owl leaned back in his
chair with his chin up as if he had all the answers. "Everything
we've seen so far is very impressive. Did you build these goggles
yourself?"

He reached one hand up and adjusted his lenses. "I did."

"It must've taken a lot of skill to do that."

"I worked for years to put them together, traveling the globe to find just the right stones. Obsidian, a stone that defies its own matter. They had to work perfectly—any flaws would break the connection between our worlds—but I finally brought us together, and my ladies shared in my discovery, although the words of the skeptics still tug on their ears. They get impatient, and the liars try to lure them away from me. Don't they know that time doesn't exist?"

"He says time doesn't exist," Sarah whispered to Finn, who sat only inches away.

Owl gestured to Sarah. "Who is the young woman?"

"She's my friend."

"Did you die together?"

Emmie didn't answer, fearing an argument with the spirit.

"For you are dead. You must know it." Owl continued, "And see how your friendship has endured, and will endure, forever. Is that something to fear?"

"What is he saying?" Finn asked.

Sarah passed along the conversation to Finn through whispers.

Owl formed a puzzled expression and strained forward while glancing around. "I see the spirits of two young ladies. Is there another spirit present?"

Owl can't see Finn. "Just us."

Finn is right. The goggles are a two-way device.

"Ask him what happens to those who don't believe you?" Finn said.

Emmie repeated Finn's question.

Owl frowned. "They are free to follow their own path."

"Do you harm them?" Sarah asked.

"For what purpose? Only the lack of Truth can harm them. It's the way of the universe, and whatever you discover inside yourself, deep inside, behind all the false narratives and deceptions, is the essence of who you are. Your Truth can be found deep within that hidden darkness, and it longs to be released to the universe. Truth is emotion. Emotion is material."

Sarah continued whispering Owl's words to Finn. Would the ghosts hear their whispering too?

"Is that why you forced that woman to kill that man here?" Sarah asked. "To set him free?"

Owl frowned. "Young lady, I never killed anyone. Each soul who follows me is free to act as it wishes until the Truth finds it. Then it's not my place to interfere. I don't control anyone against their will. That idea is repulsive to me."

Emmie cut in. "Do you know the young man she is referring to? A woman killed him here in this house recently."

"I'm not aware of any murders in Miss Carter's home. If such a thing happened, then it is truly a tragedy. My concern is life." Owl tilted his head. "Where did my ladies go?"

"They're still here in the house, but they're dying, just like you. Do you see that?"

Owl glanced down at himself. "Dying?"

"One of your followers must have possessed the girl who killed the man here," Sarah said. "She must have poisoned you all. Do you know who might have done something like that?"

Slowly, Owl shook his head. "Joan has never mentioned anyone having died in this house. Except, of course, her own boy. Certainly you are mistaken."

"It happened," Emmie said, "and we need to know why it happened. There's something hidden in this house, behind all the whispering and chants. A murderer."

"We need the chanting and whispering to stop," Sarah added. "It's doing something to us, and to others who visit the house. You talk about truth and something peaceful in your beliefs, but one of your followers has taken things too far."

"Truth cannot be taken too far," he said sternly. "You would be lucky for it to find you."

Owl heaved forward suddenly in his seat as if about to throw up, and a little white foam seeped from the corner of his mouth. He wiped it against the back of his hand and continued while his face turned white. "I feel so weak and cold. The Truth is all that

I have talked about. You are here chanting the vibrating sounds of the universe, so you must understand."

Shuddering, Owl wobbled in his chair as if he might fall over. There wasn't time to listen to his philosophy anymore. They needed to get to the bottom of things.

"Something happened to you all," Emmie said. "Someone must have poisoned you. Did one of your followers do this? Was it Joan?"

A pained expression crossed his face, and more white foam erupted from his mouth. He gurgled.

"You're dying," Emmie said. "We need to stop anyone else from getting hurt. Can you please stop the chanting? It's preventing us from seeing everything clearly in this place."

Instead, Owl sank into his chair and choked until his form faded away.

Emmie slipped off her goggles, and Sarah did the same. Finn shook his head after Sarah finished telling him everything.

"Why do they always disappear right when we're starting to get somewhere?" he asked.

"That's just how these things work. Maybe they sense we're trying to force them to pass on, or they start to remember their own mortality and it scares them. But without intervening, they'll just keep going in their... loop." Emmie leaned back and sighed.

Sarah shook her head. "It hurts so much. They're all still feeling it. They need peace."

Finn stared into the space where Owl had sat. "Do you believe him when he says he wouldn't harm anyone?"

Sarah and Emmie looked at each other. "Yes," Sarah said. "I think he was telling the truth."

"Then it was one of the women," Finn said. "It must be Joan. She was the one growing poison."

"We don't know that for sure," Emmie protested.

"But it *is* her house," Finn pointed out. "Her hemlock. She was the impressionable, artistic, obsessed with her boy's death.

Putting mirrors everywhere so her living son would obsess over his brother like her, and painting her dead one."

He cut himself short, biting his lip as if keeping from saying more. He seemed disproportionately angry. Emmie suddenly wondered about his relationship with his own mother—and father. He never, ever spoke of them, and that didn't bode well.

"You said hemlock might treat depression and insomnia." Finn spoke more calmly to Sarah. "Maybe that's why she was taking it until she snapped and fed it to everyone."

A cool breeze passed through the room, followed by a faint whisper, soft and melodic. The same chant they had just finished. There were other women in the house they hadn't come across, but Emmie knew that the gentle whispers now filling her ears came from Joan. What had sounded before like an obscure mix of voices now became one clear, melodic chant.

"That has to be her voice." Emmie turned to locate its source, but the house echoed the sound off every wall. It had to be Joan, still grasping at Owl's philosophy like a desperate prayer.

Finn turned to Emmie. "So where is she?"

Emmie nodded slowly. "In the only place she could get away."

28

The large windows of the sunroom showed a serene autumn afternoon with dried leaves spread out over the withering grass. Emmie lifted the goggles for a moment to compare what she was seeing with reality. There was a stark contrast between the two. In the present, thick dark clouds blocked any chance of guessing if the sun had set or not, and the snow was pouring down in a torrent of white feathers that obscured the landscape.

She slipped them back on again and the snow disappeared. But in the distance, between the trees near the lake, she spotted puffs of smoke rising from the chimney of the lake house.

"Finn." Emmie turned to him, raising the goggles to her forehead. "Did you get the power restored in the lake house?"

"I couldn't find the circuit breaker. Why?"

"I'm sure someone is out there now. They're using the fireplace. At least that's how it appears through the goggles. I'm guessing it's either the boy or Joan. Or both." Emmie stopped herself from asking Finn to look again for the circuit breaker out of fear that he might bring up the reason it was blown. Better to just let it go. Even with the power on again, it would still take too much time to warm it up anyway.

"We need to go out there," Emmie said.

Sarah pulled on Emmie's arm and stumbled. "Em…"

Her face was distressed and paler than before.

"Sarah? You okay?" Finn had moved to the door but now he stopped. He walked to Sarah, slipping his arm around her with a concerned expression. "What are you feeling?"

"Nothing too bad. It's not getting worse."

He stared into her eyes. "You're feeling what those women felt, and Owl. Someone should check on you. The chanting might lead to something serious for you if it's strong enough."

"It's the same I always deal with." Sarah looked at Emmie with tired eyes, then at Finn. "I should go out there with Emmie. The idea is to find spirits. That's what I'm here for as well."

"Let her decide, Finn," Emmie said. "You don't understand how it is. We know how to take care of ourselves."

"You're not an empath, Emmie," Finn said curtly. "You know about yourself, not about her."

"Finn!" Sarah said sharply. "She is right. I *do* know."

"All right." Finn held up his hands and let go of Sarah. He shot a quick, narrow-eyed scowl at Emmie before walking away. A few seconds later, his voice came back from the end of the hall. "I'll stay here and focus on trying to decipher some of those books I found earlier. There's got to be something in there about how to neutralize the sounds. Careful with all the broken glass around the door over there. I'll clean up the mess tomorrow."

Emmie waited until Finn was out of earshot before speaking to Sarah. Her friend was looking a *little* better now; her eyes held a sparkle again.

"Life of an empath, right?" Emmie said with a nervous laugh. "Though I can't say I envy what you go through."

"Finn will get used to it at some point," Sarah said. "I guess he means well."

Emmie held on to her as they moved along. The whispering rose in the air again on their way to the front door. It was getting louder, and it pulsed within Emmie's mind like a finger prodding her to do something very important—a vital task she'd forgotten to complete.

Moments after they reached the entryway and grabbed their jackets from the coat rack, a loud crash reverberated through the house. The sound came from the séance room.

Emmie and Sarah ran back and found Finn hunched forward on the floor with the séance table flipped over on its side.

"Finn! Are you okay?" Sarah rushed to him and reached down to help him stand.

Finn groggily rose with their help until he sat in a chair, still leaning forward as if trying to get his bearings. He ran his fingers through his hair. His face was strained and red, and he didn't look at them but at the floor. "I sort of lost my balance there."

"How..." Emmie looked at the massive overturned oak table.

Finn grumbled. "I grabbed at the edge of the table when I fell over."

"Not spirits this time?" Sarah watched his face, but he wasn't smiling.

Finn wavered in his chair as if he'd downed one too many drinks.

"Should we stay with you?" Emmie couldn't see or sense any spirits. She lowered the goggles over her eyes again and still saw nothing.

"Don't worry about me. I don't have the goggles, so they can't hurt me. Right? You girls just go take care of things. I'll be here."

Emmie tugged at Sarah's arm as they left the room. "It's better to get it over with, so we three can get back together before nightfall."

Sarah hurried to her jacket and scarf, then looked back over Emmie's shoulder toward Finn, her face full of concern. "We shouldn't leave him alone again."

"We won't be gone long."

They finished preparing to go outside and stood by the front door for a moment as Sarah whispered to Emmie, "I don't think the spirits can harm him, but still..."

Emmie glanced into the house, as if Finn might hear them. "He's probably safer than us. It looks like they can't see him if he's not wearing the goggles, and he hasn't even heard them."

"It's almost too much..." Sarah frowned. "Everything that's happened in this house."

Emmie stopped and listened. Silence. "And I think things are winding down. I can feel it."

Finn would be fine.

29

They slipped on their goggles in the doorway, but Sarah struggled with the strap. "The buckle is stripped. It doesn't stay tight."

The leather was cracked and worn down after a hundred years of neglect. Amazing that it had held together for so long. And aside from that, Sarah's face had become paler.

"Sarah, are you truly up to this? Maybe Finn is right." Emmie met her gaze.

"It's the same as always, Emmie. I guess as my powers grow, so will the impact on me until maybe I find some way to deflect it. Nothing that I can't handle, though. We can't stop now."

Emmie worked with the strap a little more, tightening it again after Sarah slipped them over her eyes.

A moment later, Sarah pivoted her head. "Do you hear that?"

"Whispers?" Emmie asked.

"Yes." Sarah removed the goggles, then slipped them back on. "That's strange. I can't hear them without these."

"Interesting. If you're hearing the same thing I do, they'll come and go. I try not to think about it."

"We'll get to Joan and stop all this."

The frigid winter air chilled Emmie's skin as they hurried

down the porch steps, knocking through a thick accumulation of snow that contrasted with what her goggles showed. She felt the resistance of the snow pushing against her feet, but none of it appeared through the goggles. Stumbling a moment later, she grabbed the handrail and paused.

"This isn't going to work." Emmie stared down through her goggles. Only lush green grass beneath her feet. Yet the reality of the snowstorm was undeniable while trudging ahead.

"What isn't?" Sarah's arm slipped away from Emmie's side.

"Wearing these things in this weather." Emmie removed her goggles and adjusted her eyes to the surroundings. "I can't see where I'm going."

But Sarah didn't appear to be holding up well in the blistering wind. Her scarf shrouded her face, but she struggled to keep the hood of her jacket over her head as the gusts of wind blasted into them. She staggered and extended her elbow toward Emmie as if *she* needed help. Sarah was too used to taking care of everyone, even when she was ill.

A flurry of snowflakes blew around them, carried by powerful gusts of wind that pelted their bare faces. The snow had already obscured the steps and sidewalk leading out to the driveway and around to the back of the house.

Emmie pressed forward into the wind and cradled the goggles against her chest. Her hair whipped in every direction, and each step plowing through the snow magnified her resolve to stop whatever was harming Sarah. A clump of snow flew up under her left pant leg and chilled her bare skin, reminding her of the miserably inadequate ankle socks she was wearing since she hadn't known she would be sinking into the snow like this.

It was impossible to follow any particular path to the lake house. But despite the heavy snow cover, a row of shrubbery defined a narrow garden, lining what she assumed was the sidewalk leading toward the backyard. Dozens of dead or hibernating plants and small trees filled the area, some of them having accumulated a crown of snow.

As she moved along beside the garden, the toe of her shoe caught on something buried beneath the snow and she stumbled forward before catching herself. Pausing to shake it off, she glanced back at the object. A section of garden hose snaked up over the snow.

Sarah turned toward her. "You okay?"

"I'm fine." She continued, but stepped a little more carefully.

Some of the areas in the backyard had drifted up to two or three feet already, with the wind cutting between the trees in surges that forced them to stop and look away. Emmie huddled beside Sarah as they made their way toward the wooded area surrounding the lifeless lake house.

Weaving through several large oak trees, Emmie looked out at the vast, white, open field of snow that was the lake. She could see across to the lights on the opposite shore, but they were blurred within the melting snow over her eyelids. The dark gray skies would grow darker as the sun dropped below the horizon soon.

Sarah lagged, clutching Emmie's arm as they pushed forward through a snowdrift beside a row of hedges.

The wind battered Emmie's face, and she gasped for breath until Sarah's arm fell away and she screamed. Emmie stopped and turned back. Sarah lay face down in the snow with her arms sprawled out like a snow angel.

"Oh my God, Sarah, are you all right?" Emmie kneeled beside her and held her arm.

Sarah groaned and curled forward as she turned to face Emmie. "It's getting worse."

"Let's go back inside." Emmie helped her stand again.

"No, we better do this now. I don't think I can do it again."

Nothing covered her eyes. Her goggles were missing.

"Where are your...?"

Sarah's hands flew up to her panicked face. "Oh my God, where did they go?" She turned and dropped on her knees, pushing her hands into the snowbank. A gust of wind thrust them to the side as Sarah moaned while searching for the goggles. "Where are they?"

Emmie slid her shoe through a mound of snow but felt nothing solid. The snow was falling so fast that it could have covered up the goggles within seconds. "I'll come back and get it later. We can use mine for now."

"I hope I didn't break them. Finn will kill me." Sarah drooped forward with her head down.

"It doesn't matter right now. Let's just see what's out there, then get you back inside the house." Emmie pulled her up again.

They continued toward the lake house, weaving between several trees, and she held Sarah against her side as she leaned forward and lost her balance a few times along the way.

It was the worst way she had ever seen her friend react to the spirit. How far could that go? Was Finn right, and could Sarah's empathic connection with the spirit world drain everything from her? Maybe even take her life? Was it like draining a battery with no hope of recharging it once it was gone?

"We're almost there," Emmie reassured her.

Emmie slipped on her goggles when the lake house came into view. The smoke still rose from the chimney, but there was no sign of anyone else in the house. If Joan was there, at least she wasn't aware of them approaching. Perhaps Joan had taken the goggles from the séance out to the lake house with her, so they would need to approach her with caution. If Joan was behind the murders, there was no telling what she might do to them.

Emmie reached the steps to the front door. The goggles showed well-constructed wooden steps with potted plants sprouting a variety of flowers beneath the handrails on both sides. A cast-bronze ornamental thermometer was mounted beside the door displaying the temperature: 72°. It had been a perfect day when they'd died, a beautiful afternoon for such a tragedy.

Emmie paused, then peeked under her goggles to have a look around at reality again. The snow shovel that had fallen across the door was there, but Finn had pushed it off to the side. Glass covered the steps, and the shattered storm window sent a pang of guilt through her.

Finn could've been seriously hurt.

But that's what you wanted, right?

Either way, I should have gone back and helped him.

Too late now.

Emmie held Sarah back from stepping up to the door. Instead, she led her friend around the back of the house and peered in the massive picture windows overlooking the lake.

They had a clear view of everything in the main section of the house. Through the goggles, everything was calm and warm and pleasant, with the light coming from a lamp beside the side window. There was another light across the room, a tall floor lamp, and it illuminated a large painting canvas propped up on a sturdy wooden easel. A woman sat on a stool before it, throwing down thick strokes of deep red paint. In a loud whisper, she chanted the same melodic words Emmie had heard during the séance.

No mistaking the woman's face. It was Joan.

＃ 30 ＃

The wind off the lake was particularly harsh against Emmie's face, whipping at her as she adjusted her position to get a better view of Joan. She shielded herself with one hand while also straining to hold her friend upright beside her. The stunning scene of the lake as it had appeared one summer afternoon a century earlier lay behind her, with the waves rippling across the surface within a gentle breeze. The tree branches barely stirred, starkly contrasting with the blasts of freezing wind that threatened to knock her down.

Joan slouched on a stool in front of the canvas without looking at them.

Emmie stepped through dried, cracking shrubs to get a better view of the canvas. An assortment of brushes and pallets surrounded the woman, some of them thick with paint and others untouched. The walls were vibrantly painted with vast murals that stretched from the floor to the ceiling.

On one wall there was a scene of a mother tucking her child into bed as she kneeled beside him with her arms draped over his chest as if she were crying. The painting's tone and style resembled something that might be found in an old church, like Mary comforting the baby Jesus, although in this scene the child's complexion revealed that something was very wrong. The boy's eyes were closed and his face white. Dead? The woman in the painting was clearly meant to be Joan and the boy her child, but another boy stood in the distance, watching them as if he were too afraid to approach.

The twins. And Joan had painted the heartbreaking event after William had died.

Against another wall, between towering shelves of books, a different mural showed a boy staring at himself in a full-length mirror, his sullen expression fixed on his own reflection. The boy's surroundings within the painting were familiar: one of the upstairs bedrooms. This had to be Edgar. His hands were pressed flat against the mirror as if trying to pass through the glass, just as Emmie had seen him.

Emmie caught her shoe on a frozen branch on the ground and it snapped in half. The noise broke the tension and silence.

"Do you think she knows we're here?" Sarah whispered, her voice barely audible in the wind.

"I think she would have already turned around and reacted if that were the case. She doesn't have the goggles on. You need to see this." Emmie removed the goggles.

Sarah slipped them on with a dramatic shiver while adjusting them. "These things are like ice!"

She glanced around at her surroundings, then turned back toward the window and stared silently for several seconds until she said, "Her paintings are so... strange."

Emmie watched her reactions. "Like many of the designs on the property."

"It's just so hard to see her face from out here. And I think she's saying something."

"Chanting?"

"I don't think so. Looks more like a conversation... with herself. We should go inside and listen."

"Are we ready to confront her? If she poisoned everyone, things could quickly get out of hand."

Sarah removed the goggles and handed them back to Emmie. "But she can't hear us, right? She's not wearing goggles, so maybe we could walk in there to get a better view of what she's doing and saying. We wouldn't rush anything—just get out of the wind, if nothing else."

Emmie agreed and they circled around to the entrance. Seeing the shattered window in the storm door stirred Emmie's guilt at the pain she must have caused Finn earlier, but she continued toward it without stopping. Trudging up the steps, the broken glass buried beneath the snow crunched beneath their shoes. Another reminder of what she'd done.

Moving cautiously inside, Emmie put on the goggles again. The lake house transformed back to Joan's charming sanctuary beside the lake while the woman still sat hunched forward on a high, wooden stool in front of her painter's easel. As expected, she hadn't reacted to their entrance, but Emmie still kept her distance.

Joan straightened a little and dipped her brush into the red paint before smearing it across the top edge of the painting. The color added more brilliance to an already ominous red sunset. The painting showed a cemetery and an open hole at the bottom of the frame with dirt walls and grass around the rim. In the image, Joan was kneeling beside the grave, peering down into the hole with her arms stretched as if whoever lay inside might reach up to her before the gravedigger filled in the hole.

Until that moment, they hadn't gotten a clear view of Joan's face, but after Emmie inched closer Joan flinched her head to the side, then adjusted her gaze until she stared straight into Emmie's. Joan's face was flushed, and tears streaked down her cheeks. A deep desperation filled her watery eyes, as only something like the death of a child could evoke.

Joan's gaze remained fixed on the spot as Emmie moved to the side. Maybe the woman *had* seen or heard something, like the almost supernatural senses of a cat reacting to an imperceptible noise in the darkness. Frozen in position like that for a few seconds, she slumped forward again a moment later before climbing off her stool.

"Did she see us?" Sarah asked.

"I don't think so."

The closet across the room was wide open, and the mural Finn had mentioned was there, although most of it was hidden in shadow from that distance. Despite the lack of details, a couple of faces stood out: the twin boys playing together near the shore of the lake. One of them had lifted his trouser leg to dip his toes in the water while the other boy danced on the shore. Their mother lounged in the grass a short distance away.

On a table near the window beneath them, several bound books lay open, along with an assortment of jars like those Emmie had seen in the kitchen—the ones Sarah had identified as containing hemlock.

But Sarah was visibly shaking, and they were out of time.

Emmie took her arm. "I've seen enough. We'll come back later when you're feeling stronger."

Sarah pulled back a little. Her teeth chattered as she insisted, "We shouldn't stop now. It'll just get worse."

Before Emmie could argue, Joan lifted one of the books on the table and hurled it across the room; it smashed into one of the bookcases and thudded against the floor. She smeared her tears across her face with the back of her hand and held her brush against the canvas as if to continue painting, but drooped forward instead. Her brush slipped from her fingers and dropped to the floor. She seemed not to notice.

Emmie inched back, and at the same time Sarah lost her balance, slamming her hand against the side of the house near the window frame.

Joan spun around and faced them, staring with wide eyes as if completely aware of their presence. Her face was full of pain and terror. "Go away!" she screamed.

Emmie winced at the woman's deafening outburst and stumbled back, pulling Sarah along with her, though her friend couldn't see Joan.

"What's wrong?" Sarah asked, although there wasn't time to explain.

Emmie moved them toward the door, her heart racing. They weren't prepared to face a woman in that frame of mind—not in Sarah's weakened state. "Get outside."

They hurried out the door and gripped the handrail on the way down to keep from slipping over the broken shards of glass on the steps. As they reached the trail connecting the two houses, the storm door flew open behind them and slammed against the metal railing.

The commotion only fueled Emmie to move faster. Had Joan actually *seen* them without the goggles? Or had she simply *felt* them as someone alone in a house might sense someone watching them from the shadows? In any case, the woman was clearly disturbed and too dangerous to deal with for now. Better to take it slow under the circumstances.

"What did you see?" Sarah asked after they'd passed a few trees.

"She's *very* upset."

"At us? Do you think she poisoned everyone?"

"I'm not positive yet, but... I don't feel safe."

A moment later, Joan's voice erupted again from behind them. A different cry this time—no sign of the terror from a moment ago. Now her cries were long, drawn-out wails, full of pain and desperation.

Emmie slowed and turned around. Through the trees, she spotted Joan staggering to the bottom of the steps, clutching her throat and wheezing as white foam flowed over her chin. Her panicked eyes bulged as she gasped in each breath.

"Oh my God." Emmie grabbed Sarah's arm. "She's dying."

Emmie led Sarah back toward the lake house. She approached Joan cautiously as the woman struggled to stand upright, clutching the handrail while curled forward.

"Em," Sarah said, "it's getting much worse."

"Someone poisoned her too."

Emmie instinctually reached out to help Joan, but the woman shuddered and backed away as if still aware of their presence.

"My poor child." Joan spoke between gasping breaths, staring out across the lawn while still holding her throat. "What have you done, Edgar? May God have mercy on your soul for your evil deed." She looked at the sky. The white foam left trails down her chin and neck. "How could you have done this, my sweet Edgar? Murder... and just a boy. I am to blame for what you've done. It's *all* my fault. My fault..."

Joan dropped to her knees, collapsed onto her side, then faded away before Emmie could say anything else.

Emmie removed the goggles, her mind still reeling from Joan's words.

Edgar... murder. He had poisoned everyone.

She repeated what Joan had said to Sarah.

Her friend sighed. "I felt it."

Emmie's heart beat faster. "We have to warn Finn about Edgar."

"At least we know the truth now."

Slipping the goggle's strap around her arm, Emmie trudged across the snow toward the house beside Sarah. They moved more slowly on their way back as the winds thrust them sideways. Both lost their balance a few times. Sarah paused and warned that she might throw up again.

"Try and wait until we get back inside." Emmie stroked her friend's shoulder. "We're almost there, and you'll be more comfortable."

Sarah nodded and lumbered ahead several more steps, then gestured toward the spot where she had dropped her goggles. "I think the goggles are around here somewhere."

Emmie pulled her forward. "Don't worry about that. Let's get you inside. We'll find them later."

The snow had covered in the area where Sarah had fallen anyway. It wouldn't matter if they searched for them now or the next day, after the storm had passed.

"But Finn..." Sarah pleaded.

"He'll be more worried about you. Of course, he'll understand. The goggles aren't lost."

Sarah shielded her face against the wind and they huddled while a blast of cold ripped around them like a small tornado. After it had passed, something caught Emmie's eye about twenty feet away. Two figures standing beside a pine tree. An adult and a boy.

The adult was leaning down as the boy whispered something into his ear.

❧ 31 ❧

The table hadn't flipped over by itself.

Finn had watched himself lift it in a moment of impulsive rage, digging his fingers into the bottom edge as he stood, and he hadn't even considered if any of his electronics or the books would be damaged. He hadn't lost his balance, and no unknown entity had taken control of him. He had lifted the table himself, violently hurling it onto its side.

The strange thing was... it had felt good. Really, really good. Something deep inside had gone out of him like a toxic breath he'd been holding for years.

He had flipped it upright again after the girls had left. But the way Emmie had stared at him... with eyes that wondered what was up with him.

Do you really want to know?

Too much fire burning inside of him, as if someone had pumped propane gas into his chest, and someone else had tossed a lit match down his throat. The blaze had run out of fuel moments after igniting, yet the ashes still smoldered in his chest.

Leaning on the table's edge with his knuckles pressed into the wood surface, he stared forward at the black and white portrait of an old Spiritualist séance in progress, complete with the "ghost" of a woman standing behind the psychic. The photo helped him to snap out of the bubble of emotion. It led his mind back to reality, to rational thinking.

He hadn't lost it like that since his younger brother Neil died.

After Neil's funeral, his parents had put on a so-called "brave" face, as if the most horrible of things had never happened, or as if "getting on with life" was the right thing to do.

They had never treated Neil with an ounce of dignity, anyway, calling him a loser for dropping out of college and humiliating him on many occasions for losing his job. They had refused to believe depression was a real illness. *People chose how they felt,* they'd said. Neil had begged to move into their basement during one of the darkest times of his life, and they had acted like he was making it up to take advantage of their wealth.

And the afternoon after Neil's funeral, before Finn had even had a chance to grieve, his father had quite casually asked the handyman to go into the basement and paint over the bloodstains.

The request had shocked Finn at first, but the message was clear. *Erase any sign of my son.* The son who was fresh in his grave.

Then the rage had surged through Finn like a bolt of lightning. He hadn't held back after that.

"What was it like finding Neil down there, Dad? And you, Mom? After you drove him into a corner, literally into a basement corner. What was Neil supposed to do? He just needed a little more time, but that was too much for you, wasn't it? All the cash stuffing your bank accounts and you couldn't cut him a break even once. Not even once. That blood down there is yours! You *own* it and *you* can clean it up! But God forbid you should do it yourselves and really see what you've done. You'll pay some stranger to do it for you, clean *your* blood off the wall *because he was your flesh and blood,* so you won't have to face the truth. You killed your son! You killed your boy!"

It didn't matter that they'd stood there, saying nothing. He'd wanted to say all of it every time they had shamed Neil by shoving Finn's accomplishments down his throat. Trying to turn brother against brother. It had been cathartic and... *terrifying* to lose control, but he didn't regret it one bit. Not seeing them since then had been liberating too.

And he didn't regret flipping over the table now.

You would have regretted it if you had broken something. But he hadn't.

You need to get out more, old man.

Cabin fever? Probably. Too much sun at the beaches had come back to haunt him, and now he was going through withdrawals. The Cabo San Lucas shakes.

He picked up the book he'd been reading off the floor and pulled his chair before sitting down. He didn't feel like reading anything at the moment, but he hated wasting time too.

Okay, just a little tirade to blow off some steam.

Sarah and Emmie had scrutinized him before they'd left, eyeing him as if a spirit might have possessed him or he'd lost control of his sensibilities. No, nothing like that. Just a little tantrum. Or just *the truth*.

All better now. He took in a deep breath and let it out slowly as he opened the book in front of him. He skimmed through the text without taking the time to comprehend what it said. The words flowed across the page while his mind wandered back to his goggles. The girls had taken both sets and left him there to read. Yes, the house was quiet, perfectly conducive to reading, but a little time to play with his new toys was what he needed.

He glanced at the clock on his phone. They'd only been gone for five minutes, yet he was already sick of staring at those words, words, and more words.

"Just a couple of minutes," his voice echoed within the room. He had only used the goggles for a couple of minutes before they'd taken them away. *He'd* found the goggles. It had been the most spectacular sight in his life, and they'd robbed him of it.

He closed his eyes.

There will be other ghosts. You're making too much of this.

Grow up, Finn. We're a team, and they're just doing their job.

But, damn, it had felt good to throw the table. He rubbed his biceps. They still ached from the sudden surge and his head still throbbed, although he was coming down from the high, cooling down with each breath.

He rubbed his forehead and pushed the book away. It slid almost to the other side of the table. Enough reading for now. Maybe a drink or a long walk would be wonderful under normal circumstances, but...

No chance of getting outside now. The wind pushed against the window across the room. Maybe not even possible tomorrow, by the look of things. The snow had piled up along the bottom edge of the windowsill and the glass had frosted over.

This wonderful Minnesota winter captivity. Couldn't have planned it better myself. Oh, wait, you did *plan this yourself.*

Yes. Yes, I did. I planned all this; I pressured them to take the job and... He yelled, "Now I'm stuck!"

The throbbing in his ears grew louder. *Okay, okay. More of that withdrawal thing. So let's just think about this. The girls are out exploring the backyard for any signs of the spirits which they'd all seen through the goggles. A fascinating, mind-bending experience. If only they'd allowed him to relish the moment a little longer.*

You'll get plenty of time to mess with the goggles in the next house.

It was like he had two opposing voices in his head, both his own, and neither would shut up. Wasn't this schizophrenia? Finn stared out the window again. It was getting dark now.

Emmie had taken Sarah into that cold, and Sarah was not well. *Far* from well, and Emmie kept pushing her. He shouldn't have allowed it. Of course Emmie had stopped him from being with Sarah so that he couldn't speak for her and protect her. But he'd put an end to her interference.

Pushing his chair back so hard it went crashing to the floor, he hurried to the front door and put on his coat and gloves before heading outside into the blistering cold. The wind whipped around him as he circled around to the side of the house. He could find the lake house easily enough, despite the darkness and snow blasting into his eyes. And the girls would have turned on a light out there by now.

He paused.

Oh shit. I told them I would find the circuit breaker and reset it.

They'll be back sooner than expected when they find the house still frozen and dark. Then we'll all go out there together like a cozy little family.

He moved toward the trees, and the only light guiding him came from the windows of Whisper House. Something bumped against his thigh and he remembered the sculptor's hammer was still in the pocket of his coat. He patted it softly, like comforting a child. Better to bring it along. Never know when he might need to break something. He put a hand over it as he walked, however, or he would end up with a bruise.

His shoes kicked through the snow that crept up almost to his knees, and something caught his ear. A scratching sound, like a bug scuttling. He swatted his hand beside his ear and then paused again. Bugs didn't survive Minnesota winters so well. Maybe an animal in the distance? Maybe a small bird had flown by? But most of the birds had already flown south. *To Cabo San Lucas, if they're smart.*

And the sound came back again, this time a little clearer. It came from the trees not more than thirty feet away.

"Someone out there?" he yelled.

No one responded. He tensed, considering that a wild animal might be staring back at him, sizing him up to decide whether he'd be a good meal.

Finn continued on his way, trudging through the snow until his shoe thumped against something buried beneath it. Whatever it was caught on his shoe and he almost tripped. He stopped to pick it up, brushing off the snow from the item he'd almost crushed. The strap connected to the object was unmistakable. The goggles. *His* goggles. His one-of-a-kind goggles, the precious artifact the girls had promised they would take care of.

He clenched the strap as his face warmed in the freezing air. "Son of a bitch."

Before he slipped the goggles on, he knocked the snow from the lenses and cleared the strap. The freezing, rigid leather fit snugly, and the icy metal frame stung his skin, but he could see his surroundings clearly, better than he would have imagined. Looking down at himself, he saw the ghost again, just as he had back in the séance room. Yet all around him was a bright autumn day, as it had been long ago.

He lifted and lowered the goggles a few times to compare his surroundings between Owl's portal to the past and reality. Everything was in the same place, generally, and if he was *really* careful, he'd be fine. Leaving the goggles on, he resumed his way to the lake house.

The girls had discarded them like a piece of trash. Why should he ever do what they said again?

Never.

The sound came from the forest. Not just a wild animal. This time, the noise was clearly human. The familiar whispering chant rose and fell, the same as he'd heard inside the house.

Without the snow and wind to obscure his vision, he spotted the source of the chant immediately. A figure stood staring at him from beside a pine tree. The boy.

"Edgar?" That was his name, wasn't it?

The boy's flawless brown pants and button-down white shirt reflected his upper-class status, but his face was pale and he hunched forward as if on the edge of vomiting. He was wearing the goggles now, peering straight back at Finn.

Finn's pulse thumped in his ears. He could run back inside Whisper House or hurry ahead to the lake house and get the girls so they could try to communicate with him.

Or, for the first time, he could do it himself.

What would he say to a spirit? Before he could decide, the boy gestured for Finn to approach him.

"You want to talk?" Finn asked.

The boy nodded and gestured again for Finn to come closer.

Finn stepped forward, although his legs shivered, either from freezing or fear. "All right, sure."

Edgar staggered as Finn arrived within a few feet of him. "You want to tell me something, little guy?"

Edgar opened his mouth and gasped in a breath before answering. "She locked you in there."

Finn tried to make sense of his statement. "What? Who locked me in where?"

"The taller woman. When you were in my mother's studio, that woman saw the shovel was blocking the door, but she just left it there and walked away. She wanted you to be stuck in there."

The events of Finn's escape from the lake house replayed in his mind. Sure, the shovel must have fallen in front of the door after they'd left, but could Emmie have gone back to the house knowing full well he was trapped in there?

A deep rage ignited. That propane tank in his chest was filling again.

He could have died in there. Had that been her intention?

"How do you know?" he asked Edgar.

Edgar coughed and leaned forward for a moment before turning his face up. "I saw it happen. The tall one is mean."

Finn opened his mouth to argue, feeling the snowflakes land against his tongue and melt, then snapped it shut again. Emmie had locked him in the lake house. To freeze.

As white foam dripped from the corner of his mouth, Edgar shook his head. "What are you going to do?"

The boy's words hung in the air for a moment like a strange dream.

Finn met the boy's gaze, and it was all so clear. "You'll see."

32

"**F**inn?" Emmie called out to him as he stood beside the pine tree, staring back at her through the goggles. He must have found the ones Sarah had lost on their way out. Was he angry?

Edgar stood beside Finn, staring at them with a solemn expression. The boy adjusted his goggles, then moved behind Finn.

"There you are," Finn grumbled. He removed something from his coat pocket and tapped it against his leg while taking a step toward them.

"What are you doing out here?" Sarah asked him.

He gestured to Edgar. "I found someone."

Edgar's pale, gaunt face reminded Emmie that he was desperately sick. He leaned toward Finn and whispered something in his ear.

Finn nodded to him, then turned back to them. "I can see him just as plain as day through these things." He touched the goggles. "Can hear him too."

"I'm sorry about the goggles. I tripped, and they fell off," Sarah said. "I was going to find them."

"That's okay, Sarah. I know you wouldn't have left them out

here," he said softly as he pushed his goggles up onto his forehead. "But you know what else I discovered?"

Finn's expression was unlike any Emmie had seen on his face before. He was giving them a tight smile, but his eyes told another story.

He focused on Sarah but gestured to Emmie. "A little bird told me our friend here locked me in the lake house on purpose."

Sarah gasped, her breaths streaming out like puffs of smoke. "That's not true."

Finn turned to Emmie. "Isn't it?"

When she didn't respond, Sarah turned toward her. "You'd never—"

"Would you, Emmie?" Finn asked.

Emmie shivered and looked away. "It's cold. Let's go inside and talk about this."

"Yes, let's talk about this. Let's talk about all the bullshit I had to go through to get out of that little house back there and how you trapped me in on purpose. You wanted me to freeze to death, didn't you?"

"No, Finn, it wasn't like that."

"Emmie, what is he saying?" Sarah seemed horrified. "Why don't you tell him you'd never do that?"

"Because she did." He nodded slowly. "Edgar told me everything. When the shovel blocked the door, you just walked away, knowing full well that I was trapped. And it wasn't just a little practical joke either. You wanted to hurt me. Kill me."

"That's not true!" Emmie cried. "Never!"

"Oh, yes, it is. Do you think I haven't seen that look in your eyes? You're crazy jealous that Sarah and I care for each other and you're getting left behind. Are you so miserable now that you'll do anything to rip us apart? It's just eating at you, isn't it?"

"Finn!" Sarah cried. "Don't say things like that. They aren't true."

"She wants everyone to be miserable like her."

Emmie shook her head. "No, I don't. I—"

"You tried to kill me!" He took a step forward.

She took one back. "It wasn't like that. I swear. I was horrified when I saw you coming in all cold and hurt." She rubbed her forehead. "I don't know what came over me."

"The devil made you do it, right? Sure, blame the house, Emmie. This has been going on since the trip to Mexico. It's not the house. It's *you*."

"Finn, please!" Sarah said.

He stretched his free hand toward Sarah. "Get away from her, Sarah. She is not the friend we thought she was."

Stepping sideways, Sarah took Emmie's arm. "You're scaring me, Finn."

"Something's gotten into you." Emmie extended her palm as if to stop him. "You're not yourself."

Finn's eyes widened, and he shook his head. "Oh, this is me, all right. Pure, unfiltered Finn. And I've never, ever felt more myself than today."

The confrontation had paralyzed Emmie for a moment, but as her heart beat faster and her mind raced to process what he was saying, the danger became clear.

Finn lifted the object in his hand. It was a *hammer* with a black metal head. He lifted the hammer to his chest and charged toward them.

In a second, Emmie had yanked Sarah along and headed toward the house as he came straight at them. On the way, she grabbed the back of an oversized wooden lawn chair and swiveled it into his path. Something thumped against the chair and he let out a loud curse, words she'd never heard him say before.

Sarah screamed and stumbled but kept pace with her. Emmie hoped Sarah understood that wasn't really Finn back there, and that he intended to use the hammer if he got the chance.

He would kill her.

Whatever had come over him, they couldn't deal with it in that weather. They needed to get inside and separate themselves from him until he calmed down. Maybe they knew the house better than he did, but her mind strained to remember which rooms had locks on the doors. Not too many. And maybe that wouldn't be enough.

"Sarah!" Finn limped behind them. He'd obviously hurt his leg, but it wouldn't slow him for long. "Sarah, come back to me. She's not the friend you think she is. She's just like that girl who killed her boyfriend, except I got away. I'm tougher than she thought. And she'll hurt you too!"

"No, Finn." Sarah glanced over her shoulder without slowing. "Stop this!"

They reached the front door and Emmie rushed inside the house, pulling Sarah and locking the door behind them.

Sarah turned back, trying to look out the window on the door.

"We don't have time," Emmie said, still pulling her. Their snow-drenched jackets and shoes left wet trails across the floor on their way toward the stairs.

Emmie pulled out her phone and started dialing 911 until Sarah cupped her hand over the screen.

"Don't call the police." Sarah was near tears. "They'll kill him. He's not himself right now and we can help him by restraining him in some way and then forcing the spirit out of him. Can't you see it in his eyes?"

"I can see it all right, but we can't argue with a man of Finn's strength... and that hammer."

Drained of color, Sarah's face begged her not to make that call as she slumped against Emmie. She'd begun to sob, and it broke Emmie's heart.

This is my fault. And there was no denying what Finn had said outside. She hadn't wished him to die, but she hadn't acted to stop what might have been a tragedy either.

"We'll be all right, I swear." Emmie tried to comfort her friend while scanning the area. "We won't hurt him—"

Finn rattled the front door, then pounded against it. They

jumped and Sarah shrieked. The wood cracked under his weight, but it didn't open. But for how long? His face peered in at them.

"Trapping me outside in the cold again, Emmie? Edgar was right."

"He was wrong!" Emmie screamed back at him.

He would get in eventually, but how would they protect themselves until he calmed down? They had to get to whatever had taken hold of him.

Emmie glanced around the house.

Where to hide?

Finn had broken out of the lake house through the storm door's window, and all the rooms in the house had windows, except... the basement? But even then, how could they get him down there and *keep* him there? They would need to knock him out or tie him up. And they could do it if Emmie and Sarah worked together, but Sarah was in no condition to help wrestle Finn to the ground, despite her skill at dealing with difficult patients at the hospital.

She glanced at the top of the stairs. Maybe a bathroom? Only one small window in each of the ones up there. If they could get him inside and block the door like she had done at the lake house, they could talk him down. Or Sarah could.

"Where are your car keys?" Sarah asked in a weak voice.

Emmie's panicked mind strained to remember. Had she left them in her jacket? She touched her pocket, but they weren't there. In the kitchen? No. She couldn't remember. Emmie pointed up. "Maybe... upstairs?"

"I'll wait here," Sarah said. "We can get out the back door and sneak around to the car in front after we hear him enter the house."

As if hearing their plan, Finn thumped against the door again. This time the whole house shook and cracked; it felt like the structure might collapse at any second.

Emmie lurched toward the stairs, then turned back. "I can't leave you down here alone. He might get in."

"Don't worry about me. He thinks he's protecting me."

"We don't know what crazy idea might get into his head." Emmie grabbed Sarah's arm, and they trudged up to their bedroom together. Arriving at the beside table where she thought she'd left her car keys, she groaned. They weren't there either. Emmie met Sarah's gaze just as Finn crashed through the front door.

"Can't keep a good man down!" Finn shouted. Glass shattered and crackled across the wood floor. Several booming thumps followed as he pounded up the stairs.

Emmie's heart raced, and she rushed toward the bedroom door pulling Sarah, slamming it shut, then tried to lock it, finding there was no lock. Her eyes stopped on the antique oak dresser. It would work if they moved fast.

She jumped around to the opposite side of the dresser and strained to push it in front of the door. Sarah helped, but the effects of the poisoning had drained her.

After the dresser was firmly in place, Emmie dragged her bed across the room and jammed it in against the dresser to add to the obstacles between them and Finn.

Despite their unique dilemma, if Finn didn't calm down soon, she *would* call the police, although Sarah was right, and she feared the consequences of getting outside help. Once that ball was in motion and the police were on their way, there'd be no turning back. But there was no telling how far Finn would go under the spirit's influence. She clutched the phone.

"Talk to him when he gets here. Try to calm him down, if you can."

A moment later, Finn rattled the doorhandle. Sarah got as near to it as she could.

"Finn, I'm frightened."

There was silence for a moment until Finn spoke. "I know, and that's why I need you to open this door and get out of there. Emmie's not the same person she was a few months ago. Our relationship has changed her. She's just taking advantage of you now."

"Finn, it's not like that," Sarah said gently.

"It is. You can't see it because she's tricked you too, but I can see it. Everything is so clear now. Please come out so we can be together and let me keep you safe."

Sarah leaned forward and reached over the dresser, then placed her hand on the door. "I don't feel safe now, not with you attacking us like this."

"I'm not attacking you..." He continued in a whisper, "... only her."

With her palm flat against the door, Sarah bowed her head. "That's what I mean. We should all take some time and talk about this, somewhere far away from this house."

"Yes, I like that idea." The frame cracked as the door bulged in. "I can take you away from here, just you and me, and we can be done with her."

Sarah slumped. "No, Finn. That's not what I mean."

Pushing on the door a little harder, Finn rattled the handle again. "What have you got blocking the door? I know you couldn't have done that, since she made you so weak."

"She didn't do that to me. The pain is from the spirits who died from poisoning. It has nothing to do with Emmie."

His voice exploded in a shout. "It has *everything* to do with her. She can't stand to see us together, and now she's put your life in danger too. She doesn't care about you."

An answering scream rose in Emmie's throat. *I do care!* She swallowed it and clenched her teeth.

Sarah's soft voice countered Finn's rage. "She cares about both of us so much, Finn. She's faced so much evil, standing between us and all the spirits that tried to harm us. Do you remember?"

He said nothing, and Sarah continued, "And that's why I need you to lock yourself in one of the rooms. Please do it for me, just until we can sort all of this out. Things have gotten so... out of hand."

Finn grumbled. "You still don't get it, do you?" His weight shifted against the door, moving from one side to the other, as if searching for any signs of weakness. "Emmie? How does it feel to be locked in? To be helpless?"

Emmie's voice cracked. "We're in this together, Finn."

"Now you want that to be true, don't you? How about I put *you* out in the cold?" Finn cursed under his breath. "Sarah, sweetheart, open the door... please."

Sarah stepped back. "No, Finn."

"She's going to kill you. She's been trying to ever since we stepped into this place."

"Fight against that thought, Finn. We need you to protect us from this house."

Emmie stepped forward and pulled Sarah away just as something slammed against the door, cracking a section of the wood as it pushed in. The frame splintered and creaked.

The house's aging wood might hold Finn off for a while, but nothing would keep him separated from Sarah for long. Love would find a way. And if there's anything Emmie had learned about him over the past few months, one trait stood out—the trait he had mentioned himself: He was relentless.

It won't be long now.

33

Finn slammed the hammer against the door. Sarah shuddered and Emmie held back a scream.

"Emmie," Sarah said, hunched forward on the edge of the bed, hugging her stomach. "Call Jason Reeves."

Jason. For the first time ever, she associated his name with hope and relief. If they couldn't call the police, he was the only person who would understand what they were going through. He could be there in a couple of hours, assuming the storm didn't slow him.

But would they still be alive in a couple of hours?

"I'm sure it was the boy whispering," Sarah said. "Not Joan or Owl. They were all chanting, but he was the one whispering."

"Find your Truth..." The words lingered in Emmie's mind. "That's what I kept hearing when I allowed Finn to get locked inside the lake house. I felt like he deserved it."

"But you don't feel he deserved to die out there, did you?"

"It was like... whatever happened was destiny. It was what he had brought on himself."

"He doesn't truly think you deserve to die either, but he's capable of putting you out in the cold, I guess. This house is affecting us all. Whatever Edgar is whispering to us is controlling us. In a way, it's possessing us."

Not you, Emmie realized. Sarah had done nothing out of character. Maybe it was still to come...

Finn's hammer hit the door's frame and Emmie jumped as the sound exploded through the room. Sarah shook and Emmie dug out her phone.

With cold, trembling fingers, she flipped through her phone's contacts and found Jason. She unblocked him and hit dial.

Her mobile network was unavailable.

"No!" Her heart raced faster.

"What's wrong?" Sarah's face was so pale, and her eyelids almost closed.

"The signal." Emmie lifted her phone, moving it through the air, but the signal bars didn't appear. Not even one little bar.

The hammer slammed into the door again and Sarah winced. She was near tears as she folded her arms over her chest. "There's got to be something we can do. Some way to snap him out of it."

Despite the lack of a signal, Emmie typed a text message, summarizing their dilemma and begging Jason to get there as fast as he could, along with something to restrain Finn. She sent the text and stared at her phone's screen, waiting for the sound that her message had gone out.

She met Sarah's pleading gaze for a moment, then returned to the phone and added to her message: *And, if we don't make it, tell Finn we don't blame him, and not to blame himself.*

"Finn, please stop." Sarah's voice cracked.

The snow was piling up outside the window. It would cushion their fall—but even if they managed to get outside, Finn would almost certainly hear them escaping and be waiting for them on the ground.

The sound of his huffing breaths echoed in from the hallway, although the hammering had stopped. No footsteps to indicate he had left the area, but at least he wasn't forcing himself inside anymore. Maybe the struggle had worn him down, or maybe Sarah had touched his heart, or maybe he was having other ideas.

As quietly as possible, Emmie slid a stool under the window as their last resort to escape if things got really bad, even though that plan was far from ideal.

Sarah shivered and balled up on the bed in the meantime, and Emmie threw a blanket over her. Her wet shoes poked out and hung over the edge, dripping the melted snow on the floor, where a small puddle had formed.

Sarah closed her eyes and her face contorted with pain, although she didn't complain.

Emmie had seen that same expression on the poison victims. Sarah had absorbed all the tragic pain that filled the house. Would she have enough strength to recover? They all needed to get out of the house as soon as possible.

The wind rattled the glass on the window again. The storm was getting worse, and there was no sign that Finn had left his post behind their door.

How long could they wait in there? How long before Finn made another attempt to get inside the room?

Emmie lay beside Sarah on the bed as the commotion subsided.

After a while in silence, the room's serenity and the steady drone of the wind battering against the window lulled Emmie to the edge of sleep, although she forced herself to stay awake. So much had happened that day. Despite the real danger of being killed by her friend, she was exhausted. Her mind jumped to thoughts of food and water, and she licked her dry lips, often imagining herself opening the window and letting the snowflakes land and melt on her tongue.

Sarah stirred and sat up. "Em, sorry to say this, but I need to use the bathroom."

Emmie glanced around the room. There was nothing suitable to use as a bathroom in their room. *Worse than a prison.*

As her frustration grew, Finn thumped against the door and

groaned. A moment later, his footsteps echoed away down the hall. She went to the door and pressed her ear against a small section that wasn't blocked by any furniture. Only silence.

She hurried over and whispered into Sarah's ear, "He's gone. He went downstairs."

Sarah opened her eyes drowsily. "Are you sure?"

"Positive."

If they were careful, *very* careful, they could slide the furniture aside and get out. She cleared her parched throat. The nearest bathroom was two doors down the hall on the left. They could make it there and back in five or ten minutes if they hurried. And whatever had distracted Finn might keep him busy downstairs for a while. *Probably grabbing something down there to prepare for a renewed attack.*

Sarah wavered as she stood. "Do you think we can make it to the car?"

"Not with him downstairs, even if he is worn down. But if we can make it to another room down the hall near the stairs, and he thinks we're still in here..."

Taking great care to push the furniture aside silently, they moved it back far enough to squeeze through, then opened the door a few millimeters at a time to minimize any noises.

Her stomach churned at the destruction Finn had left behind. All the wood was cracked and splintered. The doorknob was bent, although it hadn't snapped off. Maybe he had spared it, thinking the door might not open at all if he removed it. The hammer had gouged deep streaks down the frame. A modern door would have shattered in minutes, but this massive old thing had survived the attack.

Squeezing through the opening, they made their way out into the hallway. Emmie's ears perked at every squeak and crack.

The bathroom's doorway was just fifteen feet ahead and the light was off. All Emmie's senses focused on signs that Finn might be headed back upstairs. Her mouth hung open as she struggled to keep each breath slow and light. Sarah moved behind her, keeping pace and stepping in unison.

Arriving inside the bathroom, Emmie closed the door and locked it. After taking turns with the toilet, Emmie savored the cool water from the faucet, using a souvenir cup she had taken from their hotel room in Cabo San Lucas. She took a moment to stare at herself in the mirror.

Her face reflected the pain and exhaustion that filled her body.

"When you get out of here," Emmie mumbled to herself, "you're going to take a break from all this. Understand?"

Understood.

A nagging hunger made her stomach rumble, and a wave of dizziness swept through her. *I haven't eaten in... many hours.* Low blood sugar.

She gripped the edge of the counter to steady herself, following the hand-carved wooden designs on the edge of the mirror down to the cabinet beneath the sink. It flowed all the way to floor and became a painted design. All the designs resembled the same mandala theme she'd seen throughout the house.

It's everywhere. Can't escape it.

Sarah stepped over and stared at the bathroom door before whispering, "Where is he?"

Good question. Had he really given up? Had he come to his senses?

Emmie guessed that ten minutes had passed. Maybe Finn wasn't coming back, but she couldn't count on that hope.

"Look, I remember now I left my car keys in the sunroom after we got back from town yesterday. We're both tired, but I'm sure we can get down there, out the back door, and around to the front in no time. Then we should make it to the car, if we run like hell."

Sarah frowned. "What if he gets there first?"

"We need to think positive," Emmie said, and as Sarah grimaced, she added, "Old Owl said thoughts materialize, or some such thing. We've dealt with some bad stuff, Sarah. We will get out of this, and Finn too. All right?"

Sarah nodded. "All right."

"On three. One... two..."

Emmie stopped. The power to the house went out.

❧ 34 ❧

"What happened?" Sarah asked. "He must have switched off the power."

The room was dark, except for the afternoon's gray, cloudy light streaming in through the window. Emmie adjusted her eyes to the faint light, but it wasn't enough to get around. She pulled out her phone and checked the battery. Less than half full, and she needed that message to go off to Jason whenever the signal picked up.

"Do you have your phone?" she asked Sarah. "I can't let my battery die."

Sarah was still hunched forward, but she reached inside her jacket, unzipped a pocket, and took out her phone, handing it to Emmie. "It's affecting all of us—whatever energy Owl stirred up."

Emmie met her friend's tired, pale face. "Yeah. Everything is freaking out."

The wind pushed against the window, and she watched the glass rattle for a few seconds. Maybe it *would* be better to climb out the window than to face Finn. The power had switched off only moments earlier, but the warmth had already faded around them.

Emmie looked at Sarah again. No, she wasn't in any condition to climb down.

But she might die. Both of us could die.

A noise echoed through the house. The door to the basement? Finn had gone to the circuit breaker, and they could make a run for the front door in that moment, but he was still downstairs and would certainly confront them by the time they arrived. The creaky old stairs would give them away.

Maybe there was something in the room they could use to defend themselves from Finn just long enough to escape. A weapon that wouldn't kill him, just knock him out of the way.

She stepped around the bathroom's perimeter focusing in on every item, but found nothing. Of course there were no weapons after what had happened in the house recently—nothing even resembling a weapon.

Pushing aside the rug in front of the sink in desperation, she scanned the floor with the light from Sarah's phone and spotted the edge of the same concentric mandala design she'd seen on the hidden door leading to the tower. Only a corner of the design was visible at first—she hadn't seen it earlier, as the rug had obscured most of it—but it was there.

She pulled back the rug as far as she could.

A trapdoor.

It wasn't much wider than Emmie, probably the same size as the one hidden door she'd found in the sunroom. It just looked like a small section of the floor someone had cut through and then sealed back up. But she slipped the goggles over her eyes for a moment, and through them she saw the edge. Using her fingernails, she pried it up enough to grab, then opened it all the way.

The opening was dark and clean within the goggles, but removing them revealed a myriad of very real cobwebs and a dense darkness that dropped down a couple of feet to a wooden surface before making a sharp turn to run parallel under the bathroom's floor. It led toward the center of the house.

Not really a great space for an adult to explore, much less the ideal way to escape from their current predicament considering how weak Sarah was, but it would have to do. Joan had probably built the tunnel through the house for her boys, and there was no guarantee it would lead them to safety. It could go anywhere, including a drop into some blocked shaft—or send them crashing through the ceiling of one of the rooms below. Not much space to maneuver either. The idea of getting stuck in there churned her stomach; she wasn't claustrophobic—but with no room to maneuver, getting trapped would be like pushing herself into her own coffin.

Yet what were their choices? They could climb out the window, falling two stories, and probably break a bone or two. Or wait out Finn's psychotic episode, which might never happen. She couldn't even call 911 with no signal...

No, whatever lay in that tunnel was their best hope of getting out of the house alive.

Slipping her arm through the strap of the goggles, Emmie squeezed down into the hole, testing the wooden base and sides of the structure with her foot. Would it hold their weight? Again she switched Sarah's phone into flashlight mode and peered down into the darkness. Within the cobwebs, a few small black dots scurried away.

I guess a lair of spiders is better than a hammer to the head.

Sarah was leaning against the door to the bathroom. Emmie whispered, "We'll go out this way."

Her friend gave a weak nod and walked over to Emmie's side. Sarah leaned forward, examining the opening, then whispered, "Do you know where it goes?"

Emmie couldn't lie. "No."

Wrapping her arms around Emmie, Sarah nodded. "It's such a mess, Emmie. We can't let Finn hurt you, and we can't leave him behind."

Emmie held her friend for a moment, squeezing her. "You just stick with me, okay? We're going to be just fine. If this leads to the tower, like I think it does, then we'll just climb down into the sunroom and make a run for the car. Simple as that."

"Yes."

"We'll come back for Finn with reinforcements." She moved back and looked at Sarah. "I don't think he would ever hurt you, but I don't want to risk it."

"All right."

Emmie moved down into the hole first and climbed headfirst into the tunnel that ran parallel with the floor. Still using the phone as a flashlight, she inched forward, trying to avoid kicking her feet against the walls of the structure.

A few more black dots scurried around her.

Damn those spiders. Funny how it's the little things that scare me the most.

She crawled on her belly, the toes of her shoes propelling her forward a few inches at a time. The wood cracked and creaked around her. It might hold up, but would Finn hear all the commotion and be waiting for them on the other side?

Her jacket scraped against the scratchy surfaces, stirring up dust that threatened to make her sneeze. The wood now sank under her weight, but she didn't feel that it was in danger of collapsing. Was it true that they made things of a higher quality back then?

I guess we'll find out.

After squirming through the narrow passageway for a couple of minutes, Emmie realized that her friend had stopped. She glanced back, although she only could turn her head far enough to see Sarah from the corner of her eye. "Sarah? You okay?"

"Yeah." Sarah moaned. "Just give me a minute."

Emmie's breath hung in the cool air. No circulation. Maybe the tunnel didn't actually lead anywhere. The thought gave her chills. Or was it just the cold? Her elbows ached from knocking against the wood beneath her, but she was sure she could make it to the end unless they encountered something along the way.

Like a spirit? It didn't matter which one it was, she would move right through it.

Sarah's coat scraped against the wood again. She was moving forward, and Emmie continued, taking it slow and careful to allow Sarah enough time to keep up.

Sarah gasped and her jacket rustled. "It's getting worse, Em."

"Hang in there. We're almost there," Emmie lied. She focused on the light ahead. She couldn't see a thing. Maybe another fifteen or twenty feet.

Gripping Emmie's ankle, Sarah insisted, "I just... don't have any strength."

Emmie paused and flipped over onto her back with great difficulty. The wooden structure cracked more loudly as she adjusted herself to the new position. Running her hand along the wooden frame around her, she discovered that every foot or two there was a section of wood that jutted out just enough for her to hook her fingers around it. She could get enough leverage to pull a little extra weight.

She extended her leg toward Sarah. "Hold on to my leg. I'll pull you."

Sarah didn't argue, but her grasp on Emmie's leg was anything but secure. Working together, they moved along in sync a little at a time, and they continued ahead for several minutes before Emmie paused to look over her shoulder into the darkness up ahead.

"I see it," Emmie lied again. "Just a little more." She put away the phone and then continued; both of them were breathing heavily, and every muscle in Emmie's body was aching. She couldn't imagine what Sarah was going through.

"Whatever is causing this," Sarah said between exhausted breaths, "it's coming from everywhere, every direction, not just one person."

Emmie continued dragging her friend along several inches at a time with short bursts of energy, although her muscles were on fire and her fingertips numb in the icy darkness. They were making more noise than she'd wanted, but they were also running out of time. Sarah wasn't one to complain, having dealt with the weakness caused by her gift so many times, so Emmie knew her friend was in serious trouble.

After another five minutes, the sound didn't echo as much, a sign that they *were* nearing the end. A short time later, Emmie's head bumped into a wooden surface that was blocking the end of the tunnel. She let out a gasp, from relief and also distress that they might need to crawl all the way back to the room if they hadn't reached safety—but after turning over onto her chest again, she pushed against the cold surface and it snapped open away from them. A doorway leading back into the tower.

Oh, thank God.

A rush of energy flashed through her as she pulled herself through the doorway. She stretched out over the tower's floor, immediately turning back to help pull Sarah out.

Sarah struggled to stand after squeezing through the door. Emmie wrapped her arm around her lower back, but Sarah was limp. She still managed to prop her friend against the wall—no way to stay there long without freezing—but Emmie needed to get her bearings and find their way out.

The freezing air stung Emmie's damp face. The tower's windows were dark gray and frosted over, allowing only a little light to get through.

After reassuring Sarah one more time—this time with sincere hope in her voice—she slipped the goggles back on. What she had imagined the space looked like long ago was different from how she viewed it through the goggles.

Joan's astounding display of painted artistry was everywhere. The familiar themes and designs that had appeared throughout the house covered the center pillar and every wall. She hadn't left one inch of the space unpainted. There were massive mandalas full of vibrant colors blended next to smaller, more intricate designs, some of which Finn had pointed out in Owl's book. No doubt, Joan had spent a great deal of time and effort to paint the area.

But in the small room, a delicate whispering voice grew louder, chanting the same sounds she had heard in her room on the previous night. She held her breath, forcing herself to remain still though her body shivered as the cold air sank beneath her clothes and encompassed her.

... *AAA LL MM UU WW OO YAA MEE LLL MM FEE WOE SSS...*

Even through the goggles, there was no one in the room.

Until a pale face poked out from behind the center pillar. Edgar.

❧ 35 ❧

Edgar's face was just as strained and pale as the women's and Owl's at having been poisoned, although he continued chanting between labored breaths, wheezing out the same repetitive sounds Emmie had heard throughout her time at the house. His mouth opened and closed robotically, a movement broken only by gasps of breath and random convulsions. He stared at them through his goggles while his hands dug into an open jar he held against his chest.

Pulling out a handful of dried leaves from the jar, he extended his open palm as if offering a gift to Emmie. "This is for you."

"That's poison," Emmie said.

"It's my Truth to you."

"I'll die if I eat that. You poisoned all of them, didn't you?"

Edgar smiled warmly. "I had to share it with Professor Cromwell, mother, and all the ladies, and you need to take this too so we can all be together."

Emmie's legs weakened, and she clutched an exposed beam, bracing the wall of the tower for balance. She wavered on the edge of fainting. How could such an innocent face—not an ounce of evil in his eyes—offer up death with such a loving gaze?

218

The boy continued, still holding out the leaves. "I'm helping you to your Truth, to end your suffering. We can all be together again, and mother won't miss William so much, and all the ladies won't cry anymore. Take it, and you can join us as we find our Truth!"

Edgar stepped forward, but Emmie retreated. "We shouldn't eat that. Nobody should."

He formed a puzzled expression. "Professor Cromwell understands the secrets of the universe, and he said we should all share our Truth with others. And this is mine."

"What are you talking about?"

"I'm a liberator. I freed them all from the burden of Professor Cromwell's shortcomings, but I succeeded in sharing the Truth with them. We will always be together, never leave like my twin brother did. Mother was so sad, but I've done it! I've kept us together. Why are you so surprised?"

Emmie inched back. "You poisoned them to keep them here with you?"

"Professor Cromwell couldn't bring my twin brother back to mother, or fulfill any of his promises to the ladies—he's a fraud—so I did it. I knew I could."

"How can you mistake murder for liberation?"

"But you were the one who told me that!" he said.

Emmie widened her eyes. "Told you what?"

"Souls that die a peaceful death pass on. The lesson you shared with me was clear. We can be together only through an unnatural death. That's what you said. And I was chosen to make that happen. It's my Truth. It is done."

Her heart sank. The words she had spoken to the boy came back to her. She had only meant to soothe his anguished heart in her earlier conversation with him, to ease the pain of losing his twin brother, but somehow he had misinterpreted her.

Even more disturbing, in his reality, somehow, she was the ghost telling him all this in his present but way in the past for her. They had all, a hundred and thirty years ago, been sitting around a séance table and seen her and Sarah and Finn. And a hundred and thirty years ago, she had told this boy that it was impossible for him to ever see his brother again. That only unnatural deaths kept people together. And he had accomplished exactly that.

With a muffled sob, Emmie stumbled back. Her own words had directed him to kill. She had been responsible for those awful deaths! Whatever energy Owl had released in the house would cause the tragic events to loop like a scratched record, repeating the same section of song without someone to step in and nudge the needle.

Time doesn't exist, Owl had said.

Emmie's tears streamed down and dripped off her chin.

Edgar lowered the leaves and extended his other small hand to her face. He caressed her cheek. "Don't cry anymore. Just take my gift. It will hurt a little, like when I go to the doctor, but it's for your own good. Mother always tells me that."

"I—I can't," Emmie said.

Despite what the boy had just told her, she needed to get Sarah out of that house, away from all the toxic energy that was literally poisoning her friend. And for Finn, at some point the nightmare had to end, as it had for her. The spirits would always be trapped there without intervention from the one person who might help release them, but Sarah might not survive the night if they didn't leave, and Finn might still kill them.

Carrying the awful burden of the knowledge that she had provoked the poisonings, Emmie stepped toward the ladder. But now she had to deal with the living—with Sarah and... Finn.

Sarah, who had heard nothing of what Edgar had said, had stood up and now stepped forward, although she stumbled along the way. Her wavering steps reminded Emmie that the end was near.

Emmie whispered in Sarah's ear, "You just need to make it down the ladder. We're almost there. I'll be right behind you." She helped Sarah along by wrapping an arm under her shoulder.

Sarah nodded. "If we meet Finn—"

"We'll die if we don't leave now. But I won't hurt him."

Edgar's words had made her more determined than ever to see Sarah and Finn survive. How could she live knowing she'd been responsible for their deaths? She stepped down the ladder first, her feet touching each step with all the stealth of a burglar. Still the wood creaked, and it was impossible to think they would make it out of there silently.

Where are you, Finn?

The house was quiet. He could be anywhere, but she pictured him waiting for them at the bottom of the stairs, or just on the other side of the hidden door, hunkered down with his hammer and thermal camera, having followed their heat signatures through the walls of the house all along. If he had taken the time to hunt them in the same way he hunted spirits, they wouldn't have a chance. Their only hope would be that he hadn't taken the time to think it through, that his mind was too clouded by the distorted reality that filled the house.

Sarah groggily moved down the ladder a couple of steps after Emmie, her feet and movements generating more noise than expected. But they could be outside within minutes... *if* everything went smoothly.

Emmie opened her mouth to encourage her friend, then closed it. No need to add to her despair.

A minute later, they reached the bottom of the ladder and Emmie removed her goggles, hooking the strap around her wrist before opening the small hidden door leading out into the sunroom. She cracked it open gently, as her hands trembled both from fear and from the freezing stillness of the tower that had numbed her bare fingers to the bones.

Finn wasn't in the sunroom, as far as she could see, but there were plenty of darkened corners where he might be waiting for them to lower their defenses. Emmie scanned every corner before continuing forward.

Sarah wavered beside Emmie, clutching her arm as she

followed without adding to the noises that threatened to give them away.

Now it would be a simple matter of crossing the sunroom and stepping out the back door. After opening the door, the wind and air pressure would flood in, whipping through the whole house. It would create some noise, jarring some loose doors to shift on their hinges as far as upstairs, but that was just the way it had to be. No turning back. And once outside, they would need to run fast—faster than they had ever done in their lives—to make it to the car before Finn got to them.

Emmie stepped out into the sunroom, helping Sarah and creeping along the squeaking wood floor toward the back door. She found her keys right where she'd left them the previous evening, which was a miracle. Finn, in his normal state, would have thought to take them. She clutched them carefully to avoid making noise. When her hand touched the back door's handle, a rush of relief swept through her. She clicked open the metal lock and paused before opening it.

Edgar's voice whispered into her ear—not the chant this time, but the words: "You can't run from your Truth."

Emmie turned back, but Edgar wasn't visible without the goggles, which were still dangling over her forearm. He wasn't visible, yet she could hear him.

No time to talk.

She pushed the door open, and the wind grabbed it violently, as if someone were playing tug-of-war with her on the other side. At first, she imagined it was Finn, wielding his hammer like a drunk construction worker after a long day of demolition, but there was no sign of anyone. No footsteps in the snow or shadows approaching.

Still, by opening the door she had blown their cover, and they needed to run. Emmie charged ahead down the back steps with Sarah gasping for breath at her side.

She turned right, toward her car in the driveway, and made it as far as the edge of the house before stopping in her tracks. Her car was there, thirty feet away and buried in snow, but a shadowed figure stood beside it with a raised hammer.

Sarah let out a restrained gasp.

Finn.

❧ 36 ❧

Finn slammed the hammer down into the car's windshield
with a sharp crack, leaving a dark patch embedded within
the blanket of snow that covered the glass. Even without the
torrential snowfall, it was clear that their plan to escape in her
car wasn't going to happen. While she stared, Finn raised the
hammer again in his right hand and threw down another strike.
Half the windshield disappeared.

Emmie held in a gasp with her mouth hanging open and
started to turn back, but Finn paused after a few more blows and
leaned down sideways as if... listening to someone whispering in
his ear.

Edgar.

"Come on," Emmie spoke softly in Sarah's ear while pulling
her friend toward the back of the house.

"The chanting." Sarah's voice rose above the wind, rushing
into Emmie's ears. "The chanting. Do you hear it?"

Emmie focused on a faint voice blurred within all the other
noises battering her ears. As Edgar continued whispering to
Finn, she pinpointed the source of the sounds. It was Edgar,
without a doubt, but the boy wasn't directing Finn at all, not
with words anyway; he was simply repeating the haunting,

tuneful chant she had heard earlier. Finn swayed within the power that had overcome him. Whatever energy Edgar had picked up from Owl's twisted ideas allowed him to direct the whispering chants and keep Finn prisoner. It was not possession, but something deeper that Owl had conjured from the dark corners of the universe and called Truth. Finn had lost control of himself.

Emmie led Sarah behind the edge of the house and paused, glancing back at Finn for a moment. As if he sensed her staring at him, his gaze snapped toward her.

Pulling Sarah further into the darkness of the backyard, Emmie decided to run to the lake. The closest neighbor she had seen was there, on the other side, and there must be some way she could get their attention. They wouldn't be safe anywhere if someone didn't come to help them.

In the blistering cold of the winter afternoon, she paused for a moment and got the goggles, placing them over her eyes. Through them, the sun sat on the lake's horizon and a beautiful gold sunset gradually faded into brilliant shades of red and orange. It would have warmed her heart under normal circumstances. Her surroundings within the goggles were clear, and the lake house was straight ahead, behind a thick cluster of trees. She plotted a course that way, as she could find the other house from the shore if she stood right in front. There were plenty of differences between the two worlds, however, and she raised and lowered the goggles over her eyes repeatedly to compare them.

Smoke still rose from the chimney of the lake house. Joan had returned. They could stop and confront her again, but the image of her sent a deep chill through Emmie. The woman was mad, and she had driven her boy mad. It wouldn't be worth the effort to convince her to help them stop Edgar's chanting. Her grief had consumed her thoughts. They were on their own.

Emmie glanced back as her shoes kicked through the snow. No sign of Finn or Edgar, but it wouldn't take Finn long to make it around the house.

Sarah made Emmie stop and meet her gaze for a moment. Her face was barely visible within the storm, but her deep distress was clear in her voice. "Finn won't survive. I can feel it."

"I said I won't hurt him. I promise I'll let him kill me first."

"Not you. The boy will. His power is only getting stronger."

"Then we need to get away, or lead Finn out of here."

At Sarah's nod, Emmie began weaving between the trees and she passed the lake house with her heart racing and her stomach churning.

Sarah was right. The boy's hold over Finn had driven him to extreme violence, and maybe there was no coming back from that. Maybe he couldn't stop until he hurt someone—even himself.

Finn's voice called out from the backyard, but his words were muddled in the wind. Something about teaching her a lesson.

Emmie hadn't had the chance to think how to attract the attention of the house across the lake. Yet, the light was on in the present; someone was home. Emmie looked at the lake and knew there was only one direction they could take. She yanked on Sarah's arm.

"The ice?" Sarah said. "We won't make it, Emmie! Let me try—"

"The lights are on." She pointed to the house across. It seemed so far. "It's not totally dark, and they must look out the window every now and again. They might see us running and screaming."

Without hesitation, she pulled Sarah toward the frozen lake. It would take a lot of effort, and balance, to make it across, something she wasn't sure her weakened friend had in her. But they had no other option now.

The phone buzzed in her pocket. Her fingers were almost frozen, and she would only lose their last lifeline if she dropped it, but she managed to pull it out and read the message on her screen. *On my way.*

The message to Jason had gotten through, but when had he

read it? When had he written back? Just now? It would be too late if he were coming from Minneapolis.

Emmie held back a frustrated scream and lumbered down to the shoreline with Sarah, then paused before stepping onto the ice. Through the goggles, the water gently rose and fell with each wave, but her foot found a hard, icy layer.

But another strange thing filled her vision. Owl's reality was darkening as they fled, as if the goggles' lenses were fogging over. Moving forward, she stepped cautiously onto the ice even as it cracked beneath their feet and the warm summer landscape faded even further.

A limit. That reality must only still exist in and near the house.

Would that be enough to break Edgar's hold on Finn?

A renewed hope filled her. "We need to lure him away from the house."

"What?" Sarah asked feebly.

"Edgar can't control Finn way out here. Just like my phone, the signal of their reality only works within a certain radius. It doesn't reach out here."

"Are you sure?" Sarah's face brightened. "Then let's keep going. We can make it!"

The ice cracked louder with Sarah's next eager step forward, but that was no surprise. It *was* December in Minnesota. It would be a couple of feet thick by then in most areas of the lake, and a few diehard fishing enthusiasts had even towed out their ice fishing houses along the shore of the far side. Emmie *wanted* to believe that it was safe, although she'd lived in Minnesota long enough to know that every year a few impatient souls ventured onto the ice only to break through a thin section and drown.

Yet the ice was solid where she stepped. Plenty thick to hold their weight—theoretically, as Finn might say.

The wind blew the snow across Emmie's face, although her bare skin was numb.

Finn's voice drifted out to them. "You can't escape your Truth."

The Truth is, I have to.

The women looked behind them to find Finn on the shore. A gust of wind surged and the edge of her pants flapped as Emmie steadied herself. The snow covering the ice provided a false sense of security, suggesting they could get through the thick accrual without sliding, but reality was unforgiving.

One wrong step and we're on our backs.

The wind whooshed in Emmie's ears as they trudged toward the house on the opposite shore. A long, slow trek ahead. If Finn reached them before they arrived at the other side, well... She tried not to think about it.

A few minutes later, her vision within the goggles had darkened to the point where it made no sense to continue wearing them. She pushed them down and hung them around her neck, despite her instinct to discard them in the snow. Maybe she would still need them.

Emmie glanced back. Finn was on the ice, still wielding the hammer, showing no signs of slowing down. Edgar was still influencing him.

Shit.

She raised the goggles and looked. The boy was walking by Finn, *over water.* How far could Edgar venture away from his mystical—or cursed—home? At some point, the boy would turn back. That only made sense.

Right, Em?

I guess we'll find out.

The way ahead, however, was still black. She and Sarah had passed the limit a minute earlier, so Finn *should* be okay after arriving where they now stood, depending on how long it would take for Edgar's control to wear off. *If* her theory was correct.

The wind drowned everything except her racing thoughts and their heaving breaths as they moved ahead. After another few minutes, Emmie's legs weakened, while Sarah could barely stand. They were still a long way from reaching the opposite shore from Joan's house, and she hadn't looked back at Finn in a while. He might be only a few feet behind them by then, but she hadn't heard his voice. Wouldn't he have taunted them when he got close enough?

She couldn't help it. She had to look back. And when she did, she gasped.

Finn was gone.

❧ 37 ☙

E mmie squinted within the blur of wind and snow whipping
up off the ice and pelting her face. She could see all the
way to the shoreline and almost to the house, yet Finn was
nowhere in sight. But he had to be there somewhere.

"No, no! Emmie, where is he?" Sarah cried, gaining strength.

Putting on her goggles again, Emmie saw Edgar on the shoreline, staring out at them with a gentle smile. His lips were moving.
No doubt he was still chanting, even from that distance, like a
child reciting a nursery rhyme over and over with unstoppable zeal.

Emmie lowered her goggles again just as Sarah screamed and
began running back toward the shore, though she was sliding.
"Finn!" she cried hoarsely.

Something stirred in the water halfway between them and
the shore. A man was struggling, splashing, and crying out for
help between gasps of breath.

Finn.

He clung to something in the water, hoisting himself up
above the surface, throwing his leg over for a moment before
dropping back down. His goggles were gone, and he stared at the
women for a moment with one hand reaching out.

"Emmie, help me!" Finn cried.

He was calling her name, not Sarah's. *He's back.*

Sarah had managed to hurry in his direction faster than she had escaped from him.

"That's him, but it's too dangerous," Emmie pleaded, reaching for her and trying to hold her back.

"No!" Sarah said, shaking her off. "I won't let him die!"

But Emmie had no plan. She ran and slid after Sarah, whimpering as she watched Finn struggle at the edge of the collapsed ice hole.

It's my fault, my fault. Her heart ached watching him disappear and appear again. How long before hypothermia set in?

As they approached, Finn waved them away. "Don't..."

It's definitely Finn.

He thrashed within the water, pulling himself up onto his chest. "Don't come over here. It's not..."

The edge of ice holding him up broke, and he disappeared again.

Sarah screamed, a sound that ought to have caught the attention of anyone within miles.

They weren't far from the shore, maybe only fifteen or twenty feet, but panic swept through Emmie as she scoured the area for anything she might use to save Finn. No branches or objects that might help. Without hesitating, she slipped off her jacket. They dropped face down on the ice and slid forward the final few feet toward Finn, tossing out the jacket toward him. It was the only lifeline they could offer.

The ice numbed Emmie's body within seconds, but nothing was more important now than Finn. Edgar was certainly watching them even now from the shoreline, but there was no sense in seeing him. At least the separation from Edgar had cleared Finn's mind.

Finn clutched the arm of Emmie's jacket, although his fingers were white and stiff. The ice around the hole broke away in his futile struggle. He would drown soon, if the icy temperature didn't get him first.

"Finn, hang on." Emmie helped Sarah hold her jacket, but Finn wasn't rising beyond the top of his chest. He was shaking, and his arms flailed more slowly with each second. His body was shutting down.

"Hold on!" Sarah pleaded with him.

Something in the backyard caught Emmie's attention. A figure running toward them, bounding through the snow with a long rope-like object.

Not a rope, but the garden hose she had tripped over earlier.

And Jason.

38

Emmie almost cried as Jason arrived on the scene. The yellow sprinkler attached to the end of the garden hose that he dragged with him acted as a perfect hook for Finn to grab hold of after Jason tossed it into the water.

Finn managed to wrap his arm around the sprinkler, although his fingers must have been ice by then. Most of the life had gone out of him. His mouth hung open, choking in gasps of breath as he shivered throughout the rescue.

Working together, the three of them hoisted him out over the ice, then dragged him to shore. Without pausing, each person grabbed one side of Finn as they carried him back into the house.

Jason led the way inside, flipping the light switch near the front door. "Lights don't work."

"Power's out." Emmie looked around the room. Where had Finn gone to turn off the power? She hoped he hadn't permanently sabotaged it in his altered state of mind.

"What? Why?"

Without answering his question, Sarah gestured with her head toward the living room. "Put him on the couch... and get a fire started."

Jason's phone became their only light as Sarah directed them through the freezing, dark house.

Placing Finn's damp, chilled body on the couch, Sarah shivered while checking on his condition endlessly. She never left his side while talking to him in a soft, yet firm tone. She pointed to the fireplace and asked no one in particular, "Get that started." The nurse in Sarah had taken over, and they didn't argue.

Jason hurried over to it and loaded in some wood. "I'll do my best."

Emmie helped Sarah remove Finn's wet clothes down to his underwear, then stepped back and looked around. "I'll find the circuit breaker."

"Basement," Finn mumbled.

"Finn!" Sarah said joyfully.

Emmie studied his face for a moment. Influenced or not, Finn wasn't a danger to anyone now. She hurried away to the basement, found the breaker in a corner near the furnace and switched it on to cheers from upstairs.

Returning only minutes later, Jason had started a small fire in the fireplace, and a somewhat purple Finn sat upright in Sarah's arms. His wet clothes lay in a dripping pile beside the couch, and he shivered within a thick maroon blanket. His eyes were open, but he didn't smile or meet her gaze.

"I'll call 911," Emmie said.

Sarah nodded, her expression somber. At least the panic had subsided.

Emmie rushed outside again to the end of the driveway with her phone out to search for a signal. After only a few seconds, she got through. The operator stayed on the line after getting her information, but it was too cold to wait out there just to stay connected. Emmie walked back inside, warning the operator that the signal might die. It did.

Help is on its way, Finn.

Returning to her friends, she stood beside the fire next to Jason.

Sarah pushed the wet hair off Finn's forehead. "You got through?"

Emmie nodded and stared at Finn. "Is he still..."

Sarah opened her mouth to answer but Finn interrupted.

"A m-m-madman?" He met Emmie's gaze, his body still shaking. "I'm so sorry. I–"

Emmie held up her hand, but smiled warmly. "We can talk about it later." She looked at Sarah. "How is he doing?"

"Stable."

Emmie's smile widened. "Wonderful. We still need to finish a few things before the ambulance gets here."

Sarah looked to Finn.

He nodded. "I'm fine. Do what you need to do before that kid whispers in someone else's ear."

"Now if we can just find him..." Emmie turned to Sarah. "Why did you say I needed to bring William? You know he can't come back."

Looking over her shoulder at Jason, who had stepped over and sat beside Finn as he lay next to the crackling flames, Sarah motioned with her head for Emmie to follow her.

She led Emmie into the séance room.

"There's something I want to try," Sarah said. "Something I read about."

"What is it?"

"It's called mirroring."

Emmie made a wide gesture with her hand. "You mean something to do with all the mirrors in the house?"

Sarah shook her head. "Different." She sat at the table, and Emmie took a chair next to her. "It's like what I did with Daniel Hyde, channeling a spirit to allow them expression through me, but not quite the same. All the mirrors reminded me of something I read. It's something empaths can do."

"All right... But if you're suggesting to allow Edgar to—"

"Not like that. No channeling with this. The whole twin thing with Edgar, and with Finn and his brother. I feel that,

235

Emmie. I can imagine it so well. How it must hurt." She stretched out her hand to Emmie, and it was dry and warm. Emmie squeezed it. "I would feel that loss if it were you or Finn. I know that loss."

Emmie looked into her friend's eyes, which now held a subtle blue glow. She had more questions about what Sarah intended to do, but stayed silent.

Sarah nodded reassuringly. "Close your eyes."

Emmie did, though she opened one after a moment and saw Sarah smiling with eyes shut, as if she were lost in a dream. Again, Emmie closed hers, and behind her lids the room brightened a few seconds later.

The light flooded Emmie's sight, despite her closed lids, until she couldn't resist the temptation to peek at her friend again. Cracking her eyes open, the light blinded her for a moment, forcing her to turn her head sideways to avoid looking directly at the source of the radiance.

But Emmie's eyes adjusted to the light, which now encompassed Sarah. Her friend's body radiated shifting colors from red to orange to green and deep blue. The auras that Sarah had talked about so often, the ones Emmie had never seen before.

The feeling was exhilarating as the glow passed through Emmie, warming her own heart with a deep, calm presence.

This is what her patients must feel before passing away. No wonder they go to her.

Only a moment later, Edgar appeared in the room. He moved to Sarah, staring at her, transfixed by her aura as it shifted and transformed into a mirror image of himself.

The twin.

Sarah had now become William, and Edgar stepped toward her, extending his hand to her face. "William? Is that you?"

"I've come to get you, Edgar," Sarah said in a small boy's voice.

"What about Mother?"

"She will be with us soon. Come!"

Edgar stared into William's eyes, then reached out and embraced his twin before merging with Sarah's spirit for a moment. Edgar became part of the light and escaped in the air above Sarah.

The other spirits in the house had also been drawn by the brightness. They appeared around the table: the ladies, Joan, and Owl. Each of the ladies moved toward Sarah, their faces filled with bliss as they passed through her as if she were a door. They rose into the air in a burst of light. Only Joan and Owl remained.

Joan reached out longingly to William. "You came back."

"I was always here."

Kneeling, she embraced her son, her cheek to his, until she became light too and passed through Sarah.

Owl spoke to the room, though his eyes could not leave Sarah, who was now only light in no shape at all. "You see?" he said, to no one and everyone. "I was right. I was right all along!"

"You were right," Sarah whispered back.

Owl disappeared in a burst just as Finn walked into the room, still wrapped in the blanket and with Jason propping him up. The light burned even brighter, having absorbed all the souls and their bliss, until they could make out Sarah's shape again, shining like the sun.

"Isn't she beautiful?" Emmie said without taking her eyes off her friend.

"Yes." Finn's eyes were full of wonder. "Yes, she is."

Someone knocked on the front door before a loud voice called out, "Emergency 911!"

The light in Sarah dimmed and disappeared within seconds, and she was herself again, just as Finn dropped into a chair.

"We're in here!" Jason called.

Emmie stood as the paramedics entered and scrambled around Finn. Jason took charge of answering most questions in a way that sometimes distorted the truth but didn't break it. It was difficult to keep from laughing at the calm confidence of his expert schmoozing, though they had done the same thing a couple of times themselves.

No one needed to go upstairs, to Emmie's relief, or they might have seen the damage Finn had caused and questioned them further. After the paramedics claimed that Finn was doing remarkably well considering that he had fallen through the ice, they put him on a gurney and rolled him outside. He made an obscene gesture to the house before they slid him into the ambulance, but the paramedics only looked at each other and shrugged.

Sarah insisted on going with him, having stood at his side every moment until then, but Finn gestured her away. "Isn't there one more *thing* you need to do?"

She glanced back at the house, then moved away from him. "You're right."

"That's what I like to hear." Finn grinned. "Jason can go with me to the hospital. It's all his fault."

Raising his eyebrows, Jason didn't protest. He climbed in instead.

"Where are you taking him?" Emmie asked.

"St. Luke's," one of the paramedics said. "It's ten miles south of here. You won't miss it."

Another paramedic nodded at the women and pulled the doors of the ambulance closed.

"One more thing..." Sarah repeated.

"Maybe this time we can find him," Emmie said.

❦ 39 ❧

Walking upstairs to the "murder room," Emmie found the air clear—not in the physical sense, but in the greater sense of energy. It had changed since Edgar's whispers had stopped. Whatever energy Owl had created over the house with the vibration of chanting had now disappeared.

She glanced at Sarah, who looked peaceful and healthier than ever, but decided not to ask about all that... *light*. There would be time to talk about it later, and to explore whatever phenomenon Sarah had tapped into.

Now, even before she opened the door to the murder room, Emmie sensed a presence inside.

Emmie opened the door and Sterling was there.

His zombie costume startled her, although she had seen much more gore on the real living dead as spirits. The blood drained from a single slit in his chest near his heart, and his expression was a mix of confusion and horror.

"Where am I?" His voice was hoarse. "Who are you?"

Sarah spoke first. "We're here to help you."

He stared down at his wound. "Michelle... stabbed me. I need help!"

Emmie nodded sympathetically. "Can you tell us why she did that?"

Sterling glanced around. "Where is she? I need to apologize."

"*You* need to apologize?"

"It's my fault." He cringed and pulled at his hair. "She found those messages from Ella on my phone. I should have listened to Diego and just denied it. But it's too late—she's so upset now. I messed up, and I just want to say I'm sorry."

Emmie met Sarah's gaze and heaved a deep sigh. Jealousy. What a motive for a murder. But then again, Emmie had almost killed Finn just to keep him away from Sarah. And Finn had attacked her with a hammer after finding out.

The Truth wasn't as wonderful as Owl had imagined, especially if it was filtered through a child with no concept of boundaries yet. An angry child lashed out at anything it didn't like with no sense of the consequences of its actions. It would kill what it loved without a second thought.

"We can tell Michelle what you told us," Emmie said. "That you're sorry for what happened."

"I never meant to hurt her."

"I'm sure that she feels the same about what she did to you," Sarah said. Emmie wasn't so sure.

Sterling ran the tips of his fingers across his wound. "I deserved it. I broke her heart."

"Nobody deserves this much violence," Sarah said softly. "But we can help make this right. You can move on to a better place. You won't feel so lost."

Sterling stared at them for a moment and nodded. "I'd like that."

Without wasting time, Sarah stepped in and encompassed him in the same brilliant light before he rose through the ceiling and disappeared a moment later. The process of releasing him was so simple, yet it had been so tragically difficult to get to that point.

They had been through so much to discover the truth of that house.

Sarah sighed. "Mission accomplished, I guess. Audrey will be pleased that we cleared out her house, that she won't need to worry about another murder or a malignant spirit."

They walked out together, hand in hand. After a moment, Emmie said, "She loves this house so much, though. And she loves Joan. Should we—"

"Tell her that Joan was half mad and made her poor son mad?" Sarah shook her head. "No. We should not tell a woman who is a mother and brings her sons here that story."

"I agree," Emmie said softly as they descended the stairs. It was funny that they didn't need to rush now—no panic, no fear —when only hours earlier the sound of their footsteps would have sent Finn into a rage.

"How will we explain the damage to the house?" Sarah asked.

Emmie laughed nervously. "Well..."

They moved into the kitchen and Emmie headed straight for a bottle of whiskey. She needed a stiff shot of something, and that would do nicely. "Considering we now have a second smooth operator working with us, let them come up with something."

She filled two shot glasses with the whiskey and handed one to Sarah. They clinked glasses.

Sarah laughed. "They'll probably try to outdo the other's explanations."

Letting the whiskey warm her throat for a moment, Emmie said, "I think Finn lost his goggles in the water." She gestured toward the kitchen table where she'd tossed the other pair of goggles while searching for the circuit breaker. "I wonder if we should tell him the other pair survived."

Sarah stepped over to the table and sat in front of the goggles. Her fingertips touched the strap as she sipped her drink. "He's reckless, that's for sure. But the goggles are worthless now, right? No more energy in the house to power them."

"Still. Might be better to keep them out of his hands. He *does* like to tinker with things like this, and the books are still available."

"Agreed. But I'm sure he's learned his lesson. Despite all that's happened, I know that Finn loves life. I'm sure he feels awful about what happened. I could feel his pain after we pulled him out of the water."

"I forgive him." Emmie took a big sip of whiskey.

Sarah watched her with a grin and did the same. "I forgive him too. We'll need to tell him that so he doesn't bury himself in guilt. He's already got plenty of that in his life. And I was thinking how difficult it must be for him."

Emmie understood. *To go on without a brother.*

Sarah continued, "Do you think we could find Neil one day? Help him?"

Emmie thought about it. "I'm more than willing to help, but how would we even bring up the subject with him? You probably know better than me how Finn avoids that subject more fiercely than anything else in his past."

"So much pain." Sarah drained the rest of her glass in one gulp. "He deserves relief."

"It'll come up," Emmie said, "one of these days."

Sarah glanced around the house. "Yes. I guess the truth comes out eventually for everyone. But I suggest we don't tell Audrey the truth about this house. Just this once."

Emmie nodded back. "Sometimes a lie is better than the truth anyway."

☙ 40 ❧

E mmie knocked on Finn's bedroom door and waited.

No answer. Not a surprise though. He'd slept a lot over the last few days since returning to the warmth and safety of Caine House, rarely coming out for anything other than food and necessities. But Sarah had elicited laughter from him that morning—the first time he'd laughed in over a week—and they hadn't *really* talked about what had happened at Whisper House yet. Not in any meaningful way, anyway. It was time.

She listened for his voice behind his door and knocked again. Still no answer.

"Finn?" She cracked the door open and peeked inside. "You awake?"

He was tucked under the covers up to his chin with his face off to the side. "Hi Emmie. I'm awake. Come on in."

She stepped inside slowly and asked in a lighthearted tone, "You... decent?"

He turned his face toward her a little, and a glimmer of a grin spread over his face.

Good, a step in the right direction.

He sat up and pushed himself back against the headboard while throwing aside the blankets, revealing that he was fully dressed. His left pant leg was bunched up above the brace around his ankle and foot. "I decided to get dressed today."

Emmie chuckled. "Sarah did say that you were doing better."

"Better is relative in my case. Did she send you up here to check on me?"

Emmie shook her head. "I was hoping we could talk for a bit."

His smile faded. "Sure, no problem."

She'd taken away his smile. Still, it was better to talk and get past the elephant in the room. Emmie sat on the edge of his bed. "I just wanted to talk about what happened."

Finn swallowed. "Should we get Sarah in on this?"

"This is more between you and me, right?"

Finn met her gaze. His eyes studied her face. "I could say I'm sorry a thousand times and it'd never be enough. From the bottom of my heart, I'm sorry."

"I'm sorry too. But we've said that before to each other and there's still something between us. You've disconnected from me. I can feel it. Sarah feels it too."

Finn nodded slowly. "You're probably right. But what am I supposed to do—what am I supposed to *feel* after acting like that in Whisper House? All that stuff about my Truth... I don't like what I discovered."

"I'm not here to judge you. We've both done things we're not proud of. But that wasn't the complete, wonderful Finn in there. That was Finn without brakes, without inhibitions. It wasn't really you—"

"But it *was*. And I can't stop thinking about it."

"You're wrong. Everyone has a dark side in them. But everyone has a lighter side in them too. We all survived our darkest moments, and I want you to forgive yourself for what you think you did."

"I don't *think* I did it. I absolutely did it. No question about it."

"Then let's accept that and move on. Sarah and I have

completely forgiven you for all of it. And I hope you can forgive me for acting hurtful too."

"I do."

"Then it's settled." Emmie stood, but stayed beside his bed.

"But please give me a little more time to work this out. Okay? It's really knocked me down." Finn stared expressionless at the brace on his ankle. "Literally. And I wouldn't be surprised if we all have PTSD after that experience. A psychologist would probably help, although I doubt I could find one who would truly understand my bizarre issues and, frankly, I'm not sure I would even confess what I was *really* thinking in that house or they'd probably throw me in jail."

The doorbell rang.

Emmie's heart quickened and Finn looked at her curiously. "Expecting someone?"

"Jason asked if he could stop by and see you. I told him okay." Emmie extended her hand and Finn accepted it while pulling himself up from the bed to stand beside her.

Finn limped forward. "I thought you never wanted to see him again."

Emmie paused to consider the question. "Things have changed... after how he came to the rescue like that and saved your life. I owe him a second chance."

Finn nodded. "You're a courageous woman, Em. I could learn a lot from you."

Emmie stepped with Finn toward the door until Sarah knocked and peeked her head inside.

"Jason's here." Sarah's gaze dropped to Finn's leg brace. "You need pain meds today?"

He shook his head. "Got anything I can take for my aching soul?"

She smiled sympathetically. "No medicines for that. I could rub your back..."

Finn paused, then limped forward while looking down. "Thank you, but not today."

Sarah hurried forward and moved in beside him. "I can take it from here."

"Sure." Emmie backed away as Sarah slid her arm around Finn's waist.

"We'll be right down," Sarah said.

A moment before Emmie stepped into the hallway, Finn spoke up, "Thank you for reaching out."

Emmie turned back. So much sadness in Finn's eyes now, even after their talk, although she sensed hope in his voice. "We all need to heal now."

JASON WAS STILL STANDING IN THE ENTRYWAY WHEN EMMIE arrived downstairs. He hadn't removed his coat yet, as if someone might ask him to leave at any moment.

Her heart still beat a little faster at seeing him, although she didn't hesitate to step over and gave him a brief hug. Pulling away, he met her gaze and smiled warmly. "That means a lot."

"We've still got a lot to talk about, but at least it's a start, right?"

"A very good start. How are you feeling?"

"As well as can be expected, I guess." She gestured toward the living room. "Please come in."

He stepped forward and finally removed his coat. "How's Finn?"

Walking beside Jason on the way to the living room, she continued, "Luckily, the injuries aren't too serious. A sprained ankle and some cuts—" An image of Finn's bloodied hand after breaking through the lake house's storm door popped into her mind and she winced. "—but nothing too serious. We're all lucky to be alive, thanks to you."

Jason touched Emmie's shoulder. "I'm sure you would have done the same for me."

"I'd like to think so."

He grinned. "I understand. Trust needs time to grow."

Sarah and Finn came down the stairs while they were talking and walked over with outstretched arms toward Jason. They greeted each other with hugs then found a place to sit. Finn sat beside Jason on the couch. Emmie sat in the recliner near the fireplace, and Sarah sat alone on the loveseat.

Jason's expression was solemn as he leaned forward with his elbows on his knees and clasped his hands. "It's wonderful to hear that everyone is doing well, although I wish your time at Whisper House had been a more pleasant experience... Look, I never would have imagined—"

Emmie held up her hand. "Don't stress over us. It wasn't your fault, and we certainly don't blame you."

"I appreciate that," Jason said.

Finn's eyes watered while meeting Jason's gaze. "I haven't had a chance to say this with everyone together, but *thank you* for saving me." He turned and faced each of them. "All of you. *Thank you.*"

Jason nodded. "If you ever accept another assignment from me, I promise I'll do more research... I just hope you won't throw in the towel after this."

"We haven't really talked about it yet." Sarah looked at Emmie, then Finn.

Emmie turned to Jason, but hesitated to ask, "Do you have something in mind?"

"Nothing at the moment. But I wouldn't think of bringing up a job again so soon after Whisper House. You should all take it easy for a while. But when you *do* decide it's time to use your skills..." Jason's gaze stopped at Emmie.

"We'll let you know." Emmie nodded once. Despite the suggestion of working again with him, the mild pressure didn't scare her, and in a way it reassured her to know that she could turn to him for work if she really needed it.

"Call me any time." Jason focused on Finn again. "And I'm sure that you'll be up and around sooner than you think."

Finn cleared his throat. "About that... I haven't mentioned this yet, but as soon as this brace comes off, I'm planning to take a nice long vacation, at least a month, somewhere far away from here."

"You just got back from Mexico, I thought?" Jason asked.

"We did."

"Where to this time?"

"Haven't decided yet." Finn looked toward Sarah. "But I'm planning to go alone and reflect on my life and all that sort of thing. Maybe I'll just sit on a beach in Rio and stare at the ocean or climb a mountain in Tibet. I just don't know yet."

Sarah's eyes widened at hearing the news, and Emmie couldn't help but feel her friend's heartache. Sarah had grown so close to him in recent weeks. It must have hurt.

Finn continued, "Not that I need to get away from anyone here..."

Sarah nodded and slumped, putting on a brave face. "I'm sure that will help."

"You like to climb?" Jason asked.

Finn shrugged. "Don't know. Never tried. But it's not about the climbing really, just finding myself." He looked at the floor. "My *real* self."

"Go for it," Jason said. "Just keep in touch."

Emmie shook her head, watching Finn until he glanced up again. "Just don't think that what happened in Whisper House is your *real* self, Finn, no matter what you heard from any whisper."

He narrowed his eyes and stared. "But how can you be *sure?*"

His question and intense stare caught her by surprise. A chill swept through her. He was trying to unnerve her to make his point, but she swallowed hard. "I just am."

Finn nodded as if he had won. "Your reaction is exactly why I need to get out of town for a little while. Get my head straight. If that was my true self, or one side of it, then I need to *seriously* deal with it."

Emmie met his gaze. "Nothing like that would have

happened, ever, without Edgar influencing us. I met my Truth too. I'm ashamed and appalled at what I did. But I would never do something like that, trap you inside a house knowing you might freeze to death in any normal situation."

"I believe you." He looked at Emmie with a warm smile, then glanced at Sarah. "But I still need to get away."

"I'll miss you," Sarah said to him.

Finn nodded, then formed a curious grin. "So what about you? How did that house influence you?"

Sarah's eyes widened. "I... didn't feel different."

"But you heard the whispers, right? Edgar must have influenced you in some way. Who did *you* try to kill?"

"Nobody," Sarah said with playfully suspicious narrow eyes.

"You said it yourself, Finn," Emmie said. "When you saw her right after releasing the spirits, and you said she was beautiful. You couldn't see her the way I could, but she was glowing with a beautiful aura, and that's her Truth."

Finn watched her for a moment as if expecting that beautiful aura to appear. "I just hope Emmie's right; that I never see that side of myself ever again."

"Or from me either," Emmie said.

Sarah glanced down at her hands, then turned to Jason. "Can I get you something to drink?"

"I better not." Jason shook his head and gestured at Emmie. "I need to save room for her."

Sarah and Finn both turned to Emmie with confused expressions, but Sarah spoke up first. "What's this?"

"He's taking me out for coffee after this," Emmie said. "Just *business*. I want to hear what he remembers about that psychic organization we visited as kids. Dr. Albright and all that."

Jason grinned at her. "I've got *tons* of stories to tell you."

"Things *have* changed." Finn's expression brightened. "That's good to see."

"My past has always bothered me," Emmie said. "I figure I better take this opportunity to get some answers."

"I'm sure I can help with that." Jason's phone buzzed. He pulled it from his pocket and glanced at the screen. "Sorry about that. They never leave me alone."

"Who?" Sarah asked.

"All the collectors and my business associates. They keep me plenty busy. Tomorrow I'm heading out to meet with a guy in California." He looked at Emmie. "One of Dr. Albright's former students, coincidentally, but that's a long story and—" He stood suddenly. "—we need coffee."

Emmie chuckled and also stood. "I'm ready when you are."

"Well, all right then." He made a wide gesture. "Lead the way."

They all stood and walked to the door together. Finn and Sarah hugged Jason again as he put on his jacket, hat, and gloves.

"Thanks again," Finn said. "We'll keep in touch."

"We will—definitely—and I'm so glad that you're recovering well." He gestured to Emmie and Sarah. "You're a lucky man, Finn, to have friends like these at your side."

"Very lucky." Finn stood with his arms crossed and his gaze dropped to the floor.

Jason looked at Emmie and opened the door, letting in a burst of icy air. "I'll warm up the car."

Emmie nodded as he hurried outside, and she put on her jacket and a scarf. By the time she was ready to leave, Finn had already started trudging up the stairs, leaving Sarah standing alone in the doorway.

Sarah called up to Finn, "You need help?"

He turned back without expression. "I'm feeling better now. You don't need to stay. I'm all stabilized."

Sarah nodded slowly, her eyes full of disappointment. "I'll head back to Betty's house—our house—then."

"Probably a good idea." Finn continued on his way up to his bedroom and closed the door.

Sarah smiled, although her watery eyes told a different story.

"Just give him some time." Emmie moved forward and hugged her friend.

Sarah tightened their embrace. "I hope time is enough."

Stepping back, Emmie met her friend's sorrowful stare. "I'm sure a vacation will clear his mind. And Christmas is on the way. After I get back, I say we take some of that money from Whisper House and go shopping."

Sarah glanced back toward the stairs as if contemplating whether she should leave Finn on a low note. She turned back to Emmie and nodded with a bright, childish smile. "I can't wait."

GET BOOK 5 IN THE EMMIE ROSE HAUNTED MYSTERY SERIES on the next page!

Read more in the Emmie Rose Haunted Mystery series on Amazon.com!

Temper House: An Emmie Rose Haunted Mystery Book 5

PLUS, get a **FREE** short story at my website!

www.deanrasmussen.com

★★★★★
Please review my book!

If you liked this book and have a moment to spare, I would greatly appreciate a short review on the page where you bought it. Your help in spreading the word is *immensely* appreciated and reviews make a huge difference in helping new readers find my novels.

Shine House: An Emmie Rose Haunted Mystery Book 0
Hanging House: An Emmie Rose Haunted Mystery Book 1
Caine House: An Emmie Rose Haunted Mystery Book 2
Hyde House: An Emmie Rose Haunted Mystery Book 3
Whisper House: An Emmie Rose Haunted Mystery Book 4
Temper House: An Emmie Rose Haunted Mystery Book 5

Dreadful Dark Tales of Horror Book 1
Dreadful Dark Tales of Horror Book 2
Dreadful Dark Tales of Horror Book 3
Dreadful Dark Tales of Horror Book 4
Dreadful Dark Tales of Horror Book 5
Dreadful Dark Tales of Horror Book 6
Dreadful Dark Tales of Horror Complete Series

Stone Hill: Shadows Rising (Book 1)
Stone Hill: Phantoms Reborn (Book 2)
Stone Hill: Leviathan Wakes (Book 3)

ABOUT THE AUTHOR

Dean Rasmussen grew up in a small Minnesota town and began writing stories at the age of ten, driven by his fascination with the Star Wars hero's journey. He continued writing short stories and attempted a few novels through his early twenties until he stopped to focus on his computer animation ambitions. He studied English at a Minnesota college during that time.

He learned the art of computer animation and went on to work on twenty feature films, a television show, and a AAA video game as a visual effects artist over thirteen years.

Dean currently teaches animation for visual effects in Orlando, Florida. Inspired by his favorite authors, Stephen King, Ray Bradbury, and H. P. Lovecraft, Dean began writing novels and short stories again in 2018 to thrill and delight a new generation of horror fans.

ACKNOWLEDGMENTS

Thank you to my wife and family who supported me, and who continue to do so, through many long hours of writing.

Thank you to my friends and relatives, some of whom have passed away, who inspired me and supported my crazy ideas. Thank you for putting up with me!

Thank you to everyone who worked with me to get this book out on time!

Thank you to all my supporters!

Printed in Great Britain
by Amazon

36746903R10148